DEATH OF SENSEI

LIFE AND DEATH OF SENSEI
LOREN W. CHRISTENSEN

ISBN: 9798592038280
First print edition January 2021

Interior and cover design by Kamila Miller kzmiller.com

THE LIFE AND DEATH OF SENSEI

LOREN W. CHRISTENSEN

ACKNOWLEDGEMENTS

A rose to my bride, Lisa, for her support.
Ron Sloan for looking over the Vietnam
scene—and welcome home brother
Kevin Faulk for his keen editorial eye and story suggestions
A'lyse Langroodi for her help with the cover photo
Kamila Miller for her always excellent
cover design and interior layout

The battle between good and evil runs through the heart of every man

Aleksandr Solzhenitsyn

~

Only the dead have seen the end of war

Plato

CONTENTS

PROLOGUE

Grant sat down in the chair indicated by Sensei and quick-glanced around the office. He hadn't been in it before. When he signed up for lessons three months earlier, he had talked with a pleasant senior student who explained the system, the cost, and answered questions. Sensei had visited only one of Grant's beginner classes, which were led by advanced black belts. His understanding was that Sensei, due to health issues, taught only the black belt classes.

Unlike other martial arts schools he had visited before settling on this one, there were no trophies in the windows, no displays of diplomas, and no group pictures of students. Instead, each wall displayed a single framed quote. Likewise, Sensei's office walls.

Directly to his front: "The Mind is everything. What you think, you become."

To his right: "The distance between your dreams and reality is called action."

To his left: "The trouble is, you think you have time."

Sensei was sitting behind a small desk that separated them, so Grant didn't want to turn around and see what was on the wall behind him.

The man—Grant didn't know his real name; everyone just called him Sensei—was wearing a faded black gi, threadbare around the collar, and a battered red belt around his waist that denoted his rank, 10th dan. Grant knew he held advanced degrees in other fighting arts besides American Free Style Karate. Sensei folded his hands and rested them on his desktop, the knuckles of both hands enlarged and overlaid with thick calluses.

As this was the first time Grant had seen him within six feet, the white belt was captivated by the teacher's eyes, which were at once warm, amused, and intense. Maybe "intense" wasn't the right word… Full of history. Yes, that described them. There were 72 years reflected in those eyes (Grant' teacher had revealed Sensei's age the first day of class), and Grant guessed they weren't all easy ones.

But those eyes were damn intense too.

Grant was a writer. He had been published—a book and a few magazine pieces—but he was still relatively new at it, still learning to play the role of being an author. At 33, he was too old to change his manner of dress to a tweed sports jacket with patches on the elbows, blue jeans, and a scarf draped flamboyantly around his neck. Instead, he strived to be eagle-eyed, keenly observant, penetratingly analytical, wonderfully imaginative, strongly disciplined, and curious as a cat about everything and everyone. And he needed to stop using so many adjectives.

So far, he had only written nonfiction, but like most writers, he felt, no, he knew, he had a great novel in him just bursting to get out. About what, he had no clue.

Even at 72, Grant observed, Sensei's bearing was imposing. Well over six feet tall, 200 hard pounds, a thick neck and muscular chest partially revealed by his gaping gi top. His hands were large, as were his wrists and fingers, and those daunting knuckles looked as if they could punch through a bank vault.

"How goes your training, Grant?" Sensei asked, his voice low, gentle.

"Humbling, sir," he said, a little uncomfortable under the man's gaze. His eyes seemed to draw him in as if only the two of them existed in all the world.

Sensei nodded. "That's normal. I hope you keep that humility as you improve."

"Yes, sir."

Sensei studied Grant for a long moment, his hands still clasped, his thick top thumb rubbing his bottom one. Then he said, "I read your book, *Surviving the Second Tower.*"

Grants mouth dropped open.

Sensei's eyes smiled. "I read it about eight months ago, long before you joined us. I saw your name on our roster and wondered if you were the same Grant Perry who wrote the book. I looked on

Amazon, and there was your handsome photo."

Grant closed his mouth and struggled not to smile. This was the first time someone had recognized him. And by Sensei no less. Got to stay cool, he thought. "It was a fascinating project, sir. She was an amazing woman."

"I agree. Her tale of enduring the Twin Towers attack, her eight days spent trapped in the rubble, the loss of her legs, and her psychological problems, her PTSD, after she was found, was, I thought, a true story of survival. I was mesmerized."

"Wow. Thank you, Sensei. That means a lot to me."

"Have you written other biographical books?"

"That's the only book. But I've written a few magazine pieces about people. One in *Reader's Digest,* two in *Men's Health,* and a long newspaper piece segmented into three consecutive days. That one was an American soldier's experience in Afghanistan and his troubles after he got home."

"It was in *The Oregonian.* Read it. And the one about the painter in *Reader's Digest.* I missed the other one, I guess. What was it about?"

"*Men's Health* is a bodybuilding magazine. It was about a person with paraplegia, a female competitor who uses a wheelchair."

Sensei jotted something on a notepad. He looked up. "I like your writing style. Good clarity, excellent research, and keen observation skills. The latter is a mature attribute not always seen in young writers. And you don't glorify your subjects, either. Your story on Alfred B, the painter, revealed his moody, cantankerous side. His criticism of other painters to the point of making him sound jealous of their work."

"Well," Grant said with a weak smile, "he didn't mind my comments about his moodiness, but he was upset about my comments about what I perceived as his jealously of other people's work."

Sensei nodded. "I think it's important to show the humanness of a person, a complete picture. If not, the work is just fluff."

"Yes, sir. Thank you."

"And I liked how you showed… I forgot the woman's name in the second Twin Tower…"

"Elizabeth Dempsey."

"Yes. I liked how you told of how Elizabeth Dempsey, in her desperation, pushed slower-moving older people out of the way in the smoke-filled stairwell as she ran down thirty floors. And I liked what you wrote about her being more concerned about her lost wages because she couldn't work than she was about the deaths of nearly three thousand people."

"Actually, the first part was what Elizabeth wanted. She wanted me to tell of her aggressiveness in the stairwell to show the effect of fear on her actions. She considered herself a caring and compassionate person. But her absolute terror from the impact of the airliner eight floors above her, the way her floor swayed and trembled, the panic and chaos all around her, it, well, it shocked her how she acted so selfishly. She said it made her a complete stranger to herself; her actions, she said, weren't who she thought she was." Grant shrugged. "She was okay with me writing that, but she wasn't about me editorializing negatively about her concerns about money more than the loss of so many lives."

Sensei jotted on his notepad again for a moment, leaving Grant to wonder what this meeting was about.

The instructor stopped writing for a moment and looked at Grant, his eyes seemed lost in thought. He looked down at his pad again, shoved it to the side, and leaned back in his chair. This time his eyes focused on Grant.

"I would like you to write a biography about me."

"What? Write a…"

"A bio on me. Yes. Flaws and all. No sugar coating."

"But…but there are biographers out there who have more experience—"

"Of course, there are," Sensei said, nodding. "But I like your writing style. It's fresh, you have a sharp eye, and you have a working knowledge of the martial arts. By the way, I hope you're not thinking about quitting. The first two or three months are the hardest for beginners because their thoughts of being the next Bruce Lee fade when they realize how much work it is. I insist that you continue to train so you can better add the martial arts perspective to the story."

Sensei studied Grant. "I can see those wheels turning in your head. May I take that as a yes?"

Two weeks later, Sensei died from cardiac arrest.

CHAPTER ONE

THE FUNERAL

Grant was standing under his burgundy umbrella atop a sloped manicured lawn dotted with grave markers of every size and shape. It was mid-spring, and the grey drizzle underscored the smell of freshly mowed grass and blooming life on the many trees on the sprawling acreage where thousands of departed rested just beneath the surface. Grant had only been to three gravesite burials, his father's, cousin's, and a friend he had known since he was nine years old. The one happening 50 yards below him among a copse of pink flowering cherry trees was for a man he had barely known for about three months.

There were at least 200 open umbrellas bunched together down there, many of them protecting two people. They stood solemnly around an American flag-draped coffin, their heads bowed as the minister prayed into a hand-held microphone.

Grant contemplated that there wouldn't be more than ten people at his funeral, maybe 15. More, if some of them brought a date. That was okay. He didn't care about being popular or famous, anyway. He just wanted to be a successful writer.

After Sensei surprised him with a request to pen his biography, they spent a good two hours talking about the project. Sensei reiterated the importance of telling the truth, and he provided a shortlist of people he believed would do exactly that. Sensei put a number after each name to indicate the order the interviews should appear in the book. But after he handed him the list, he said, "That's if you tell my story linearly. If you deem it to work better some other way, I won't argue. You're the writer, and I'm too close to the subject."

The more they talked—Sensei did most of it—the more enthused Grant got, hoping the story would be general enough to appeal to nonmartial arts readers.

They agreed to meet two times the following week. They had the first meeting after Sensei's last black belt class on Tuesday, but he canceled Friday because, as he put it, "I'm a tad under the weather." Grant waited for a reschedule call, but none came. He didn't learn of the man's passing until he went to class on Wednesday of the following week. He had died the day before.

Grant was shocked, to understate it, and disappointed. Then a day later, he received a letter from Sensei postmarked two days before his death. It included only two sentences about his health. "I've been feeling profoundly weak of late. I don't seem to be improving."

At first, it was strange to Grant that he would share something so personal with him. But when he thought about it, personal was what the bio was all about. The next two paragraphs made it clear that he wanted Grant to continue with the book. "If the book makes less than $10,000, keep all of it. If it makes over $10,000, I want you to give 35 percent to Leo Ichiro, who will use it to keep the four schools running. I have notified him of my wishes." A strange will, Grant thought, but it was okay with him. He would talk with this Leo Ichiro about it.

The next paragraph began with, "I think I was a good man, but I must admit there were times I wasn't. I like to think I've been moving toward doing good in such quantity to make up for the bad. I only hope it works that way. It's been said that a good man never dies."

Two sentences made up the next paragraph. "I hope what little good I have done has helped and inspired others to do the same. Forgive me if that sounds like ego talking."

The last paragraph was a single sentence. "I'm feeling sleepy.

There would be no further correspondence.

Grant positioned himself on one end of the horseshoe-shaped gathering of mourners. He wanted to see as many faces as possible given the number of people and the many umbrellas angled against the light wind and rain. A wheelchair sat near the center of the gathering, the occupant's umbrella turned downward, making it impossible for Grant to know if the person was male or female. He studied others while the black-robed minister spoke, his grave tone well-practiced.

"Nathaniel Stone, the incredible man everyone called Sensei, was loved by all those he met, all those he touched with his caring, his grace, his kindness, and his guidance. So many people, thousands perhaps, have a Sensei story…

I hope so, Grant thought, looking at a 50-something woman standing in front of the crowd, centered on the flag-draped coffin. Her face was tight, the tension apparent in her bunched brow and pursed lips. He didn't know her, but if he were to guess, he'd say there was more anger in that face than sadness.

"…of how Sensei helped shape their lives for the better," the minister continued. "At six feet tall, his stature, his devotion to fitness, and, of course, his treasured study of the martial arts, made him an imposing figure. Nonetheless, to those who were close to him, he was a teddy bear." The mourners reacted to that with nods, chuckles, and sobs. "He was indeed a protector to everyone he loved and everyone he deemed needing help." More nods.

"Many of you have heard the story of Sensei coming to the rescue of a young boy behind a 7-Eleven about a dozen years ago. In short, four young teenagers were pushing the boy around, kicking him in his behind, and threatening to do worse. Sensei saw what was happening and quickly positioned himself between the twelve-year-old and the bullies. When they tried to get aggressive with him—the emphasis on tried—they soon found themselves, all four of them, sprawled on the grass. He didn't hit, kick, or judo chop," the minister made a chopping gesture with the side of his hand, "any of them, but there they were nonetheless unceremoniously dumped on the grass.

"Sensei sent the victim off to his home then commanded the boys to sit up, cross their legs, and listen to what he had to say. He spent nearly an hour with them, first talking to them, then listening to what they had to say, and then talking with them. Well, it must have been an amazing and inspiring time because three of them joined his karate school and went on to graduate from college. Today, one is a major in the Army, one is an attorney, and one is a police officer right here in Portland, Oregon. He is also an assistant instructor in… Which school is it, Martin?"

"Sensei's Watkins Street Dojo, sir," a voice said from the gathering.

"Martin, raise your hand, please."

A tall, good looking man behind the sour woman Grant noticed earlier shyly lifted his arm. Heads nodded their respect, and a young, attractive woman standing by him leaned into his side and tightened her grip on his arm.

There is a Martin on Sensei's list, Grant remembered.

"Miss Lindsay Graham," the minister said, stepping up to the 50-something woman Grant had zeroed in on a moment earlier. She was on the list, too. The woman was dressed in a smart dark grey suit, holding an umbrella of the same color. The minister gave her an I-understand-your-pain smile as he patted her upper arm, the gesture knocking drips from her umbrella down onto his face. Someone behind Grant chuckled at that.

The minister said, "With a loving heart the size of all outdoors, Miss Graham provided Sensei's wife, Roni, love and care for the last months of her life. Roni passed on to the loving arms of Jesus two years ago." With his white gloved hand still on her upper arm, he stepped aside as if to give her space to step forward to say a few words.

She shook her head once, but that was enough considering her hard expression.

"I heard she's hired an attorney," a woman's voice from behind Grant whispered. "She's a gold digger."

"Live-in caretaker," another female scoffed. "His wife wasn't the only one she was taking care of."

Oh really? Grant thought.

The minister surveyed the gathering. "Mister Ichiro? Ready?"

A hand went up behind the person in the wheelchair. He was an older man, 70s, his face showing subtle Asian characteristics: wide, full lips, and almond-shaped eyes. He was on the list; the name Sensei wanted to receive 35 percent of the royalties. The minister gestured for him to come forward.

Mister Ichiro wore a dark blue raincoat without an umbrella. He had a buzz cut and a heavy jaw that looked like it could take a mule's kick without blinking. He didn't react to the increasing downpour smacking against his face.

He touched the person's shoulder in the wheelchair as he stepped around it and moved toward the coffin. He placed his palm on the lid and lowered his head slightly. Grant could see his lips moving, but his words were inaudible. After a moment, he pressed his palms against the sides of his thighs and slowly bowed, his back straight, his head in perfect alignment, eyes cast down. He held the 45-degree angle for the traditional three seconds Grant was taught, then straightened.

Nice touch, the writer thought.

The man turned around, looked at the minister, who nodded.

Ichiro's eyes scanned the crowd, his feet together, his back straight, hands at his side. He inhaled sharply and barked out what sounded like "Kee-oh-skay!" Grant knew it was kiotsuke, the Japanese word that calls for attention at the beginning of each karate class.

People throughout the crowd began moving toward the front, excusing themselves as they maneuvered through the crowd. As each person—men, women, teens, and children—neared the coffin, they formed a half-circle around it, standing at attention, their heads angled to look at the place where Sensei lay.

Well-rehearsed, Grant thought, looking at what he estimated to be 60 plus people. Sensei's students, he assumed, somber, military-like, many openly weeping.

"Sensei!" Ichiro thundered, looking at the coffin.

"Thank you for teaching us!" the group called out unevenly.

They stood in silence for a moment, the only sound rain spattering on umbrella tops, the caw of treed crows, and lots of sniffing.

"*Rei!*" the leader snapped.

As one, the 60 slowly bowed toward Sensei's coffin, held it, then straightened.

Mister Ichiro turned to face the other mourners. "My name is Leo Ichiro, one of Sensei's instructors. This small formality is how

Sensei ended each training session. And after we thanked him for teaching us, he always responded with 'And thank you for teaching me.' This wasn't false humility. He told me many times that he learned as much from the students as they learned from him." He looked down at his feet for a moment. When he looked up, his eyes were wet. "I… I will always treasure my memory of him."

He turned back around and nodded at the students. Without being commanded, they bowed at the coffin one last time and rejoined the other mourners.

Grant couldn't decide if that was corny or the most impressive thing he had seen in a long while. He was anxious to interview Mr. Ichiro.

When the gathering was intact again, the minister asked if anyone else would like to say something.

"I do," a male voice said from the back on Grant's side of the gathering. A moment later, another older man stepped forward with a slight limp. He was distinguished-looking, in his late 60s, with a lived-in face. He held a clear umbrella above him to protect his fine, black overcoat and the lush black scarf tied around his neck. In contrast to the upscale attire, he wore a beat-up baseball cap with what looked like, from where Grant stood, a row of red, yellow, green, and purple rectangular military ribbons across the front. Grant moved a few feet closer and squinted. Embroidered in blood-red above them: "Combat Veteran, Vietnam."

Interesting, Grant thought.

The man moved up to the coffin, removed his cap, and laid his palm on the lid. He closed his eyes for a moment, opened them, and said something. Grant couldn't hear what it was, but he read the man's lips. "Thank you."

He turned around and faced the gathering. Still holding his cap in his hand, he said, "My name's Ben Walters. My friend didn't go by 'Sensei' when I met him in the Army. We called him 'Sarge' then. He was a damn good leader and a damn good man too. One night in a jungle…" Ben Walters closed his eyes and shook his head. He opened them a moment later. "One night in a jungle, we spent time in hell together." He inhaled and exhaled raggedly. "If it were not for him," his voice cracked, "I wouldn't be here…and…I…"

He looked down, took another deep breath. "I wouldn't be here, and neither would my four boys and my seven grandbabies. Sarge's actions… allowed me to have these gifts, these joys." He closed his eyes.

The gathering stood silent, motionless as Ben Walters fisted his free hand, then opened it. His eyes seemed to look at nothing, as he said, his voice staccato, "That…Goddamn night."

He stopped there as if the three words said it all. He looked back at the coffin. "Thank you, Sarge." He turned to the mourners, his jaw trembling. He nodded for a long moment, his eyes scanning the crowd. He put on his cap and moved through them to where he had been.

Damn, Grant thought. The way he had looked at everyone. It was as if he were thinking that they would never understand.

Ben Walters was on the list too.

A neighbor spoke next, telling how well he took care of his yard and how he helped her dig up a stump. Another old-timer said he knew Sensei in high school. They both went to work at a lumberyard after graduating. Sensei quit the job three years later to go into the Army. Both people had nice things to say, all of it was uninteresting to Grant.

As the minister made a few closing remarks, the rain stopped, and a ray of sunshine punched through the fir trees and onto the gravesite. Several mourners applauded happily at the sight as others choked back their sobs to laugh and then sob again.

Okay, Grant thought, that's freaking weird.

‹0›

"Sir," Grant called out, walking quickly to catch up to the dapper man wearing the cap displaying the military ribbons. "Excuse me, sir," he said again as the man continued to walk toward the long line of cars parked on one side of the road that wound through the cemetery. Other mourners were heading to their vehicles or talking in groups on the lawn. This time the man turned around.

"Thank you, uh, Mister Walters?" Grant said, wheezing. When he didn't respond, Grant said, "Whew, that's quite a hill. I got asthma."

"What hill? Oh," he said, looking at the long grade he had walked up without effort despite his years. "Ben Walters. What can I do for you, son?"

Grant handed him a black business card. "My name is Grant Perry. I'm a writer, and I'd like to interview you for a book I'm writing on Sensei."

Walters glanced at the card. "What are you going to write about him?"

Grant smiled, noting the suspicion in his voice. "I haven't written the first sentence yet, sir, but from what I can tell and from what I saw here, he was an amazing man loved by a lot of people. What you did was touching, powerful. I really want to hear about his Vietnam experience."

Walters studied him for a moment, looking for what? Grant wondered.

"If it helps, sir, Sensei authorized me to write his bio and put your name on a contact list."

"He did?"

"Yes. We had just been talking about it when he got sick. We had two meetings, but Sensei canceled the third, complaining of not feeling well. I didn't see him again. But he sent me a letter explaining that he still wanted his story told, warts and all."

Walters nodded, still studying him. "You have a slant?"

"No, sir. Other than showing all sides of him. As I said, that's what he wanted the book to convey."

The man's face relaxed a little. "Okay."

Okay, what? Grant wondered.

"I'm guessing, Mister Walters, that you knew Sensei before most of the others here today. Plus, you knew him in a war. And after listening to you a while ago, I'd love to hear the story behind what you told us about that thing he did for you in Vietnam."

Walters nodded slowly, pensively. "I would like to tell you about my time with him. Sarge was a warrior, a real one. He saved me, and..." He looked over at a fir tree where a half dozen crows just landed, all of them facing the grave. He looked back at Grant. "The word hero and warrior have been overused in recent years. The press called the nearly three thousand people in the Twin Towers heroes." He shook his head. "No, they were victims. The police officers and firefighters who went up to help those trapped, they were the heroes." He squinted at Grant. "Okay, I'll talk to you."

Grant thought he heard a hint of a threat in his agreement. "Yes, sir. May I get your phone number to make an appointment?"

Walters looked down at Grant's card. "I'll call you in a couple of days. Maybe tomorrow."

With that, Walters turned and headed for a black BMW.

Grant smiled and shook his head. "Oookay then." He spotted the woman who didn't want to say anything to the gathering. Lindsay Graham.

"Miss Graham, excuse me. Miss—" She turned around, closed her umbrella, and shook the water off. She looked at him. A very attractive older woman, Grant thought. But I can feel the cold emanating off her.

"Yes?"

"Sorry to bother you," he said, extending a card to her. "Grant Perry. I'm trying to contact people before everyone disperses. I'm a writer, and I'm working on a book about Sensei. I'm hoping to ask you a few questions about your relationship with him. You have a unique perspective, one that I would certainly treat with the utmost respect. Would you have an hour or so in the next few days?"

She frowned. "'Utmost respect.' What do you mean? Is that an option?"

Whoops, Grant thought. "I… I, uh, just meant that in my experience, I know that people sometimes say things in interviews that they wish they hadn't. And I would work around that." He gave her his best understanding look.

"What kind of questions?"

"Oh, uh, my understanding is that you cared for Sensei's wife when she was ill, and I think a little info about that experience would help color the man's relationship with her. That sort of thing."

"That's personal."

Grant studied her tense face, wondering if she was being protective of the man or hiding something. Someone behind him earlier said, *His wife wasn't the only one she was taking care of.* What did that mean? Cruel gossip? Or something else?

Grant nodded. “I understand your concern. I was a student of Sensei’s.” He left out the part that he had only trained at the school for a dozen weeks, and he had missed several classes. “But I know from my personal relationship with him that I want to protect him too. And I will do that by being respectful of the man, his past, his life.” Hey, that was pretty good, Grant thought. “That said, he was very clear that he wanted his story told accurately, even if it showed some blemishes.” She looked at him without expression. What the hell, Grant thought. “I actually have your name on a list he gave me. Maybe he didn’t have time to contact you.” And Ben Walters for that matter, he thought.

She looked at him for a moment. “Why a book?”

“One night after class, he asked me how I was liking the classes. We ended up talking for quite a while, mostly about my writing. I didn’t realize he was sort of interviewing me, so when he asked if I would like to write a book about him, I jumped at the chance. But I had had only two sessions with him before he turned ill a week later.”

“I see,” she said. “Did he tell you anything about me?”

“No, ma’am? Just gave me your name.”

Lindsay Graham nodded. “Really?”

“He didn’t say anything about anyone on the list. Maybe he didn’t want to prejudice my interview.”

“Mmm,” she said, her lips pressed tight, studying him, which Grant found not just a little unnerving. He could see her in a nun’s habit beating a child with a paddle.

Her face abruptly softened, but not much. “He called me a few days ago,” she said. “Did you know that?”

“No.”

“He told me you were writing a book and asked me to cooperate.”

“I see,” Grant said, wondering why she was making him work for it.

“I’ll do it, Mister Perry. But if I don’t like the questions, it’s over.”

“Thank you. Could I get your number?”

She looked at the card. “I’ll call you.”

“Sounds good, Miss Graham. I look forward to it.” But not really, he thought. “And thanks.”

Grant scanned the grounds and spotted the man the minister said was a policeman. He looked at his name in his notebook then walked quickly toward him.

Several mourners were still at the gravesite, talking in groups, standing alone, or in pairs looking at the flag-draped coffin. The policeman and his wife or girlfriend were standing a few yards away from the casket, gazing at the expanse of tree-dotted cemetery grounds and back to Sensei's soon-to-be resting place.

"Mister Martin?" Grant said when he was about 15 feet behind him. The couple turned around. "I'm sorry to bother you, and I'm sorry that I don't know if Martin is your first name or last."

"Yes?" He said, not answering the implied question. Yeah, he's a cop, Grant mused. Suspicious. He didn't have anything against them, and he had never been in trouble, but they still made him nervous.

"My name is Grant Perry," he said, extending his card to him. He looked at the woman, distracted for a moment by her attractiveness. Seductive. Damn. He forced himself to look back to the cop. "I'm a writer, and I'm gathering information for a book on Sensei."

"I've seen you at the Fifth and Main school."

"Yes, sir. I'm new, but like so many, I was immediately taken in by Sensei. I think his story, especially how he helped so many people not just to learn the fighting arts but to be better people too." Grant realized too late that he gestured at the cop when he said, 'to be better people.'

"Like me," the cop stated.

"Sorry. I didn't mean to be specific. I was moved by what the minister said about you. I think it would make a wonderful addition to the book. A powerful one that will help a lot of people."

The man looked at Grant for a moment, long enough that he understood the term 'cop eyes.' It was discomforting, and he hadn't done anything wrong. Well, he did just lay it on a little thick. So far, everyone seemed cold about being interviewed, or maybe they're caught off guard being approached at the man's funeral.

"How many books have you written?"

"One other. A book about a woman who survived the attacks on the Twin Towers, and some magazine bios. I'm excited about this project; Sensei was such an incredible man. I should add that he asked me to write it."

"He asked you?" the officer said, his voice suspicious.

"He did. About twelve days ago. We had just gotten started when he fell ill."

"Did Sensei provide you with a list of people to talk with?"

Grant nodded. He did, and you're on it. But no phone numbers. That's why I've been boldly, and probably rudely, approaching people here."

The cop looked at the lady, she nodded almost imperceptibly. He looked at Grant. "Martin is my last name. Thomas, my first. This is Rhonda."

"Nice to meet you both. I'd like to sit down with you at a coffee place, restaurant, wherever and talk to you about your amazing experience."

"We can do that," Thomas said. "Sensei told me to be open with you."

Grant looked surprised. "Oh, he told you about me."

"He did. Actually, he left a message on my phone about it. I didn't have time to call him back right then, and two days later, he was gone."

"I'm so sorry for your loss," Grant said.

Thomas nodded and handed the writer his card. "Call me later in the week, and I'll check my schedule."

"Thank you," Grant said, watching them head for their car. They know about the book, but they're all making me dance for an interview. Maybe they're protective of Sensei.

Grant moved up the lawn toward the parking area where car doors were closing, and engines were coming to life. Tears shed, platitudes spoken, and formalities performed. How many of these people truly cared? How many will really feel his absence? Was he as loved as it appears? Why do martial arts students seem to worship their instructors? Because of their guidance? Because the teacher changes their lives, or they see in the teacher what they want to be? Or maybe because the teachers can kick their asses?

Was there a book here? Sensei the man, an icon in the martial arts world, a nice guy, but would people outside of it care?

Before Grant took his first training session three months earlier, he didn't know about the martial arts culture. He just thought it was people punching, kicking, and thrashing around on the floor. As it turned out, it was that, but what shocked him was all the idol worship. It was as if Sensei were some kind of rock star.

Students would shout "Yes, Sensei" whenever he spoke. Grant found that annoying after 30 minutes, and that was just his first class. The teacher would say something like, "Okay, assume your fighting stance," and everyone would respond with "Yes, Sensei!" Some students shouting it as if they were Marines. Sometimes the teacher would start to say something, like, "Okay, let's—" and the class would bellow, "Yes, Sensei," interrupting the man. Grant thought it had a kiss-up element to it, as if whoever shouted it the loudest and the most often would get awarded a new belt faster.

And the kowtowing bordered on silly, and so was the constant bowing. Some people would click their heels together when the teacher told them what to do as if they were part of the queen's honor guard. Others would scrunch their heads down not to be taller than the teacher when he was near. And when he praised a student, the eagerness and the barrage of "Yes, Sensei" and, "Thank you, Sensei" was crazy. No one had said, "I'm not worthy, Sensei," yet, but he knew it was coming. It was as if they saw the teachers as someone who had reached enlightenment or had acquired the ability to walk on water.

All that was just for Grant's regular teacher, a third-degree black belt named Shane Copeland. The first night he saw Sensei, the tenth degree lying in the coffin, was when he stopped in to greet the new students. Grant was astonished and not just a little amused at how the third-degree teacher was bowing and scraping as if Sensei was Henry the Eighth. The man couldn't get a word in edgeways because the teacher kept shouting, "Yes, Sensei!" every time the boss got half a sentence out.

The second night Grant and Sensei met to talk about the book, Grant asked him about the kowtowing. It was a nervy thing to do, and he wondered if that might not only terminate the book deal but also get his butt kicked out the door. To his surprise, Sensei said he didn't like it and never had, but he allowed it because the senior black belts insisted. The top ranks met three times a year, and on several of those occasions, Sensei brought up tossing out the formalities except for bowing in and out of class. But every time he was unanimously voted down.

"But they are your schools, your students," Grant said.

"They are the students' and teachers' schools," Sensei said. "The seniors argued that the pedestal was necessary for discipline, for keeping students driven to succeed, and for their need to look up to a supreme leader." He had shaken his head when he said that. "Even saying those words makes me uncomfortable. But I've gone along with it. Still, I bring it up every other quarterly meeting, and they always insist we maintain it." He shrugged and chuckled. "Such formalities were part of my roots, but even when I was just a colored belt, I always told myself if I ever became a teacher, I wouldn't follow it. I'd be laid back, casual. Well, as you can see, that didn't happen."

There were only about half a dozen cars parked along the side of the cemetery road now. Grant spotted the man who had led the students in a bow to the coffin. He was folding a wheelchair behind a minivan, its side door open. Grant hurried toward him, watching as he placed the chair into the van, slid the door closed, and began slipping off his raincoat.

"Sir?" Grant said, approaching. "Mister Ichiro?"

The martial artist turned around. Closeup, Grant still thought the man was impressive for someone in his sixties or early seventies: buzz cut, thick neck, broad shoulders, fit-looking even in an overcoat. So far, the teachers looked physically fit. Good examples, he thought.

"Grant Perry, I presume," the man said, a slight smile on his face. "The writer."

"Yes. How did you…?"

"Sensei told me about your project." He paused as he looked down the slope toward the gravesite. He looked back at Grant, cleared his throat. "Anyway, nice to meet you."

Grant extended his hand. Finally, he thought, someone on the list who tells me he knew about me and the book.

"Mister Ichiro, I thought what you did down there was very moving."

"Call me Leo," the man said shaking his hand. "Leo Ichiro." Grant scanned his face. "My father is Japanese," he said, apparently used to the inspection. "I favor my Italian mother."

Must be one tough looking mother, Grant thought. "I'm sorry. I didn't mean to…"

"I saw you talking to some of the others. Are you lining up interviews? If so, Sensei told me to talk to you."

"Oh," Grant said, pleasantly surprised. "Cool. I had to work a little on the others."

He nodded. "I'm sure many people aren't themselves today. But I know Sensei was interested in this project. He was in perfect health when he began thinking about it, at least we thought he was. This was about six months ago. I don't believe you were training with us then."

"No, sir. I've been coming for about three months."

Leo nodded. "Maybe he knew something he wasn't telling anyone. You know, about his health." He shrugged and looked back down the grassy slope. "It's hard to say. Sometimes people like to say that the deceased knew it was happening." He looked back at Grant. "Who knows, right? But whether Sensei knew or didn't know about how much time he had left, he for sure wanted the book written."

"I promise to do my best," Grant said.

"I would certainly hope so," Leo said. "In full disclosure, I questioned Sensei's choice of you." Grant swallowed. "I researched you and found that you have only written a few magazine pieces and one book. The book didn't do well."

"I've written bios for magazines and my book *Surviving the Second Tower* was a bio too. It sold nicely. Not great, but nicely. Not bad for my first and with a small publisher that lacked hustle. I have a potential agent now."

Leo nodded. "I'm free this weekend, Saturday." He handed Grant a piece of paper. "My address and phone number. Eleven thirty works best for me."

"Wonderful. Thank you, sir. See you then."

Grant started to turn when he noticed eyes through the darkly tinted passenger side window. They were barely visible, but they looked female, young, at least younger than Leo. They were looking at him. Oh, how amazing they were. So much so he nearly walked into a small street sign noting Section H.

He quick-glanced at Leo, who was moving around the front of the van to the driver's side. Grant looked back at the eyes.

Were they smiling?

CHAPTER TWO

BEN WALTERS

"Are you still working, Mister Walters?" Grant asked as they slid into a booth at Eugene's Best Eats, located in a strip mall about six blocks from the sprawling University of Oregon campus. Ben was wearing a Levi jacket, jeans, and boots, a different look from the high-end suit, overcoat, and plush scarf he wore at the funeral. Judging by his attire, Grant was surprised that the man chose a café close to downtown Eugene. Today, he looked like a cowboy who would have picked a western bar somewhere out in the farmlands.

"Why?" Walters asked with a twinkle in his eye. "Do I look like I've walked away from a senior citizen home?"

Grant quickly shook his head, his face turning crimson. "No, no. Sorry." He made a weak hand gesture at his clothing, "I assumed you owned one of the many farms down here. That's hard work even for a young man."

"A farm?"

"Morning, Ben," the waitress greeted, stopping at his side of the booth. She hip-bumped his arm. "When you going to take me dancin'?"

"Soon, Gertie, soon."

Okay, so he's a regular here, Grant thought.

"You a student, sweetie?" she asked.

"This is Grant," Walters said. "He a writer. We're going to be talking for a while."

"Okay. I'll keep the interruptions down to a minimum. You want a loaded cheeseburger and a chocolate shake?"

"Always," Walters said. He looked at Grant. "Gertie's burgers are top-notch. So's her shake."

"Sounds good," Grant said, feeling like he had dropped into Pleasantville, Ohio. When Gertie headed for the kitchen, he said, "Someone said you had a farm or ranch."

"Really?" Walters said, his eyes reading Grant's. "My duds lead you to that conclusion?"

"No, no. Someone said you—"

"How can I be honest with you if you're not honest with me?"

"What? No, I..." For the second time in six minutes, his face burned hot. "I just... Sorry. Yes, it was your Levi's."

"Thank you."

Grant nodded, feeling like a jerk that he'd blown his first impression. Then his sense of awkwardness doubled as Ben Walters seemed to be sizing him up.

"You said you had written a biography before?"

Grant nodded. "Yes, sir, some magazine pieces on people and one book titled *Surviving the Second Tower*. It's about a woman who survived the passenger plane into the second Twin Tower. Sensei had read it and a few of my magazine bios and approached me to write his. I think his story will make for a fascinating book."

"It would make for an outstanding book. But are you up to the task?"

"I am, yes."

"Got a publisher, an agent?"

Grant felt as if Walters was doing the interviewing. Maybe he was just an overprotective friend. No matter because he already had the writing job, but he had to put up with it because the guy knew Sensei in Vietnam.

Grant said, "I've become friends with one of the executive editors of one of the magazines that have published me. He likes my stuff and said if I ever decide to write a book, send it to him, and if he likes it, he'll put in a word for me with a man he knows. An agent."

Walters nodded. "Getting published is about knowing people, a lot of luck, and writing skill, in that order. Or not necessarily in that order. There is no clear path."

"Yes, sir," Grant said, wondering how he knew anything of the publishing world.

The bell over the door jingled, and two college-aged girls entered. Grant eyed them, and they eyed him. Then they saw Walters.

"Good afternoon, Professor," they sing-songed, nearly in unison.

"Big quiz tomorrow, ladies."

"We'll be ready," they said, a little more out of sync this time. The girls took seats at the counter.

Grant looked at him. "Not a farmer," he said with a half-smile.

"I'm a tenured professor at the U of O, have been for 31 years. Social science mostly, but I help with psychology when the school is desperate for an instructor."

"Holy shit," Grant said, his face reddening for the third time. "That's how you know about publishing."

"I've written thirty-two books, mostly texts, and a hundred or so articles." He smiled at the writer's reddening face. "Finish this line for me, Grant. 'You can't tell a book…"

"By its cover," Grant said, shaking his head with embarrassment. "Point made, and I'm an idiot."

"Nah, just clumsy. Sarge must have seen something in you, and I trust that."

"Thank you. And thanks for tolerating my clumsiness. You're my first interview for this book, and I'm a little nervous. Even more, now that I know you're a college professor."

Ben Walters chuckled. "You'll be a veteran writer after this project. Oh, and I like Levi's, always have. You ready to start?" Then in a slow drawl, "I gotta be up at the barn by sundown to milk ol' Bessie." He chuckled again. "You're a blusher, aren't you?"

They got their milkshakes first and a minute later their burgers. One sip and one bite, and Grant agreed that they were outstanding. He retrieved a recorder and a spiral notebook out of his backpack and set them on the table. He switched on the recorder, double-checked it was running, and centered it between them. "You called him 'Sarge.'"

The professor nodded. "As I said at the cemetery, everyone calls him Sensei now, but he was Sarge to the other guys and me, and I've called him that ever since."

"Could you give me a little bio on when you entered the Army, a little on your training, when you got to Vietnam, and when you met Sen, uh, Sarge?"

The twinkle that had been in the professor's eye since they sat down disappeared and his relaxed posture straightened a little. He took another bite of his burger, this time chewing more slowly. He looked out the window, but Grant didn't think he was looking at passersby.

He turned back, his eyes narrowed, hard. "I went to boot camp at Fort Lewis and did my advanced infantry training there too. Afterward, they sent me home for two weeks, then to Oakland for three days waiting for a flight to Alaska, then Japan, then to Bien Hoa, Vietnam. I spent the next three days filling sandbags, burning shit in 50-gallon barrels, watching choppers crisscrossing overhead, listening to far off artillery pound the earth, and reflecting on how I had been bagging groceries at Safeway five months earlier. I couldn't sleep a wink because of the constant noise, I was scared as hell, and it was so damn hot. I have a fishing buddy, a Nam vet, who says it was so hot in Vietnam that fishermen had to use potholders to pull worms out of the ground."

The professor pushed his half-eaten burger aside and looked out the window again. A good 30 seconds later, he looked back at Grant and seemed to jolt a little as if he had forgotten the writer was there. He picked up his shake. "Great milkshakes, huh?" He set it back down without taking a sip.

"The chopper ride out to the hill took twenty-five minutes, ten of which the door gunner sprayed hot death into the vegetation after two rounds from the ground smacked into the side of our bird about a foot from where he was sitting behind his sixty. He was spraying bullets; I was crappin' bricks."

The professor picked up his burger, then set it back down without taking a bite. Did he know he was toying with his food? Grant wondered. He made a notation in his notebook.

"But you want to know about Sarge, so let me jump to that.

"I had already been in camp about six months pulling missions when he arrived. Sarge was no FNG, fucking new guy in Army speak. He had been in the Nam for nine months with the Big Red

One. The three weeks before he came to my unit, he had been recuperating in Third Field Hospital in Saigon, having caught a bad infection after falling into a shallow hole and getting jabbed by shit-tipped punji sticks. I think he got sent to my unit instead of returning to his original one because we were down two NCOs after losing both on the same night about three weeks earlier. Before Sarge got assigned to us, e-fours were leading missions, not quite the blind leading the blind, but close.

"This probably sounds strange, but I've thought about it often. There was something about Sarge. He had that 'it' thing that movie directors say about some actors. The guys immediately liked him, and it was apparent that he would take care of us. The way he praised us, carried himself, finagled things we needed from supply, and talked to the captain about the most tactically safe way to carry out our missions. All this made us trust him, and this feeling intensified after our first few missions with him leading us."

"He had been with us almost two months when the incident happened. He had led us on six missions, all of them night details, and on each one, we made contact with Charlie. Charlie was another name for the VC. We never lost a man; we killed at least forty-four of them, though. Those were the ones we found. There were always signs others had been carried away. We were successful because Sarge knew what he was doing. And what we were doing was called 'attrition.' Our task was to chip away at the enemy's numbers, their strength. And we did a good job of it week after week.

"But what happened on that moonlit night in that clearing couldn't have been prevented, no matter how good Sarge was." The professor laughed, but there was no humor in it. "Well, it could have been prevented if we hadn't gone out. But that wasn't an option. It was all about finding the Vietcong and killing them."

THAT NIGHT

A squad is usually about ten guys, give or take. There were 13 of us that night. The captain gave us two FNGs to OJT on what he thought would be a low-key hike. And as was often the case, we didn't have a lieutenant, just Sarge leading us. The night was hot, moonlit, with a slight breeze. We had just crossed a massive rice paddy, which made me nervous because the moon was so bright. But we made it without incident, quickly climbed a muddy embankment, and took a knee at the edge of the jungle.

The next to last guy out of the paddy was an FNG. He stepped on a snake as he climbed the embankment and cried out when it chomped into his boot; it didn't penetrate to his foot, though. A guy to his rear punched him in the back and told him to shut the fuck up. The guy just took the punch without doing or saying anything. A couple of minutes later, the FNG turned just so in the moonlight, and I could see his cheeks were glistening with trailing tears.

The poor guy was scared shitless. I think he had already been crying when the snake freaked him out. The serpent was the cherry on the pudding, the pudding being his fear of the mission. At least he was smart enough to be afraid. Some FNGs were too stupid or too full of bravado.

I was always terrified anticipating these missions, and every second I was on them. But I got so I could function in my fear. Sarge never made any indication of being afraid, but he had to have been. He was always taking care of business: making sure everyone kept quiet, watching where we stepped, continuously checking our surroundings, and repositioning men when and where he deemed it necessary.

When we were all out of the rice paddy, he pointed at a narrow passageway, a path, that sliced through the jungle. The map showed a large clearing about a hundred yards into it and then a mile-deep of more jungle. Where that ended, there was a village we were supposed to search.

Paths were always a big question mark. They could be an efficient way to go because they were easier to traverse than hacking through vines and limbs on a 105-degree day. But they could also be high-risk because Charlie would sometimes arrange deadly surprises along the way for us to step on or trip over. Like a Bouncing Betty.

A Bouncing Betty was invented by a sicko in the nineteen-thirties and employed during World War Two. The hellish thing was buried underground, with three exposed prongs on the top covered over with vines. When a man stepped on the prongs, the mine would shoot up about three feet and detonate at groin level. Ball bearings inside blasted out and shredded groins and bladders. They were lethal for sixty-six feet but could affect profound casualties up to 460 feet.

We'd lost two sergeants and incurred three severe injuries in the last few weeks, so everyone walked like we were treading on thin ice, which we were.

"Walk the path or chop through?" Sarge asked with a half-smile, already knowing our answer. Everyone said 'path' without hesitation. We were exhausted, having humped for over twelve hours already, and we needed a break. "You're sure?" he asked with a grin.

He got a dozen "Damn straight we are," and one "FTA." The latter meant Fuck the Army, a common saying by the guys who got drafted.

As usual, Sarge took the point, and we followed him in. We had gone only 50 feet or so when I started feeling anxious for no specific reason I could detect. Reason or no reason, getting the feeling was important. When you had been in the Nam for a while and started feeling something—sensing something—you paid attention to it. Thinking back on that moment later, I don't remember there being any jungle sounds, and there were always jungle sounds, a mad racket of insects, birds, creepy-crawlies, ghosts, everything.

It was very dark too. The jungle canopy blocked the moonlight, so I was getting smacked in the face by thick vines I couldn't see, spider webs cloaked me, and everyone was tripping over roots. Every step we took, we'd wonder if this one, this damn one, was a Bouncing Betty.

It might have been a path, but it was a shitty one. And that feeling of anticipation I had was getting stronger.

A few minutes later, I could see moonlight again up ahead; it was the clearing. Sarge stopped at the entrance. Sometimes we moved across clearings; other times, we moved stealthily around them.

But before he could tell us how to proceed, a heart-stopping burst from multiple AK-47s ripped through the quiet.

I couldn't tell from what direction they were coming, but Sarge shouted, "Behind us! Get down!" Like a well-oiled machine, three guys took prone positions facing our right flank, three to the left, three to the front, and the rest, including me, dropped and began laying down fire toward our rear. That is, except for the FNG who got his boot snake bit. He stood frozen in place with eyes as big as coffee saucers until someone yanked him down onto his belly.

"Mortarman!" Sarge shouted, competing with the racket, "drop some."

Another burst of AKs ripped the vegetation from my right, and a heartbeat later, rounds came at us from my left. I heard a man scream, then another. We were hugging the jungle floor, but guys were still getting shot, lots of them crying out, "I'm hit! I'm hit!" I knew some poor bastards were already dead.

An explosion to my left was so loud it nearly stopped my heart, and dirt and pieces of tree bark struck the side of my face. It hurt like hell, but I kept firing toward our rear. I wasn't that tough; I was just on autopilot.

Then came another explosion from our right, this one so close it flipped the mortarman over onto his back and sent his tube flipping end over end into the air. When he tried to sit up, I could see at least a dozen bloody wounds on his face. I pushed him back down onto his back. "Stay down," I shouted. "You're just nicked." I jabbed my finger at his M-16. "Lay down fire to your right."

I was at the rear of our squad. Sarge was on his belly at the front of the clearing edge, trying to pull our radioman behind a big mound of dirt as rounds smacked into the poor guy's body and radio.

There were about ten other men between Sarge and me. The only ones still in the fight were laying down fire to our left and right flanks.

I spotted the radio half-buried about six feet away at my 10 o'clock. An explosion must have sent it flying back where I was. I began crawling toward it.

Another explosion showered me in jungle debris and stabbed something into my right hip, knocking me up onto my side. I didn't think it was a bullet, maybe tree bark. I'd learn later that it was a shard of bone but not mine. The doc said it was from an animal, and it looked old.

I didn't think things could get worse.

Then it did.

AKs opened up from every direction. How they avoided crossfire, I still don't know. Then explosions, grenades, mortars, the whole kitchen sink. We were in a shit storm of dirt, stones, tree branches, vines, shrapnel, and 7.62 rounds. Debris was hitting me on both sides, and all I could do was claw at the jungle floor to try to get below the surface. My hearing kept fluctuating from off to partially on.

A bullet slammed into my left shoulder, knocking me partway over. It was like getting hit by a car that was on fire. I forced myself back onto my belly only to get shot again, this time on my opposite side, my upper leg.

There were two layers to the infernal cacophony: on top, automatic gunfire, explosions, zings, thumps. Underneath, godawful screams. Mine included. It was Hell epitomized, and I knew it was my last moment alive. Then everything went black...

...I awoke.

On my back. I must have been unconscious.

My ears hurt, and so did my head, shoulder, and leg. I was so nauseous. I wished I could vomit, but I couldn't.

The last thing I remembered was gunfire, lots of it, an orgy of explosions and screams and pain.

How long had I been out? One minute, five, an hour? Dirt covered most of my face, leaving only my left eye exposed. A weight on my chest and abdomen pinned and pressed me into the earth. With the dirt in my mouth and the profound weightiness pressing down on me, I could barely breathe.

As disoriented as I was, I sensed that I should be quiet and not move. But I had to get that dirt off my right eye and nose and out of my mouth. Thank God it wasn't the rainy season, so it wasn't mud, just earth rot, animal shit, dead insects, and snakeskin.

I turned my head to the right a little, and the dirt fell away from my eye and nostrils. I pushed out the jungle filth in my mouth with my tongue, most of it, anyway. Still sensing that I shouldn't move, I chewed and swallowed the rest.

The weight on my chest was pushing me toward claustrophobic panic. Again, something told me to stay still, but I needed to see whatever it was on me. I slowly turned my head until I was face up. The particles of dirt still in my eye were making it tear so that everything appeared as if underwater. I forced myself not to blink so it would flood with more tears. I held it as long as I could, then closed my eye and opened it again, once, twice, three times. Better.

It was our medic, Stiles, the biggest guy in our squad, lying perpendicular across my upper torso, his chest on mine, his brains splashed across the ground. His legs were stretched out on the other side of me out of my line of sight.

My external focus that had been on Stiles switched abruptly to internal, to all my wounds, big and small. Some felt like bee stings, big bees; others were like red-hot coals searing into my flesh.

My mind went back to external, to Stiles' 225 pounds that had me sucking for air like a beached fish. We teased him about how everyone else in the platoon was skin and bones from the heat, lack of sleep, dysentery, and crappy food, but he had actually gained weight since he had been in the unit. He was a big man to begin with, but somehow, he gained.

My mind switched to internal. I felt as if I were in a suffocating tunnel, the weighty ceiling pushing down on me, down, down. I wanted to scream.

Back to external. The silence was strange, eerie. Heavy. Was no one else alive? Was the entire squad dead except for—

I heard breathing on my left side. Had it been there all along? It had to have been. Was it a VC? I had to look.

I slowly turned my head to the left. Sarge.

His head was about 15 inches away from mine. Before I blacked out, we had been about 25 feet apart, me still in the bush, Sarge at the edge of the clearing dragging the wounded radioman.

His eyes were closed, and a trickle of blood oozed from the one ear I could see. Was he dead?

Sarge was lying on his belly, the side of his face in the dirt. Someone's leg draped across his lower back, the man's upper body on the ground, his head twisted around way farther than it should go. It was that FNG who had freaked over the snake. There was an unattached leg lying on the other side of the man's head. It was wearing a boot, and I could see two small holes near its top: the snake bite.

There was another man, Carlson, I think, the top of his head nearly touching the FNG's twisted one. He was curled into the fetal position, and his chest rose and fell rapidly.

Sarge's eyes fluttered open and looked into mine, startling the hell out of me. I thought he was gone. I instantly felt elated and comforted that he was not only alive but next to me too. He would take care of things; Sarge always did.

"You hit, Sarge?" I asked.

"Yeah," he said quietly. My hearing had mostly returned, maybe seventy-five percent. But I was so close I could read his lips.

His eyes moved from mine to something beyond me. They widened. Why? What was he seeing?

"Sarge, what—"

His eyes returned to mine. "Don't move." Then he whispered one word at a time. "Don't. Move. Don't. Speak." His eyes looked beyond me again.

Then I heard them.

Voices.

Vietnamese.

Behind me.

Someone moaned. It came from the other side of Sarge. Sarge's eyes warned me not to move. A voice behind me called out for a medic, then screamed it. "Medic! I need a—"

Shook, shook. The sound, whatever it was: wet.

Silence.

The jungle was still as if all the animals, birds, and insects held their collective breath.

"Wait!"

A different voice, also behind me, desperate, pleading.

"Wait wait WAIT—" *Shook, shook.* That sound again.

Silence.

Sarge was lying dead still, his wet eyes intensely focused on whatever was going on behind me.

Shook, shook.

The muscles around his mouth twitched. A single tear erupted from his eye farthest away from the ground, clung to his lashes for a moment, then dropped into the dust.

The voices were closer now, at least three different ones. One of them laughing.

My claustrophobia was testing the limits of my sanity. Stiles' weight on me had doubled, tripled. I had to struggle for each breath, and when I got it, half of it was dust because the side of my face was on the ground. I wanted to cough; I wanted to buck Stiles off me; I desperately needed space to move; I wanted a full breath even if it was thick with the stench of jungle rot, cordite, blood, feces, and Stiles.

If what was going on behind me was what I thought was happening, I had to get up. I *had* to get up!

A burst of laughter.

Sarge's eyes—those wet, sad, enlarged eyes—penetrated my brain. When the voices laughed again, he took advantage of the moment. "Don't move," he uttered, barely moving his mouth. "They're bayonetting everyone… To make sure we're all dead."

I don't know what my eyes communicated, but he added, "You gotta eat the pain. Don't react. Eat it."

Shook, shook.

It was the sound of a bayonet plunging into a body then extracting.

Oh my God, oh my God, oh my God—

Laughter, followed by high-pitched Vietnamese chatter, and more laughter.

Then, as if God wanted to show His sense of dark humor—ants.

Emerging from the trunk of an uprooted tree less than ten feet away and heading my way, a perfectly straight row of a thousand ants, heads bumping butts, moving fast, jerky.

About six inches from my face, they made a 90-degree left turn and headed toward Sarge. But a stream of them continued my way to skitter over my lips, into my nostrils, and across my closed eyes. A moment later, they trailed down my neck, under my shirt, and over my chest and belly.

A college entomology teacher once referred to ants as "foolishly insignificant." But I'm guessing he never laid on a jungle floor and had the son-of-a-bitches crawl all over him, *in* him, seeking, tickling, their bites like stabs from a pin.

Behind me: "Please please noooo—" *Shook, shook.*

It was the private we called "Squeaky." Not much taller than five feet, tough as nails, funny, high-pitched voice. He was due to go home in two weeks.

The ants moved off my right eye. I opened it slowly. Sarge was still lying motionless, his eyes looking at me, his face covered with a horde of those Goddamn ants.

He must have seen something in my face—hopelessness?—because he said, *"Look at me."*

Strange. Sarge's mouth didn't move.

I swear to God, his mouth wasn't moving, but I could hear his soft, gentle voice. *"Close your eye partway and keep looking at me."*

I did as he said.

"Don't move." Ants skittered all over his unmoving lips, disappearing between them. *"We're next. Close your eyes. You can take it. Eat the pain."*

A foot—filthy, calloused, inside a black sandal made from a chunk of tire—set down in front of my face.

Shook. Stiles' dead body jerked on top of me. *Shook.* Again, when the blade was pulled free.

Jesus Jesus Jesus, I screamed in my mind. Then Sarge's gentle whispered voice filled my head. *"Don't move. You can take it. You can take it."*

"Fuck this!" It was Carlson's voice, the man lying in a fetal position close to Sarge. I heard him rolling over, I think that was the sound. I strained my partially open eye to see to my left without moving my head until enough of him came into my field of vision to see he was raising his M-16 toward the man standing above me. I closed my eye and screamed in my mind.

An AK-47 ripped loose above me, and another off to my side.

I heard Carlson's boots shuffle in the dirt and his body thump heavily to the ground.

Laughter again.

The sandaled foot by my face disappeared. I waited for the blade.

Nothing.

Nothing.

Nothing.

I opened my eye a crack and saw a bayonet on the end of an AK plunge into Sarge's back, *Shook.* Yanked out, *Shook.*

He didn't move. He didn't react.

I closed my eye and waited for the steel.

<0>

Grant had been sitting with his hands clasped on the table, his body leaning toward Ben Walters. The professor sat ramrod straight during his story, heels of his palms against the edge of the table as if he were about to push away. From the memory? Although the booth behind him was empty, as was the one behind Grant, the professor's volume had started low and got even lower as he progressed. Before his story concluded, Grant had to lean toward him to hear.

The writer had only read sterile stuff about Vietnam, its history, and opinion pieces about the politics and protests. He had seen a few war movies, most of which he thought were just Hollywood trying to entertain. He assumed the professor's story would be something like how Sensei had pushed Walters into a foxhole just before a bomb exploded.

But *this*… Holy shit.

"Could I get a cup of coffee?" Grant managed as Gertie passed their table. "Professor?" Walters looked at Grant, his face blank. "Coffee, sir?"

"You okay, hon?" Gertie asked motherly, patting his shoulder. "You're as pale as a ghost."

He blinked for a moment, then, "Coffee? Oh, uh, no. A glass of milk, please. And could I trouble you to warm it a little?"

"Of course, hon." She turned to go, but not before shooting Grant an accusatory glare as if he had done something to upset her friend.

He gave the professor a moment after Gertie left, then asked in a quiet voice, "Were you stabbed?"

Walters shook his head. "The VC, the one straddling me, stabbed Stiles the dead man on top of me. But I think when Carlson jumped up, the VC got distracted killing him and forgot he hadn't stabbed me yet. The man lost his place, if you will." He shook his head. "They were so thorough stabbing the dead, but they didn't do me."

"Was the guy over you the same one who stabbed Sensei?"

The professor shrugged. "I didn't dare look that high. I did see two of the VC, the lower halves of their bodies, stab Carlson even though they had just shot about a dozen times into the poor man's face. One VC had a fixed bayonet on his weapon, and the other had a knife in his hand. I can't be sure, but the knife looked like an American K-bar. The one with the fixed bayonet had a bloody knee and was limping badly.

"There is no doubt in my mind that they would have killed me if it hadn't been for Sarge. I would have cracked like Carlson and jumped up and tried to run. And the VC would have shot me on the spot like they did him."

"But you didn't. Your bravery came through and—"

"I wasn't brave, Grant. I was beyond terrified, scared out of mind. But it was Sarge's eyes, his calmness, his talking to my mind with his mind."

"Did you ever talk to him about that? About how he telepathically, if that's what it was, talked to you?"

"Yes. Sarge said I was crazy, imagining things. 'I whispered to you,' he told me. But I'll go to my deathbed convinced his ant-filled mouth didn't move, and I was hearing him in my head, not in my ears."

"It's all so incredible," Grant said, shaking his head. "How do you think Sarge was so courageous?"

"I asked him once about it. He said, 'Oh, I was damn afraid, Ben. I was afraid every day I was over there. But I was the only one who knew it. I was the only one who knew when we got back from those missions that I'd curl up in a ball in my hooch and shake like a Chihuahua. I was the only one who knew that sometimes before we went out on a mission, I'd spew my chow on the ground.'"

Ben looked out the window while the waitress set the coffee and milk on the table.

When she left, Grant asked, "How did it all end?"

"Charlie took a chow break when they finished the bayonetting and knifing. Well, they thought they were finished, but Sarge and I were still breathing. So we remained motionless while they ate in the clearing and laughed it up. One time, I opened my eye closest to the ground, and I saw Sarge doing the same thing. He had Carlson's blood all over his face, and the ants, a huge mass of them, were having a feast. But Sarge didn't move, and his one eye was looking at me, still encouraging me to eat the agony."

The professor raised his glass, his hand shaking, slopping the milk. He set it back on the table. "His agony had to have been ten times worse than mine." The professor clasped his trembling hands and squeezed them until they stilled.

"Charlie had booze too. They got drunk and fired some rounds, and I heard the bullets' distinctive thump hitting the already dead bodies. But they didn't shoot Sarge or me." He shook his head. "I just about lost it again, but Sarge's goddamn eye…it…calmed me. I know that sounds preposterous, but it did.

"An hour later or so, the VC left. Some wore bandages, their heads and arms. The one I saw with a bloody knee now had it wrapped up, and he was limping badly. He was walking with a stick for support.

"About an hour after that, maybe two, time in which we didn't move a muscle just in case there were VC around, a chopper found us and landed in the clearing. They got Sarge and me out first, and a couple of other birds retrieved the dead.

"Sarge and I went to the same hospital. I got fixed up and sent home three weeks later. They thought the round that hit my upper leg might not heal properly. They were right; I have a little limp from it when it's cold. The VC shot Sarge three times. The round that hit his hip made him limp for a year after he got out. He eventually had two more surgeries stateside and was good as new.

The bayonet through his back just missed a lung. He never had any lasting effects from it, physically, anyway.

"We had never talked about our homes before that night, so while we were in the hospital, we learned we were both from Oregon, me Lincoln City, and him, Portland. I later settled in Eugene, and he stayed in Portland. That's how we were able to hold onto our friendship all these years."

"What happened after you got home?"

"As I said, I got home first. He went to Walter Reed Army Medical Center in D. C. for a month before he got out of the Army. We met up about a couple of months after. He agreed to debrief with me, but only if I stopped thanking him." The professor chuckled at that. "I slipped a couple of times, and he let me know he didn't like it.

"I went back to U of Oregon working on my masters, and he got a job...uh, I can't remember what it was. Carpentry, I think. Anyway, he called me about six months later. I could tell immediately by his words and tone that he was unsettled, and he said later that he could tell I was too. We just weren't ready to relax yet; we had to get out of Dodge. Fortunately, he had a Vietnam veteran boss who understood and gave him leave from his job, and I took the winter term off."

Grant waited for a different waitress to refill our cups, then asked, "What did you do?"

"Neither one of us had a car, so we bussed it, and when there wasn't one available, we hitched or jumped boxcars." He chuckled. "Everyone was doing it then. It was nineteen seventy, but there was some of the tumultuous nineteen sixties' shit still happening, and Vietnam was still raging as if what we went through didn't count for anything. Some of the free love movement was going on too. So Sarge and I took off for eight weeks, hitting big cities and hick towns from Oregon to the Florida Keys. We drank, we got laid, and we got into a couple of fights with some good ol' boys down South.

"It cleared our heads some, and we began to believe we had left Vietnam behind us—put quotes around 'to believe' and bold it—but we were naïve. Our nightmares would come back and stay with us over the decades to come.

"Anyway, we reluctantly came back to Oregon. Sarge resumed his job and got back into his beloved martial arts. I went on to earn a doctorate."

The professor plopped back against his seat back and exhaled some stress and fatigue.

"This has been an amazing story, professor," Grant said, jotting on his pad. "It paints a picture of the man that I'm guessing few people knew. And it paints a vivid picture of what you guys went through over there and your efforts to fit back into society here."

The professor nodded and sipped his milk. "There wasn't a welcoming committee, but at least we came home, albeit to a mostly ungrateful country. Eventually, though, we were gifted with productive lives and people we love and who love us. Fifty-eight thousand guys didn't get any of that."

"For what it's worth, you have my thanks."

The professor nodded his head almost imperceptibly.

"You said you two got into a couple of fights on your cross-country trip. Many of the readers of this book will want to hear about that. Did you know he had studied karate before he went into the Army? Oh, how about in your unit in Vietnam? Did you see him do anything? Get into fights, I mean."

PRISONERS

It was around the third week that Sarge had been with us, and after a particularly hairy mission, the captain gave us three days of downtime. Most of the guys were either chugging cans of Budweiser all day, or smoking joints, or doing both. Sarge never participated in that. He read or just sat on some sandbags by himself and stared off into space. We had seen some heavy action in the weeks he'd been with us, but the scuttlebutt was Sarge had been in even worse in his previous unit. Maybe that was why he preferred to spend time by himself. One day, I got stuck helping clean artillery, and I heard this rhythmic thumping coming from somewhere. I had never heard it before, so this other guy and I grabbed our M-16s and went to check it out.

Long story short, we found Sarge behind the chow tent kicking a truck tire. He had hung it about five feet off the ground from a pole and was slamming it with his shin. He was really fast, despite wearing combat boots with steel-plates in the soles. He was punching it too, more quickly than any boxer I'd seen.

The martial arts weren't all over the place like they are now, so I didn't know anything about them. Sarge told me he had trained for four years and had earned a black belt before the Army got him. They stationed him in a couple of places stateside where he received instruction in a different karate style from what he practiced at home. He said he had earned a black belt in that one and was training for his second degree when he got orders for Nam.

He tried to teach me a little, but it was like trying to teach a pig to dance. I remember liking how he was so humble about what he could do. For example, I had to squeeze out of him the fact that he had two black belts.

I heard when he was with his last unit, he beat a VC to death. Apparently, Sarge had been out on the perimeter checking listening posts when a VC charged toward him as he was talking to a guy in a foxhole. Charlie was trying to shoot them, but his weapon jammed. The guy jumped into the hole with them and got one good butt stroke into the PFC's face and was going for another when Sarge went all Bruce Lee on him. Sarge didn't want to use his weapon because it would have drawn fire from the rest of the VC out on the perimeter. The rumor was Sarge killed the man with a heart punch and a second blow to the front of his throat. You hear many exaggerated stories in the Army, but three transfers from his old unit all told the same version.

Sarge only used his stuff one time in the weeks he was in our unit, and I saw him do it.

I think it was the mission before we got wounded. We captured seven VC that night. We killed eleven, but we caught seven. I know some units would have wasted the seven, but Sarge would never have allowed that.

Back at the compound, the prisoners were laid out side-by-side on the ground with our fat cook and one FNG guarding them. The cook was being punished for something if I remember correctly. It was crap duty and too important for a scared shitless FNG and a worthless pissed off cook.

I was about 20 yards away, sitting on a pile of sandbags shooting the bull with the lieutenant. The prisoners had been baking in the sun without water for a couple of hours waiting for a truck to pick them up when a little guy on one end, skin and bones and wearing only shorts and sandals, started making like he was going to get up. The other prisoners stayed still, including a big prisoner on the opposite end. That one was as big as Sarge, a rarity for Vietnamese.

The fat cook started yelling at the smaller guy to settle down, but the prisoner kept scooting up on his knees, lying back down, and scooting up on his knees again. The cook and the FNG rushed over to him, the cook pointing his forty-five at the prisoner, and the scared FNG pointing his shaking M-16. Then the FNG, who was only eighteen years old but looked fifteen, accidentally yanked his trembling trigger finger and fired a full-auto burst into the prisoner as he was lying back down. The prisoner was doing as he was told when he was shot.

The other prisoners began yelling and pushing themselves away from their dead buddy. All of them looked as if they were about to run for it—I mean, who could blame them?—but only the big guy stood up. The lieutenant and I were running hard over there, just as Sarge, who had just showered, came around a big stack of barrels, wearing only his fatigue pants, a towel draped around his neck, and a pair of flip-flops. He was between the FNG, who was standing like a deer caught in headlights, his trembling finger still in the trigger guard, and the big prisoner. The VC must have been so focused on the FNG that he didn't notice Sarge because he took off running and screaming across the space between them and ripped the M-16 by its barrel from the stunned kid's hands.

But he only had possession for a second, not even enough time to turn it around to position it right because Sarge was suddenly right next to him. I didn't know the martial arts then, but someone told me he did a roundhouse kick with his barefoot. It was so fast; I don't see how even an experienced person would know what kind of kick it was. He kicked the man above his privates, right into his bladder.

I learned two things from Sarge later. Kicking the bladder compresses it and shocks all the sensitive nerves. The person kicked might involuntarily urinate, defecate, or throw up. Big Charlie did all three as he flip-flopped around on the ground. He was wearing shorts, so it was pretty messy.

What made Sarge's kick extra traumatic was that he was born with abnormally short toes on his right foot. The defect almost kept him from getting into the Army, but he got a signed doctor's statement that said he was fine to join up. Other guys were trying to get out of the service with made-up disabilities, but Sarge wanted in with his.

Sometimes, he kicked the big truck tire while wearing his heavy boots for added resistance, hitting it with his shins. But other times, he took advantage of his defect and strengthened his little toes by kicking the tire all-out with the tips of his stubs. Imagine the damage he did on the prisoner's bladder that day.

In the end, the kick saved the day and made Sarge even more of an icon than he already was. The FNG left on the next chopper to Saigon, never to be heard from again. I'm sure he got punished for the command's decision to have him pull prisoner duty that day.

‹0›

Grant paid for the lunch, and they crossed the street to a small park. The sky had cleared since they had been inside, and a warm spring sun made for a pleasant stroll.

"I did notice his toes," Grant said. "Just on one foot."

"His right one," the professor said.

Grant nodded. "Did he get a medal for disarming the VC?"

"Nope. He should have, but medals in the Army were quite inconsistent, at least in the Vietnam War. In fact, I talked to our colonel when I was in the hospital about getting one for Sarge for saving my life, but it never went anywhere. The brass got medals for sneezing and yelling at PFCs, but it was harder for those men actually in the fire. Not to mention that Sarge was a pain because he was always sticking up for his men, getting them out of trouble, asking for better equipment, the kind of things a good sergeant does."

Grant and the professor walked onto a small wooden bridge that crossed a narrow, rock-littered creek. Grant said, "You said there was one other time you saw him in action."

The professor stopped in the middle of the bridge and leaned on the railing, watching the water pass beneath them. "Yes, but not in Vietnam. As I said, he was only in my unit for a few weeks before we were both wounded and medevacked out."

"Where did the other one happen?"

"Idaho, of all places. On a train, in a boxcar."

THE BOXCAR

Sarge and I had been on the road for three months. Two months would have been enough, which we initially planned, but we met up with some people in Iowa who invited us to stay in a commune near the Big Sioux River. Communes were all the rage then—anti-establishment, vegetarianism, free love, weed, and all that. We both fell for a couple of lovely hippie girls, killer smiles, carefree, with hairy legs and armpits. We even committed to living with them permanently; that's how crazy we were at the time. All was well until one night, about 20 days into the experience, I happened to slur, after my third joint laced with some other drug, that we had both served with the infantry in Vietnam.

The love and peace crowd turned on us in a millisecond, including the girls who had proclaimed one moon-lit night that the four of us were soulmates. We barely escaped from the commune with our few belongings before they would have hung from a tree branch in the name of peace and love.

The problem was that under the influence of lust and dope, we had given all of our money to the commune guru, leaving us without anything, to include bus fare back to Oregon. The only option was to hitchhike to the West Coast. But after extending our thumbs for two days in the rain without getting a single ride, we decided to do as others in the Age of Aquarius were doing, which was to hop trains.

We were quick to find out that hobos—that's what they called the homeless rail riders back then—didn't like long-haired hippy freaks. We were anything but hippies, but we hadn't had a haircut in three months. By the time we reached the Idaho border, we had had a few run-ins with hobos, mostly shoving matches and threats with sticks. They all ended without violence, but the fact they happened at all put us on edge.

We learned that we only had to monitor those riders directly in front of us when we nested at one end of a boxcar, instead of two ends when we sat in the middle. I would sleep for a couple of hours, and then Sarge would pull guard duty. Then he'd sleep, and I'd monitor the glaring hobos. If we jumped into a boxcar and found both ends already occupied, we'd sit in the middle, each of us watching an end. Then the next time the train stopped, we'd hop out and find a safer boxcar.

There weren't snakes and ants in the cars as there were in the jungle, but there were rats. I'm not talking about hobos, but the four-legged critter, sometimes dozens if the boxcar had previously been hauling something like potatoes.

Our system kept us safe until the night we were nearing Boise. Then things got messy in a hurry.

We had spent most of the day in a boxcar with four other men, old-timers who needed help getting into the boxcar. We sat against the front end of the car; the other four sat against the wall across from the door. They were an amiable group, sharing stories and laughs from the road and rails. After the sun went down, everyone but me fell asleep, though Sarge was only resting his eyes if I had to guess. Around 8 p.m., the train slowed to a crawl as it climbed a long, steep grade.

"It stops for a bit, Ben," one of the old-timers named Ed said in a low voice so as not to awaken the others. The man had tilted the brim of his hat down to cover his eyes when everyone went to sleep, and he didn't lift it to speak. Somehow, he knew I was awake. Ed said, "We call it 'First Jump,' since it's the first place you can jump off or on. It only stops for about three minutes, give or take. Don't know why. Then, about forty-five minutes after that, it'll stop again at 'Second Jump'. Sometimes we pick up other riders on one or both stops. I guess that's where it gets its name."

Sarge and I were looking forward to getting to Boise. It would be the last big stop before Portland. The final leg was 344 miles, 52 hours by train, not counting unplanned stops. We were tired, hungry for quality food, and my bullet wound had been bothering me. I could tell Sarge's hip was bothering him. The cold and the rain did it then; it still does now. Sarge didn't say anything, but he had been limping more than usual. I complained enough for both of us, though.

The train stopped with a series of bumps, clanks, and groans, the noise and erratic movement waking up the other three men. Sarge remained sitting motionless, eyes closed, but I knew he was awake. Ed and another man stood, walked stiff-legged over to the open door, and pissed out the opening. Ed held onto the door frame and leaned out, looking toward the back of the train.

He turned about and headed back to his pals. "Two no-goodniks and a big-ass mutt headin' this way."

"Slide the damn door shut," one of them said.

"Good idea," Ed said, turning back to the opening. "Glad I thought of it." He and his pissing companion tugged on the large sliding door, but it didn't move. When I jumped up and added my muscle, the door moved a little and then a lot. It had less than six feet to go when a voice from outside growled. "Hold that goddamn door!"

"Keep pushing," Ed said in a loud whisper. "I've seen these two rascals before. The Devil's spawn, they are."

The door had three feet to go when a pair of hands appeared from around the door frame, lifting a light tan colored hunk of muscle on four legs into the opening. "Watch 'em, Baby," the same voice growled.

At least 90 pounds of muscle, the dog landed on its four feet looking like a low coffee table made of thick, heavy knotted oak. Its head was a cement block, and its impossibly narrow eyes quickly scanned the three of us by the door. Then it looked over at Sarge sitting by the back wall of the boxcar—my partner's eyes were still closed—then over to the other two men sitting a few feet away looking nervous.

The animal's single bark sounded like an M-80 exploding inside of an enormous kettle drum. There was no reason for it to bark other than maybe to set the tone, which it did.

The remaining two men sitting next to the wall got up as fast as two old men could; Sarge remained seated, his eyes finally opened. "Ben," he said softly. "Back over here, slowly." To the other men, he said, "That's a Pitbull. Act subservient, don't stare into its eyes. Ben, my hip stiffened up on me. Help me up, please."

He was standing by the time the first man pushed the sliding door open wider, then tossed in his backpack. He climbed in, caught his buddy's pack, and helped him inside. They were rough-looking men, unwashed, late 30s, thick builds, bearded, both with long, unwashed hair. The bigger of the two wore a green, tattered Army field jacket.

The boxcar groaned, the train jerked, and we began moving again. The two men moved to the center of the room, eyeing the older men, then Sarge and me. "You two vets?" the bigger man demanded.

I nodded; Sarge looked back at them. The smaller man, who wasn't that small, just smaller than the one wearing the Army top, snickered at Sarge. "He must be shell shocked or sometin.'"

"That right, man?" the bigger one asked, his mouth wanting to smile. He wiggled his fingers on each side of his head. "You all mental now?" The smaller one giggled again.

The bigger man's eyes stayed on Sarge for a moment, then hardened.

The Pitbull was still standing motionless, its eyes looking at Sarge and me, over to where the old timers were, then back at us. The dog was doing its duty like a hardcore grunt and scaring the hell out of me while doing it.

"Here's how this is going to play out, gents," the big man said. He pointed at the Pit without taking his eyes away from us "This here is our third partner. Name's 'Baby.' He's got two confirmed, and he's more than happy to add to his body count."

He paused to let that sink in. His mouth was smiling like a bully tends to do when he thinks people are scared of him. But his eyes were cold, real cold. "Baby is gonna make sure we get all your valuables without argument." He held up his palm and faked another smile. "I know, I know. If you all had valuables, you wouldn't be ridin' in a boxcar. We get it. But give us what you have. And I promise we'll leave you when we stop at Second Jump, in about..." he looked at his watch. "Thirty-five minutes." He looked at Sarge and me. "Roger that, troops?" he asked without humor.

Neither of us responded.

The big man's scanned Sarge's stance. "You a crip? Stop one over there in the Nam with your leg, did yuh? Well, that's the way the ball bounces, asshole." He sighed. "If it helps, think of me as Uncle Sam. First, I don't care what happened to you, and second, you still gotta pay your taxes. So show us your bags and pockets."

The train was descending now, moving fast, the clatter of the wheels loud, the boxcar rocking hard enough to make all of us shuffle about to keep our balance. Ed, his body rigid, his demeanor angry, glared at the smaller thug.

"You got somethin' to say, you old fart?" the smaller man said, apparently taking the old man's glare as a challenge.

"Yes, sir," Ed said flatly. He nodded toward us. "These two fellas are good men who served in Vietnam. I was at Frozen Chosin in Korea seventeen years ago. Career man, sergeant first class. I killed a bunch and got shot up good too. I ain't had it easy since, but I ain't never took nothing that wasn't mine. You—"

"Sit the hell down!" the small man blared with annoyance. The dog turned its great head, its narrow eyes boring into Ed.

"Not going to do it, son. I'm tired, and I just ain't going to bow to a piece of work like you two."

The big man laughed as if this was a good time for him. But the smaller man's temper flared, and he lifted his heavy coat to expose a brown-handled hunting knife.

"Gonna cut your nuts off, hero," the smaller man said, extracting the knife. He moved toward Ed.

Later, even Sarge admitted he didn't see Ed pull his .38 caliber, Smith and Wesson. But in one smooth motion, he raised the gun and sent a round through the punk's forehead, an inch above his left eye. The man crumpled dead on the floor of the boxcar without a whimper or a dying muscle twitch.

Even with his bum hip, Sarge moved quickly toward the big man, hooked the crook of his bent arm around his neck, and twisted him in a half-circle, dumping him hard onto his back. The move went smoothly because the man had been staring in disbelief at his dead partner. But the shock of thumping onto the boxcar floor snapped him out of it. "Baby! Get him!"

Through the gunshot and the takedown, the Pit had sat unflinchingly, waiting for his orders. Now the mass of muscle sprang at Sarge before its master had finished his three-word command.

Sarge was already bent at roughly 90 degrees from slamming the man down to the floor. So when the killer dog leaped, the veteran just dropped and rolled in the direction from which the dog sprang. Baby passed over him, landed gracefully on his feet for such a thickly built dog, spun, and jumped again.

Still on the floor, Sarge again rolled in the direction of the animal's launch. But Baby learned from his first lesson and didn't leap as high or as far. When its salivating, dagger-filled mouth lowered to chomp my friend, Sarge executed three compound moves in quick succession—one of them quite innovative—that surprised the dog and me too.

The first move was a forearm slam into the beast's throat as it was about to land on Sarge's chest. The second, and almost simultaneous with the first, my friend grabbed the animal's penis in a vice-like grip. Third, and executed so smoothly and effortlessly it was as if he had rehearsed it, Sarge used his forearm slam, the penis/handle, and the dog's momentum to hurtle Baby out the boxcar door.

We must have been moving about 40 miles per hour at that point, so the Pit's yelp when his body hit the hard ground was only faintly audible inside the car.

The dog's master was practically frothing as he scrambled to his feet. I punched him in the head, but it slowed him only long enough for Sarge to stand, favoring his leg even more than before.

"Lower your weapon," Sarge growled at Ed before turning to look at the big man. "Your buddy and your dog are gone. So quit while you're behind. It's over. Sit down over there against the—"

The big man leaped at him.

Sarge quickly sidestepped, buckling his bum leg. Instead of fighting the sudden void in his base of support, he rode it down to the floor, landing on his knee just as the big man was in mid-punch.

Before the attacker could adjust to his target's new position, Sarge drove right and left hook punches into each side of the man's closest leg. Hooks were one of his most potent punches, and he sunk them deep into what he told me later was the peroneal nerve on the outside of the leg and the femoral nerve on the inside.

To add to the bully's chagrin, Sarge didn't extract his inside leg punch, but instead, he snapped his fist straight up into the man's crotch. The accumulation of hits dropped the thug down onto the knee of his incapacitated leg.

If someone had entered the boxcar at this point and saw the two men, each down on one knee facing each other, they might have wondered if they had interrupted a prayer ritual.

Sarge awkwardly climbed to his feet and backed up just out of range of the big man's reach. "Scoot yourself over and rest your back against the wall." The big man obeyed this time, pushing with his good leg and holding his injured groin with one hand. "Thank you," Sarge said. "Now stay put until we get to the next stop."

"In twenty minutes," Ed said, still standing, his gun down at his side. "We can hold him 'til the cops get here."

"You killed my friend," the big man said, glaring at Ed, his voice whiny as a child's. "And you killed Baby," he said to Sarge.

Sarge didn't reply, but I did. "You and your friend made bad choices. No doubt you've done it dozens of times; this time, it didn't work out for you."

The big man's face had turned two shades darker in the short time he had been sitting there, and his hands were fisting, relaxing, and fisting again. He was no longer looking at Sarge but instead staring hard at his friend who lay a half dozen feet away, his head in a halo of expanding blood.

"Remain sitting," Sarge said, his eyes taking in all the signals of a man about to explode. "It's over. Remain—"

The big man laboriously stood.

"Let me shoot him," Ed said, raising his pistol.

The big man looked at Ed, then back at Sarge.

"Ed, lower your gun!" Sarge growled in the same voice he used to command combat troops.

I moved past my friend to face the big man, though I knew he was out of my league physically. Sarge cupped my shoulder. "Ben," he said almost gently, "make sure Ed lowers that damn gun."

"Your leg?" I said.

"His hurts too."

The big man circled Sarge to his right, his limp not as pronounced as it was minutes earlier. Sarge turned with him, his hip making the effort laborious, though his face didn't reflect the pain I knew he was feeling.

The big man stopped short of stepping in front of Ed, who had lowered his gun, though his arm twitched, wanting to raise it to rid the world of the second bully.

Sarge side-stepped to his left to encourage the man to follow suit. It worked; the big man moved to his right, which put his back to Ed.

"No, no, don't shoot!" Sarge blared, leaning out as if looking around the man's side.

The ruse worked. The bully jerked around toward Ed, who was still pointing his weapon at the floor, his expression confused why he was being yelled at again. An instant later, he caught on and bobbed his eyebrows and smirked at the big man.

Realizing he got suckered, the big man jerked back around just in time for Sarge to slam the bottom of his fist against the side of his neck. The man groaned loudly and leaned to his left, exposing his right side, his liver.

Sarge drove two powerful hook punches into it, the blows penetrating deeply to set the many nerves there ablaze, but with control so as not to break the ribs. Sarge knew the shards of bone could puncture the liver, spilling its foul contents into the body to cause his death.

The man dropped straight to the floor, curled into a tight fetal ball, and screamed.

<0>

"Damn," Grant said. "A liver punch will do that? And he could control it so it wouldn't seriously injure the man?"

The professor nodded. "He was a killer in Vietnam. Back home, he went out of his way not to seriously hurt someone, no matter how deserving they were. At least that was my experience with him. We both had had it up to here with violence. Killing, watching life ooze out of another human being, takes a toll. We were done with it."

"What happened after in the boxcar?"

"I went up to the conductor and told him what had happened. The police came, ambulances for the dead man and the big guy who still couldn't stand. Sarge and Ed were put in jail, Sarge for just a few hours until the police heard my story and the old-timers'. Ed didn't have money to bail out, so he was still behind bars when we returned six weeks later to testify. He was found guilty but given probation since his intent was to protect Sarge."

"How about the big guy?"

"He was charged initially with menacing with his Pitbull and attempted assault on Sarge, but they dropped it when Sarge refused to file a complaint. That was the last we saw of him.

"My friend had surgery on his hip a few weeks later. They said the Army surgeons really messed him up, but they were able to fix him to, what Sarge estimated, about 90 percent of where he was before being shot. I saw him compete only once. It was about ten years or so after we got home, and I couldn't believe how he could kick. There weren't any other black belts at that tournament who came close to his flexibility, speed, and power. I can't imagine if he had been one hundred percent."

The professor stood, stretched, and sat back down again. "I have a two o'clock lecture and I'm exhausted. I've given you all I have."

"Thank you so much. I hope I can email you if I think of anything else." The professor nodded. "Any last thoughts on the man?"

Professor Watkins looked across the way for a moment. "Sarge," he said, turning to Grant, "was an amazing man. I owe him my life for keeping me sane that terrible night in the jungle and showing me by his actions what a true warrior was. He was a beast under fire, yet he guided and controlled others with a calm voice and demeanor.

"Back home, he was always kind, giving, and protective of me those months we were on the road. I was never the warrior he was. He knew I was a book nerd, not a fist-fighter.

"He didn't want to fight that man in the train, and it bothered him that Ed killed his buddy. Even throwing the dog off the train troubled him.

"We exchanged phone calls every so often, and when the computer age came in, we kept in contact with emails. Sarge came down to Eugene when I got my doctorate, and I traveled to Portland when he married Roni and years later for her funeral. In the last few years, our in-person contacts were only two or three times a year.

"I should say, and you will likely learn of this, the first year or so after I returned to Eugene, Sarge had a rough spell. All I know of that period is rumor, so I'll let you dig that up if you are so inclined. Are you interviewing Leo Ichiro?"

Grant nodded. "In two days, Saturday."

"Fine, but please, whatever he tells you of that period, remember, Vietnam sucked the life out of us, and everyone handled it differently. The compassion he showed in that train, well, maybe it didn't last."

The professor knuckled a tear out of the corner of his eye and cleared his throat. "We all backslide from time to time, no? Have lapses? We quit smoking, but two weeks later, we sneak one. We break our diet with a chocolate eclair. One time when Sarge was drunk, he told me that he stopped counting his kills after twenty-six. Can you imagine how that would tear at the fabric of your soul?"

The professor stood and swiped his sleeve across his eyes. "I think he was an amazing man, and I will think of him until the day I die."

‹0›

Grant spent the next two days listening to the professor's interview three times, rewriting his notes, and researching details about Vietnam's jungles, specifically the terrible heat and humidity, the hordes of insects, poisonous snakes, and the horrific boobytraps used by the Viet Cong. That horrible moment Sensei and the professor endured was so godawful Grant wanted to ensure he captured the misery of the jungle as best he could. He owed that to Sensei and Professor Walters.

Grant told himself he would never again complain when he strained a muscle doing his Pilates and yoga and never again whine when he got warm walking from his air-conditioned car to his air-conditioned home.

CHAPTER THREE

LEO ICHIRO

Grant called Leo Ichiro's house on the way to tell him he was 45 minutes out and to see if he would like him to bring some Starbucks coffee. A woman answered, identified herself as Brooklyn, and said Leo was in the shower. She said neither one of them drank left-wing Starbucks, but her father was looking forward to his visit.

Pleasant enough, Grant thought, and political.

Leo lived on a small farm east of Vancouver, Washington, a short drive across the Columbia River that separated Oregon and Washington. Vancouver was barely a shadow of its former self, but a newish urban sprawl of strip malls, fast-food restaurants, chain grocery stores, and hospitals stretched east for miles. It turned into orchards, berry farms, grazing cattle, and clean air at its abrupt end. Grant hadn't been out of Portland in a long while, and he found the countryside to be instantly relaxing.

Leo was sitting on the steps of a large wrap-around porch as Grant pulled up. The white three-story farmhouse looked to be 100 years old or more, immaculately kept up, to include what looked like a fresh coat of paint. The man bore a hard leanness with a chiseled face, and iron-grey buzzcut. How much of his physique was from farm work and how much from his martial arts training?

"It's a small spread," Leo said after they had exchanged pleasantries. He gestured to the classic red barn about 50 yards from the house. "We have ten cows, two dozen chickens, forty acres of corn, and thirty acres of raspberries. And we got two tractors, one old, one new. I love the old rattletrap. It's like me, dependable, ornery, with a lot of history." He was a man clearly proud of his farm. Grant asked if they had workers. "We manage by ourselves in the winter, but we hire people in the spring, summer, and fall.

"Still a lot of work for you and your wife," Grant said.

Leo leaned against the railing that bordered the porch and peered out at his grounds, his eyes far away. Grant didn't know what was going on, but he thought it was best to let the moment unfold.

"I lost my Susan three years ago in a car accident on the Interstate Bridge, he said softly, referring to one of the spans that connected Oregon to Washington. "Albert, that was Brookie's husband, had been taking her mother and Brookie Christmas shopping in Portland when a semi-truck slammed into them from behind. Only Brooklyn survived, albeit wheelchair-bound with two dead legs. She's thirty-two years old now, my reason for continuing on." He jerked his thumb behind him. "You'll meet her. She's tinkering around inside."

Grant remembered the wheelchair at the gravesite and the eyes looking at him through the tinted van window as Leo climbed into the driver's seat.

Leo crossed the porch and opened the screen door. "Let's do this out in the sunroom, Grant. It's on the other side of the house and faces the cornfield."

The living room was large and pleasantly decorated with a woman's touch. His daughter's or his late wife's? They passed through a large kitchen filled with modern appliances. The counters and island were unusually low, designed, no doubt, to accommodate a wheelchair. Leo pulled open a sliding glass door and led Grant out into a long room, which he would learn was 15 feet by 40; the outer wall comprising eight ceiling-to-floor glass panes, each 12 feet high.

"A bitch for a young man to do himself," he said, retrieving two bottles of beer out of a small black refrigerator set against the back wall. He handed one to Grant and nodded toward two rocking chairs that faced the windows. "I'm seventy-one, so it was more than a bitch building this add-on last winter." They settled into the chairs. "I didn't install the windows, of course. A wise man knows his limitations. I had the wall of glass professionally installed. We got us a clear sky afternoon, so we'll be getting a fantastic sunset this evening."

"It's incredible," Grant said. "And you teach at one of Sensei's schools on top of working on your house and managing the farm."

He nodded. "I teach three nights a week. Farm work and martial arts is a tough grind that will either continue to keep me in shape or blow out my heart gasket. Some days I'm not sure which one will do it."

Grant could hear kitchen sounds now coming through the open sliding glass door to the house. It must be Brooklyn, Leo's daughter. "I can't imagine how much work all this is, the farm, teaching, remodeling the house. Just one of those things would be plenty."

"It is, but it's what I do. No complaints. Lots of people my age didn't wake up this morning. Carpe diem, right?"

"Yes, sir."

Grant heard the soft whine of what had to be a motorized wheelchair a moment before it passed through the extra-large doorway and into the sunroom. The driver's beauty caught Grant off guard, and he somehow managed to stop his jaw from dropping to the floor.

"This is our favorite time of the day," the beauty said, gliding her chair up to the small table that separated the two men. She picked up two bowls of chips she had been balancing on her lap and set them on the table. She turned her head to look at Grant, the move swishing her long deep-auburn ponytail about her shoulders. Her amber eyes moved around his face for a moment before looking into his. She extended her hand. "Brooklyn Ichiro, nice to meet you, Grant."

"Nice—" he cleared his throat, "to meet you too. I'm Grant." Her hand was soft, warm, and he didn't want to let it go.

"I know," she said with a smirk. She looked over at the windows. "I'm the official window cleaner in this room." She looked back at him. "Bet you're wondering how I do that, aren't you, Grant? Wash those windows, I mean."

He looked at the high windows. "Uh…"

Her smile was crooked, teasing. Grant thought it was the most incredible smile he had ever seen. "Well," she said, "I'll tell you before you strain something, I use a ladder."

"You use…" Grant said dumbly.

"She never tires of making that joke to people," Leo said as his daughter laughed.

Brooklyn brushed an errant lock of hair away from her face, the gesture ballet-like, Grant thought. "I'll leave you two to it," she said, backing her ride up to the kitchen door. "Let me know when you want lunch, dad."

"Nice meeting you, Brooklyn," Grant somehow managed, forgetting he had just said that to her. She moved under the archway of the door, stopped, and looked back at him. The lock of hair had fallen back over one eye. "You too, Grant,' she said softly. She glanced at her father, who was taking a long pull on his beer. She frowned at him a little, then rolled through the door.

Damn, Grant thought.

"She's my only child," Leo said, gazing across his acreage of dead-yellow corn stalks, their season long past. Grant looked at him self-consciously, wondering if he had picked up on how he was looking at his only child. "Brookie's dated a few times since the accident. Went out with the last man three times. It was on the third date when he hit her in the face."

"What?" Grant managed. "No."

"Just once. Brooklyn isn't one of those women who takes it and takes it." Still looking out at his corn, he smiled. "He hit her, and she mowed him down in that chair of hers. And when he fell on the kitchen floor, she whipped a cast iron skillet into his kneecap. The man's patella, that's the kneecap, shattered like fine porcelain. Knee breaks hurt like all hell. Shattered knees hurt more.

"She called me, and I drove like a cat on fire to the man's house in Vancouver, an area called Fruit Valley. I kicked in the locked door, and I squeezed that twerp's neck like I was choking a turkey. I was about to plunge my hand into his chest and rip out his black heart when Brooklyn bumped her chair against my leg to get my attention. She said, 'He isn't worth it, dad. Just take me back to the farm.' We left the SOB shrieking on the floor. She hasn't dated since."

He turned to Grant for the first time since he'd been talking. "I'm real protective of my baby girl."

"I understand, sir," Grant said, nodding that he got the message loud and clear, the communication underscored by the intensity in the father's eyes.

"Want another beer?"

"I'm good, thanks," Grant said, retrieving his notebook and small recorder from his backpack and setting it on the table. "Shall we begin, sir? Beginning when you first met Sensei."

"Just a sec." Leo stepped over to the door and pulled it closed. "Some of this I don't want Brooklyn to know about."

"But it will be in the book, sir," Grant said, not minding at all if she wanted to come out while they talked.

"I get that. But to me, there's a difference between reading it and hearing it come out of my mouth for the first time. Reading it will let Brooklyn see it on the page, give her time to ponder it, and formulate her questions. Hearing it… Well, I just think she should read it first." He looked back out the window.

Grant slid his spiral notebook closer to him, opened it to the next blank page after Ben Walter's interview, and wrote Leo's name at the top. They were stalling gestures as he waited for Leo to begin. Finally, he looked away from the old corn stalks, now swaying a little in a light breeze, emptied his beer, and retrieved a fresh one from the refrigerator. He sat back down and twisted off the cap.

"I knew him before he went into the Army. Some in our class called him 'Sensei' back then because he always helped people who were having trouble as we all came up through the ranks. But he wasn't a sensei, a teacher. Not for several more years.

"On that first day in nineteen sixty-four, we were both new karate students, beginning as white belts. We weren't close friends or anything then, just classmates who would outlast the other twenty who started the beginner's class with us.

"Sensei took to karate like a duck to water, leaving the rest of us in the dust. He made his black belt in less than three years, the only other one besides the teacher. I was still a brown belt when he got promoted, and I wasn't a very good one, to be honest. He only got to wear his new belt for a few months before he received his draft notice.

"Vietnam was raging then, and when we all got in line to shake hands with him and wish him good luck, I wondered if I'd see him again. It was strange looking at someone my age and wondering if he was going to die soon. But that's the way it was back then, the way we thought. We'd hear about guys dying every week over there on the five o'clock news. Fifty, seventy-five, a hundred of them a week. I'd already lost a cousin in Vietnam, and my brother lost a friend of his."

"Can you tell me a little about his personality then, before he went into the service?"

Leo took a long drink and rested the bottle on his knee. "Like I said, we weren't friends then, but I liked him. Always pleasant, low keyed, and never a showoff, although he was better than the rest of us. He was helpful when others asked for assistance with a technique or concept. Like I said, that's how he got his nickname, Sensei. Just a nice guy who had a personality that made you want to be around him." He gazed at the top of a huge Maple tree a few yards out from the sunroom. "He changed over there, though. He was a different person when he got back."

Leo shook his head, thinking. Then, "I didn't have to go in. Bad ticker. But I'm still here at seventy-one. I tested with a buddy who was worried that his heart issues would keep him out. He wanted to serve, see. When the results of our physicals came in, it showed I had the bad ticker, and his was fine. I always wondered if they got us mixed up or something. I was happy because I didn't want to go in the service, and I definitely didn't want to go over to Vietnam. I guess that makes me an asshole because I didn't say nothing."

Leo sighed and took a deep swallow of his beer. "Yeah, I got survivor's guilt after seeing how so many guys came back, including Sensei, and the feeling hasn't gone away after all these many years."

Grant didn't know what to say to that, so he asked another question. "Sensei was drafted, which meant he served two years. Did you keep training while he was gone?"

"He got a draft notice, but he signed up for three years. Yeah, I kept training for a little while." Leo pointed at his beer and raised his eyebrows; Grant said he was still working on his. Leo got himself one and stepped over the glass door and peaked in. Was he double checking to see if Brooklyn was out of earshot? "Anyway, I made black belt about nine months after Sensei went in. If he came home on leave, I never saw him.

"After my promotion," he said, plopping back down in his chair, "I dropped out of training. Long story short, my mother was a drunk, and one night during one of my parent's usual fights, she shot my father with his own hunting rifle. Killed him. She was sent away, and because I wasn't eighteen yet, they sent me to my mother's sister's house to live until I was eighteen, about a half year later. My aunt was a drunk too, but she was divorced, so there was no one for her to shoot." Leo chuckled at that. "Anyway, I sunk into this dark hole and got myself busted a few times for burglary, car theft, and fighting.

"I had just turned twenty-one when Sensei came home. He had been out of the service for a few months, traveling around the country with an Army buddy named Walters. He's a college professor down in Eugene now. You should talk to him for sure."

"I have, thanks," Grant said. "How was Sensei's demeanor when you saw him again? You said he was different."

Leo rolled his eyes. "Man, he was messed up even more than me."

NUDITY, A FIRE, AND REAQUAINTING

I'd been sitting alone at a corner table watching the topless dancer writhe on the small stage. The girl, who I thought could benefit from a few skipped meals, was struggling to interpret Jimi Hendrix's "Purple Haze" belching from a blown-out speaker perched on one corner of the stage. When I first sat down an hour earlier, I thought she could drop 40 pounds, but after three beers, I'd changed my mind to 20.

The dump was so choked with cigarette smoke there was little breathable air, but the drunks didn't give a shit since a glass of brew was 50 cents and hard drinks a buck and a half. Most of them slumping over their beverages were workers from Portland's shipyards; all of the women, about eight of them that I could see from where I sat, were skid row skanks, and that opinion was being kind. Everybody ranked women one to ten in those days, ten being the highest. A buddy said on a rare occasion you could find a skid row skank who was a four, but you could make her a ten if you drank a six-pack first. The world is too politically correct for that kind of humor nowadays.

Four months earlier, I'd been pink-slipped from my job at the downtown train station. They accused me of drinking while sweeping the lobby on the midnight shift. Yeah, I had been, but I didn't like the accusation, so I denied it, just as I'd done the last three times that they suspected it. When my sissified foreman said my breath "reeked to high heaven," I told him that was a stupid expression. That didn't help, and he ordered me to turn in my broom and "get out now." I did leave, but when he wasn't looking, I stole the broom.

Halfway through my fourth beer, I'd decided the dancer could drop 10 pounds, but a minute later, I decided she was okay the way she was.

There was a sudden commotion behind me. I twisted around and saw a couple of guys clinching one another and banging into the pool tables and chairs. A big black dude appeared out of nowhere, a big wooden mallet in his right hand. He said something I couldn't hear, and the two separated. I was pissed because I was in the mood to see a good fight.

I missed going to the dojo. I hadn't trained in over a year, mostly because I couldn't afford it. That, and my life had taken a plunge to the dark side.

When I turned back around, I noticed a guy dropping a buck on the stage for the same gyrating dancer, who I now thought was one hot chick. The tipper was wearing an olive-green military shirt with bellbottom blue jeans. I figured he got the shirt at Goodwill like a lot of the hippies did then.

Then I got a good look at his face when he turned to head back to his table. He looked familiar. But from where? Did he work at the train station? Maybe. Nah, that wasn't it. From a distance, he looked to be in his mid-20s. But when the strobe light hit him just so, he looked older. I thought maybe it was his eyes. Lifeless.

So were the other guy's eyes who was sitting with him. I thought that was strange.

They were both sitting on the same side of the table, their backs to the wall. I didn't know how long they had been there, but they weren't drunk, not even tipsy. The one who tipped the dancer scanned the room, and when those dead eyes met mine, they hesitated for a second before moving on. Then they returned. I thought that maybe we did know each other, so I nodded, and the guy returned it.

I was into my fifth beer when I noticed two different men, both wearing greasy white aprons, push through the crowd of drunken dancers and dash for the exit. Before they went out, they turned back to face the people, many of whom were looking at them with blurry-eyed curiosity. That's when I recognized them as the cooks from back in the kitchen. The taller one cupped his hands on each side of his mouth to shout over the Rolling Stones singing about not getting any satisfaction. "FIRE! The place is on fire! You can't get out the back way!"

Then the cook lifted his palm and actually waved before he and the other one bolted out the door, saving their sorry asses first.

I was glad my table was so close to the door, but that thought only lasted for about a nanosecond. Because when I struggled to my feet, all those beers rushed right to my brain, making me an easy bowling pin for the panicking people to knock over. I fell onto my belly, the table flipped over on top of my back, and the last half of my beer thumped down onto my head. It hurt because it was a big-ass mug.

Every time I tried to push myself up, someone stepped on the underside of the upturned table, pressing my back into the grimy floor. Some patrons, desperate now that the room was filling with smoke, brawled at the exit. Someone got knocked down onto the table, squishing me again. When the sound of the fighting intensified, someone or something knocked the table off my back, freeing me to low crawl a few feet away from the crush.

The grey smoke was so dense now that it clogged my lungs and confused my sense of direction. I was still on my belly, but I couldn't see my hands. I remember thinking that the fire department always advised people in a fire to get down on the floor. Well, I was, and it wasn't working.

Mick Jagger's song was on repeat. I used to sing along with it, but now I was puking up my last two mugs of brew. I started thinking I would die to Jagger with the taste of smoke and cheap beer in my gagging mouth.

What they say is true: My life started flashing back in my head. But it wasn't images of some of the gorgeous women I'd known, but of me when I was ten years old with my toe caught in a pool drain at the bottom of a park swimming pool. I remembered how my lungs burned seconds before the lifeguard yanked my foot free. That lung burning experience was enjoyable compared to lying on the floor, coughing so hard that I was on my way to losing consciousness.

Then someone stepped on my head, banging my face into the floor. I tried to lift my head again, but I couldn't because I was fading out.

I felt my body convulsing.

Everything was grey.

Suddenly, my body felt like it was ascending. You know, floating up. That's better than descending down.

<0>

"You want another beer, Grant?"

"What?" the writer jerked his head up from where he was feverishly writing in his notebook. He was surprised to see Leo standing. "Oh, uh, no thanks. What happened? Obviously, you got out."

"Yeah. Whenever I remember that smoke, I get dry mouth." He stepped over to the refrigerator.

The man still likes his beer, Grant thought, and it's just a little past noon.

The sliding glass door opened, and Brooklyn rolled out, followed by a large black cat. "Ninja wanted out here," she said, looking at

Grant. The cat moved stealthily toward Grant, its head low, eyes focused on the stranger. "Dad named him," she said. "He's a good mouser, but he hates new people. Nice knowing you, Grant."

"Wait. What?"

Ninja stopped about six feet away from Grant, his full attention on the writer's face, and lowered his body.

"He's crouching. Is he going to spring at me?" That came out more screechy than he wanted.

"Where do we UPS your shredded body, Grant?" Brooklyn asked.

"Seriously? I mean, is he going to—"

Ninja darted toward him and plopped over onto his side next to the writer's shoes. The big cat rolled onto its back and looked up at him with an expression that said, "Rub my belly."

Brooklyn cracked up, and Leo shook his head, no doubt seeing her do the attack cat bit before, along with the window cleaning gag.

Grant bent to pet Ninja, but not before noticing Brooklyn's look of disapproval as her dad unscrewed the cap from his beer. "Last one," he said, looking guilty.

Her eyes smiled at Grant. "You guys ready for a sandwich?"

Her dad shook his head. "In a little bit, daughter. Let me tell him the next part."

"Can I stay?"

"Nope."

Brooklyn looked at Grant again. "Let me know if you need anything." He thanked her, and she smiled before backing toward the doorway. "Come on, Ninj." The cat rolled up onto its feet and hurried after her. Brooklyn waited until the cat went into the kitchen, then slid the door shut.

Grant looked after her for a moment before looking over at Leo. "You said you were ascending."

He nodded. "I was dying or about to, and in my smoke-choked mind, I thought I was heading toward the light; you know, ascending to heaven. But in actuality, two guys had me by my arms and were lifting me."

"The two guys at the table?"

"Yeah, but I couldn't see them, and I don't know how in the hell they saw me."

"Was the one guy Sensei?"

"It was. Man, had he changed. Older, strung tight as a violin string. I saw Vietnam do that to a couple of school friends too."

"Before we get to that, what happened after you got out of the fire?"

"Well, the ambulance crew wanted me to go to ER, but I refused them, dumb shit that I am. But I did end up going in the next day because my lungs were hurting. Anyway, they pointed out the two who pulled me out of the joint. That's when I recognized Sensei. The other guy was Ben Walters. I didn't know him, but Sensei would introduce me.

"Thing is, I couldn't remember Sensei's real name, so I called him by his nickname again. He said he recognized me, but he looked a lot different than he did back in the karate classes. His quiet, humble demeanor was still there, but there was something else, something new. A darkness, I guess, would be the best way to describe it.

Grant looked up from writing on his pad. "Like evil, you mean?"

"No. More like Sensei had seen darkness, been in it, and it had clung to him." Grant liked that and quickly jotted it down. "He said I hadn't changed much, other than I looked two and a half years older." Leo shook his head. "Maybe, but I hadn't aged like he had. He seemed introverted too, like he was sheltering in the space one inch around him. Does that make sense? Like he felt safe within the snug invisible bubble or dome he occupied. I don't think I'm saying that very well, but it's what I was perceiving."

Grant said, "I think I understand. Writer Michaela Chung said, 'That's the thing about introverts; we wear our chaos on the inside where no one can see it.'"

Leo jabbed his finger in Grant's direction. "That's it. He was turned into himself and whatever was inside was unpleasant, dark. I don't know if he was hiding it or preventing it from getting out." He thought for a moment, then, "I was only twenty-one at the time, so I don't know if I could have put all that together back then, but looking at it now, that's what I was seeing."

"I understand," Grant said, writing quickly.

Leo downed the rest of his beer, looked at the refrigerator, over to the sliding glass door, and leaned back in his rocker, no doubt remembering Brooklyn's look. "Just like her mother," he said under his breath.

"The fire consumed the dump of a bar but took only one life, the dancer. Burnt some other people, but only the girl couldn't get out in time. The autopsy showed she had a broken leg. They figured she might have jumped off the stage, landed wrong, and broke it. Between the blaring music, the crackling and popping fire, and the shouts and coughs of people fighting their way out, no one heard her cries for help." He shook his head. "She might have been a skid row topless dancer, but she didn't deserve that ending. Newspaper said she was a mother of two, her daughter a Downs child." He shook his head again. "Life sucks, then you die, huh?"

Grant thought it best not to get into a philosophical question about life, especially since Leo had recently lost his wife, son-in-law, and Sensei.

"How did you and Sensei get together?" Grant asked when Leo didn't continue. "You said that you were just classmates before he left for the Army."

Leo took a breath and released it, the sound ragged. "Sorry, I hadn't thought about that fire in a long while. If it weren't for Sensei, I might have been the second victim of it."

He scooted himself up a little straighter. "No, we weren't friends or anything. But the night of the fire, we talked some, and I learned they had just got back into town from hiking around the country for a few months. Remember, this was nineteen seventy, and a lot of people were doing that sort of thing then. There were a ton of folk songs written about it, sung by guys like Bob Dylan.

"Sensei and Ben had had their fill, plus they were broke. They didn't even have a place to stay that night, so I invited them to my apartment to crash. Two days later, Ben Walters left to hitch his way back to his parent's home in Lincoln City, leaving Sensei and me to go down the wrong path.

"Now, I don't remember how we made the decision to rob a store, but somewhere during our days and nights of drinking and puffing grass, we decided to tap into all that cash just lying there in grocery store cash registers."

"Wait," Grant said, leaning toward him as if he heard wrong. "*Rob* a store?"

"Among other places. Now, we agreed we didn't want to hurt anyone; we just wanted the bounty.

"Now, here's the thing. The money was my prime motivation, but it wasn't Sensei's. But he didn't know that at the time, and I didn't know that about him either then."

Leo chuckled at the bewilderment on Grant's face. "Confused? Sorry. But like I said, we didn't figure it out until later when we concluded that his main incentive to do a robbery was for the adrenaline rush. He had been over there in the war, shooting people, getting shot, living on the edge day and night for months on end. But when he came home, it was boring here in comparison. His war-charged adrenaline needed to be fed. It was making him agitated, nervous, and giving him insomnia. Of course, our heavy drinking and puffing Maui Wowie and other kinds of weed didn't help our decision making, but there it was.

"He was twenty-four years old, and I was three years younger, full of bravado, pissed at the system, the government, and ourselves. Sensei more than me, but I had a good case of the piss-offs too. Life hadn't gone as I thought it would when I graduated from high school.

"I suppose this sounds like a lot of excuses, and maybe it is. But neither of us over the years could come up with a better reason why we got into crime. And neither of us ever saw a shrink to ask. Well, maybe he did, I'm not sure. I never did, though."

"So you robbed a store?" Grant asked to keep the conversation flowing. "Do you mean you shoplifted a bunch of things?"

Leo shook his head. "When you just steal something, that's theft. Burglary is when you break into a place at night to steal. Threatening to use force or actually using it on someone—pointing a weapon, beating someone up—is robbery. Robbery is the big kahuna of stealing, the crime that will get you serious prison time. But we didn't know these details in our very early twenties. I didn't until I researched it years later and saw how close we came to spending a few years in Oregon State Prison. But I don't think knowing it would have made a difference at the time. We had decided to rob a store, and that was that."

Grant was having trouble wrapping his head around this revelation. Sensei had to have known Leo would talk about it since he was on the list of interviewees. But reveal a crime? When he said he wanted his life's bumps and all told, Grant assumed he meant backsliding on his training, such as partying in college, putting on a few pounds, the sort of things people do on their bumpy road to success. But a robbery? A stick-up?

"So," Leo said, "we decided to do our first job on a Saturday night, mid-evening, figuring the store's cash registers would be full at that time. Neither of us had a car, so we had to take a bus to our crime scene."

"Here in Portland?" Grant asked, trying not to laugh at the idea of a bus as a getaway car.

"You don't eat where you shit, right?"

"Uh, never really thought about it."

"That was rhetorical. No, we took our crime south to Salem. A forty-five-minute ride away. We figured twenty minutes to check out the minimarket and a couple of minutes to do the crime. There was a return bus to Portland thirty-five minutes after our robbery. Smooth as snot on a doorknob."

"Was it?" Grant asked.

"Nope."

CRIMINAL ACTS

As it turned out, the bus dropped us off across the street from the Plaid Pantry about half a mile inside the Salem city limits.

"It's like it was written in the stars," I said as it pulled away. "You know, like it was supposed to happen. Look down at the end of the block that way. Another bus stop. That one goes northbound back to Portland. Like I said: written in the stars."

Sensei had said very little during the bus ride. I couldn't tell if he was having second thoughts or just a case of the nerves. He hadn't talked at all about Vietnam in the week we had spent together drinking and planning our caper. But I could see something in the man that set him apart from my other buddies. Like I said, I had known him only briefly before he left for the Army. I couldn't remember much of his personality. What I did remember was that he was just an average guy, joking, having fun with the others, training hard in class, and getting promoted faster than the rest of us. He was cool with it, though, and went out of his way to help us when asked. It wasn't long before we were calling him Sensei, though he had only earned about three colored belts, which was two more than everyone else.

That was before the Army. Afterward, the joking and fun personality hadn't shown itself in the days after we reconnected. What I saw then was a quiet. That's the only way I can describe it, a quiet. It was sort of a tightly controlled detachment as if he was keeping something in, afraid whatever it was would get out.

As we rode to Salem, I'd steal glances at him out of the corner of my eye, imagining that he had that same quiet intensity in the jungle. About two days before we did the robbery, Ben Walters came up from Eugene to visit Sensei. The three of us went out for beers one night, and when Sensei got up to use the restroom, Ben gave me a rushed version of their Vietnam experience together. Holy shit. No wonder the man was so intense and distant.

If he were doing this robbery to feel that adrenaline rush again, I didn't think it would come anywhere near what he had experienced over there.

Now we were in Salem and sitting on a bus stop bench, our heads scrunched into our jacket collars against the cold.

"Must be near freezing," I said, eyeing a car pull into the market's parking lot. A lone man got out and entered the store. There were ten slots for cars, seven were empty. A woman chomping into a donut came out of the store, climbed into a blue Studebaker, and left, leaving eight open spaces.

"We can split left or right," I said, "but going left would be best since we want to go north." I jerked my thumb over my shoulder.

"There's a closed warehouse back there. There's no foot traffic right now. There's no houses or apartments on the blocks left and right. We can't see what's behind the store from here other than darkness, but I know it's a huge empty lot. I checked everything out when I scouted the place."

"We got someone coming at our two o'clock," Sensei said in a whisper. "One person walking fast."

I looked but didn't see anything. "There is? All I see is that beater of a truck parked by the intersection across the street. "Where do you see—?"

A man wearing a heavy black coat rounded the corner across the street, a dark stocking hat pulled down past his ears, his hands stuffed inside his coat pockets. He walked quickly to the store and went inside as one of the motorists came out, a man with a steaming white Styrofoam cup in his hands. He climbed into his car.

"How did you know that guy was going to come around the corner?"

Sensei shrugged. "Just knew. I probably couldn't do it during the day, but the night, the darkness… Sometimes I can feel a presence." I thought that was weird, but I let it pass. Sensei nodded toward the store. "Someone else is coming out." It was a heavyset woman holding a steaming white cup.

"Night workers," I said. "No one drinks coffee this late unless they're pulling the evening or midnight shift somewhere." Another car pulled in, and two men got out and entered. The man on foot exited the store, unwrapping what looked like a pack of cigarettes. He crossed the lot, moved up the sidewalk in the direction he came, and disappeared around the corner.

Sensei said, "We have to do this fast." It was the first time he had said anything about the mechanics of the robbery. "If a customer comes in while we're inside, we should wait until he leaves or moves to the back of the store. Then we demand the money from the teller and split ten seconds later."

"Right on," I said. That was exactly how I'd done two robberies by myself in Troutdale, a small community east of Portland. The less time on site, the better.

The two men were still inside, but there were no new customers.

"Now?" I asked. "Or wait until the two guys leave?"

"Now," Sensei said, standing. He pulled his baseball cap bill down and cracked his neck left and right. "If we wait for them to go, someone else will pull in. By the time we get over there, they should be leaving."

I looked both ways. The street's clear left and right. We walked quickly across the lanes and onto the parking lot. I could see the two men at the rear of the store through the large pane window pulling out beer from the cooler. One was a black man, the other white. "They grabbed up some beer and now they're looking around the aisles. Slow shoppers. Do we go in or wait?"

"They're taking forever," Sensei said flatly. "Let's do it."

I noted that their car, a lime-green AMC Pacer, was running, the exhaust pouring white out into the freezing air.

"The white guy is back at the cooler again," Sensei said. "Looks too young to buy beer. Maybe they're trying to get up the nerve to go up to the counter."

I pushed open the door, and Sensei slipped in behind me. We glanced at the middle-aged man behind the register reading a magazine and at the two men looking in the cooler at the rear of the store. I looked back at Sensei. We had agreed it was his job to demand the money since he had the natural menace going for him.

He picked up his cue and growled at the clerk. "Drop the magazine, pal, and open the reg—"

"Back away from the counter, shit birds," a voice said from behind us. I about jumped out of my skin, but Sensei turned toward it as calm as can be. It was the black man, late 20s, heavy, not nervous, pointing a shotgun at us. The second man, a redhead not more than 18 or 19, moved quickly up the aisle, a .38 revolver in his extended shaky arm.

I moved quickly to the side like they said to do, but Sensei hesitated.

"You gonna be all brave, mutha fucka?" the man with the shotgun said, moving the opening of the big barrel toward Sensei's face. "I was a sniper with the Ninth Infantry, in the Nam, you hear? You got any questions shit for brains?"

"I do, sir," Sensei said calmly, moving diagonally to the man's right. He told me later that the diagonal movement creates the illusion of distance from the threat. "Snipers used M-Fourteens," Sensei said, faking confusion. "Could you be mistaken about your job there? That you were a sniper, I mean. Or, perhaps mistaken that you were in Vietnam at all?"

"What?" the shotgun man said in a high-pitched voice, his eyebrows bunching in confusion. Then he acted nervous and shouted, "WHAT!" He looked out of the corner of his eyes toward his partner. "You coverin' him, Bert?"

"Y-yes," the younger one said, his gun hand shaking even more.

"Hi Bert," Sensei said, looking at him.

The young robber looked as surprised as I must have. He probably hadn't noticed that his partner had called him by name. Bert looked at his buddy, his eyes wide with fear and confusion, no doubt wondering why Sensei was so calm and collected.

His partner ignored him and moved the shotgun barrel back toward the clerk who was standing with his hands up next to his head, the index finger of one trembling hand thumping the side of his ear. "Open the register, shit for brains!"

"Ye-yes, s-sir," the clerk stammered. "But I have to lower my hand down to the register to open the drawer."

"Then do it!" the holdup man blared. He looked toward Sensei, who was standing calmly, his raised hands at chest level. "Raise your hands, man."

"What?" Sensei asked.

Don't mess with this guy, I wanted to say to Sensei. Don't m—

"Raise your fuckin' hands, you retard!"

"Oh, sure, I can do that for you," Sensei said with a pleasant smile. Then he glanced at me.

While I didn't know Sensei that well—though apparently, I thought well enough of him to partner up to do a store robbery—we communicated without words during that two-second glance. He wanted us to take out the other robbers, something he called "to neutralize" when we talked about it later.

The old store clerk grabbed a fist full of bills from the register drawer and laid them on the counter.

"How much is that?" the young white crook snapped, jabbing his pistol toward the clerk, though they were at least eight feet apart.

"A-about s-seventy dollars, s-sir," the clerk managed, thrusting his hands high in the air again.

"What!" the white crook blared, exhibiting more courage than he had since the moment began. He took three quick steps toward the clerk, leading the way with his arm fully extended. "Seventy… Well, fucker, you're gonna die for that seventy." The harsh words sounded unnatural like he was a poor actor. "You understand, you old—"

Sensei snapped his hand out as quick as a snake strike and grabbed the young man's gun hand. The kid resisted by pulling his gun hand back, a response Sensei told me he anticipated, and allowed his own hand to go along for the ride. When he felt the man's muscles and tendons tighten on the gun, he forcefully cranked the man's hand around until the barrel pointed at his pelvis.

The crook's nervous finger must have curled around the trigger because the pistol discharged a .38 round into the kid's own bladder. According to the next day's newspaper, the round lodged in his pelvic bone. What it didn't say was that it was going to make pissing real difficult for a while.

All of that took less than three seconds. I snapped out of my amazement and lunged toward the other man, pushing the shotgun barrel toward the upper wall behind the register above the rack of Playboy and Penthouse magazines. The big gun discharged, the horrendous boom like a punch to my eardrums, as the pellets tore through a stack of Camel cigarette cartons, filling the air with tobacco confetti, cardboard, and wallpaper.

I ripped the big gun out of the shocked man's hands and rammed the butt of the stock right between his eyes.

He dropped unconscious next to his partner, who was writhing in pain from what I'd read somewhere was one of the most painful places to get shot. A moment later, the kid lost consciousness.

"You think he's…?" I managed, my voice sounding muffled to my hurting ears.

"He's breathing," Sensei said, leaning over the counter to check on the elderly clerk who had passed out, no doubt from fright. "This man is too." He looked back at me, studying my face.

When thinking about the moment later, I figured Sensei, with all his experience with chaos, was checking to see if I was keeping it together. I'm sure he saw I was pretty stunned, so he took control of the situation.

He scooped up the bills off the counter and pocketed them, yanked a handful of tissue from an open box by the cash register, and used them to pick up the phone. He dialed the operator.

"Listen," Sensei said into the black receiver. "My wife and I are at a Plaid Pantry on State Street right across," he looked out the window, "from a big warehouse. Greenway Packing, the sign says. There are two unconscious holdup men on the floor, one of them is shot. The clerk has passed out behind the counter, and there are guns on the floor… No, I don't know what happened… No, I don't have time for you to connect me with the police. You tell them. We're outta here." He hung up the phone and looked at me. "Let's *didi mao*."

I would hear him say those words often in the following weeks. He told me it was Vietnamese for "leave quickly." And we did exactly that.

Sensei pushed open the glass entrance door, looked left and right, and nodded to me that all was clear. We moved quickly toward the corner of the store, but Sensei stopped and looked back at the idling car, that new-looking green AMC Pacer. "Faster than the bus," he said.

"I hear sirens," I said, feeling better now. "Let's do it."

Back in charge, I slid in behind the wheel, and Sensei got into the passenger seat. I said, "All those sirens are coming from that way there, so let's take that side street." Ten minutes later, after a lot of side street zigging and zagging, we were on Interstate-5 heading north to Portland.

I was the first to speak after about 20 minutes of silence. "What are you thinking about?"

Sensei didn't answer for a long moment, then, "Wondering what I'm going to do with my half of the seventy. There are so many choices."

‹0›

"That's crazy," Grant said, shaking his head. "What did you do with the Pacer? What about the store's video cameras? Why didn't Sensei call nine-one-one?"

Leo smiled at Grant's enthusiasm. "We dumped the car in Tigard, just outside of Portland, and caught a bus into the city. We thought about taking a cab, but there would be a record. Video cameras in stores were a few years away from happening, so no worries there. And Oregon didn't have the nine-one-one system yet.

"The newspaper said one man was shot in the robbery, another received a skull injury, and the clerk was taken to the ER and released. The elderly clerk didn't mention us in his statement to the police. We figured after seeing the guns pointed at him, he had a case of tunnel vision and didn't see us at all. He said there might have been a third accomplice, which would account for the missing five hundred dollars. We got only seventy dollars. So he lied about the amount to get more from the insurance company, probably prompted by management or something. Everybody steals, you see. Everybody lies. Oh, there was no mention of the Pacer."

"That's pretty amazing," Grant said, shaking his head again. "A good first outing. So I'm curious as to how you two processed the experience."

"It wasn't my first robbery, so I was fine, although it went down crazy. It didn't sink in until I was older that it could have been us lying on the floor."

"And Sensei's thoughts on it?"

"He did have some interesting ones, which made him eventually put a kibosh on continuing. But before I get to that, let me tell you about the next three capers."

"Three more! Yes, please do."

The sliding glass door slid open, and Brooklyn rolled out partway, leaning forward in her chair to look around the door facing. She smiled at Grant. "Excuse me, dad. I heard your voices change cadence. Are you at a place where you can have a sandwich?"

"Just about, sweety," Leo said. "Give us about twenty more minutes, and then I think we'll be at a good breaking point." He looked at Grant. "Is that okay with you?"

Grant tore his gaze away from Brooklyn to respond. "Oh, uh, sure. That would be perfect." He looked back at Brooklyn. "I hope it's not too much trouble."

She affected a tired sigh. "It's a pain in the ass, but I'll do it." She laughed at Grant's shocked expression. "Kidding. It's not a problem." With that, she reversed herself out of the doorway and closed the glass door.

"The joy of my life," Leo said pointedly.

"Yes, sir."

Leo looked at the refrigerator, debated, and leaned back without a brew. "We did three more robberies over the next three weeks. We netted three hundred and eighty-five dollars on the second one, five hundred dollars on the one after that, and we got more than we asked for on the last, and I'm not talking money."

"Uh-oh."

Leo leaned back and looked out his big windows, his eyes settling on the corn as his memory traveled back over the years.

THREE MORE ROBBERIES

We committed our second robbery two weeks after the first job. We hit a Dairy Queen in Wilsonville, a short drive south from Portland. We robbed it right after their lunch crowd and made off with $385 in bills and several rolls of coins. The two teenage girls and 20-something manager were frightened to death, so much so that the young man fainted, pulling a rack of hot French fries down on top of him.

Our third robbery took place in Tigard. The target was a small porno theater that showed adult movies to the overcoat crowd 24 hours a day. My theory about the setup there, admittedly based on nothing but a hunch… Okay, full disclosure. I'd been there a couple of times, so I knew the place was a one-man operation—doorman, concession stand, and projectionist—who couldn't leave the theater to deposit the proceeds at a bank. It turned out I was right, and we pocketed a little over $500 for our effort.

Let me back up a little. We never used a firearm, nor did we simulate one. I figured using a weapon, loaded or not, or implying we had one would add years to our sentences should we get caught. So we relied on Sensei's intense glare. Crazy, I know. I came up with that after I witnessed him intimidate bar bullies twice in one month just by standing outside of their punching range and melting the flesh from their skulls with his eyes.

I completely understood the power of his it. While he never looked at me the same way he had when shutting down the men in their tracks, I saw his laser-like glare whenever he sat staring off into space, probably into some Vietnam jungle.

Since he had "the look," I figured we shouldn't waste it.

Take the Dairy Queen job, for example. One of the teens working there told the press she just knew "the bigger holdup man, the one with the really, really scary eyes, was carrying a machinegun or dynamite, something like that." That was the morning edition. The afternoon paper reported: "It was believed the men were armed with high-power weaponry and explosives. They should be considered armed and dangerous."

For two reasons, the fourth robbery turned out to be our last. The first reason is that about three weeks after we did it, I made a trip to the library on a whim to research infamous holdup people. What scared the crap out of me was that I learned that every notorious person and holdup team in history got caught or slain by the police.

The second reason the fourth robbery was our last job was because of how it concluded.

It was a city office of some kind in St. John's, a neighborhood in North Portland. That is, I thought it was a city office. The target building was across the street from a large church. The wooden sign in front of the office read "St Johns," but the rest of it had been graffitied over with "HITLER DIDN'T DO ENOUGH." My mother, Elizabeth Stein, was Jewish, so it pissed me off that no one had removed the vandalized sign.

Anyway, the idea to hit the place came about a week after we robbed the porno theater. I'd been helping two of my cousins move all of my aunt's possessions into a moving truck when I noticed two men in suits exit the St John's office across the street with what was clearly stuffed money bags. The bags didn't have a large dollar sign printed on them like in the cartoons, but I knew what they were from back when I used to deposit my paycheck at the US Bank on Monday mornings. At the far end of the line of tellers, one window displayed a sign that read, "Local Business Transactions." Most of the people lined up at the window were holding similar bags.

"Robbing a St Johns' business office would be a job for the loot and for bragging rights," I told Sensei about it. "Even if it's just a Portland neighborhood."

"But why would they have so much money?"

I shrugged. "Maybe St John's people pay their water bills or library fines there. Who knows? I mean, it's the first of the month, so it makes sense."

"But wouldn't they pay with a check?"

"All I know is the bags were full, two of them. We got good escape routes, and even if the take is mostly checks, we'll still get some cash. If it's not enough, we'll do another job. But I got a feeling about this one. Maybe we'll get enough to hold off for a while or do something else. What do yuh say, pard?"

Sensei would say later that he had a feeling about this one, too, a bad one. But he liked the idea of it being the last job. We agreed to do it on the following Monday morning since that was the day I saw the men with the bags coming out of the office.

One night, after doing some final cleaning at my aunt's place, something incredible happened. I called Sensei excited to the point of bursting. "Guess what, Sensei. Guess what I have right now. You'll never guess it but try."

When I stopped to catch my breath, Sensei said, "Well?"

"You didn't guess."

"You said—"

"Oh, right! I'll tell you. I got the green AMC Pacer! Can you believe it?"

'The—"

"Yes! I swung by my cousin's place after I left my aunt's. He and I had a beer. Three actually. And I left around midnight. I walked two blocks to the bus stop—the bus's last run of the night—and a half block from the stop, there on the corner was the same AMC Pacer we stole from those holdup dudes on our first job in Salem."

"You're telling me you re-stole it?"

"Yes! That's what I'm telling you. After we dumped the car in Tigard that night, I kept the key. I don't know why; I just did, and I put it in my wallet. But I think it's a message or something. I mean, it's like fate or something is giving us a ride after we rob the Saint Johns' business offices."

"You don't think that's reckless?"

"Noooo."

Sensei didn't say anything. I admit I was pretty crazed, but I was pumped.

"What, Sensei? I thought you'd be—"

"It all feels erratic."

"You mean, I'm a loose cannon or something?" I didn't know if I was hurt or angry. "You don't want in; I'll do the job myself." I don't remember for sure, but I might have snapped that.

Sensei would tell me later that he almost agreed to that. But when he thought about the many unpredictable missions he took in Vietnam, the robbery was nothing. Plus he felt some loyalty to me. Finally, after a long pause, he asked, "How do you see it going down?"

I told him that I drove the Pacer to my aunt's house and backed it into the unattached garage that opened to a gravel alleyway. While I was doing that, I came up with a plan that when we exited the St. John's office, we'd split up, I'd go north down the street, and he would go south. We'd cross the street at the ends of the block and proceed down the alley to meet at my aunt's garage. We'd jump in the car, roll down the alleyway, and take the 62nd Street onramp to the I-84 Freeway east.

The worrisome factor was that the job would go down at noon in broad daylight; our other jobs had been under the cloak of darkness, as the saying goes.

"We'll get everyone to lay down on the floor," I told Sensei, "which will give us time to walk quickly down the sidewalk in opposite directions. Then dash down the alley to the garage, hop in our new car, and head off into the sunset."

Sensei sighed his disapproval, or discomfort or something, and looked down at the floor. But when he didn't say anything, I took it as a go.

Sunday night, we got drunk in my aunt's empty house and passed out on the carpet around 1 a.m.

I'll admit that we were pretty crazed during this point in our crime spree, me more than Sensei. I'm not sure why other than we both sensed this was our last job, and we just wanted to get through it. I also don't know why Sensei, who had led men in Vietnam on what I assume were highly organized missions, didn't hold up his palm and say no, or at least say we needed to cool our jets and take things more slowly. I'm no shrink, but maybe at this point in his life after the war, he was in the beginning stage of his fatalistic period. That would come after we went our separate ways.

At 12:30 Monday afternoon, I looked at Sensei, who looked as bad as I felt, and asked, "We good?" My new friend's face was tight, and his eyes had a far-away look. He more or less nodded.

A little before 1 p.m., I started the Pacer to be sure it was ready to roll. Even when new, those crap cars had a rep for not starting up. I turned it off, and we just stood there outside the garage, scrunched into our heavy coats against the near-freezing weather. I bought us oversized black peacoats to conceal the money bags when we left the premises, and we wore long-billed caps to pull down to cover half our face.

Looking back on it, we should have had "Holdup Guy" embroidered on our hats. I mean, we were that obvious. But we weren't completely stupid. I taped a bandage on my chin, and Sensei had one across his nose. In that library book, I read where this famous robber, I can't remember his name, used to do that because victims always remember the bandage but not the face behind it.

I was having trouble getting a read on Sensei. He hadn't said anything for a few minutes, and he just kept scanning the alley, lingering on shadowed areas and bare-limbed trees. I remember wondering if he was looking for a VC sniper or something. I finally said, "Let's do it." It was more as a way of feeling him out.

His reply was to head south down the alley without saying anything. So I took off north as was the plan. The garage was at the alley's halfway point, so we both had about 20 yards to the sidewalk. When I reached the end, I looked back to ensure Sensei made the corner. He did. I made a left and proceeded to the next street, turned left again, and commenced heading toward the St John's business office. I saw Sensei at the far end of the block coming my way.

As we planned, I went in first, and Sensei followed, both with our bills pulled down to hide our eyes but leaving our bandages easy to see.

The office was smaller than I anticipated. Elderly white-haired women, one with a hint of blue in hers, occupied two desks. There were file cabinets along one wall, a coffee setup on the back wall, and a door that led to the back room.

"Afternoon, ladies," I said in a fake English accent. I told Sensei I wanted to take the lead on this job, using the accent for another distraction besides the bandages, but that he should still give them his hard look. "We're here to rob you." The ladies gasped. "Keep your hands on the desktops and listen carefully. We know you have bags of money. We want it. We will not hurt you."

Over the next 15 seconds, several things happened in quick succession.

My eye caught the nameplate holder on the closest desk: "Sister Hazel." I quick-glanced at the other woman's nameplate: "Sister Allison."

On the wall above the coffee maker, a large, framed photo of the Catholic church across the street. I remembered it was called Holy Angel's Church. To the left of the picture, a smaller one of Jesus Christ; his eyes were looking right at me—they looked disappointed.

A man's bald head peeked around the door frame next to the coffee pot and disappeared.

My mother had been Jewish, my father Catholic, but I quit going to the church and synagogue years earlier. "This is the church office?" I asked dumbly.

Before either trembling woman could answer, the bald man reappeared in the doorway, showing us the business end of a shotgun. Damn, I thought, two shotguns in four robberies.

The bald guy growled as cool as a cucumber, "Son-of-a-bitchin' thieves aren't going to take our church offerings a third time."

We backed up, both of us reaching behind us to turn the doorknob, which isn't effective when two hands are trying to turn it in opposite directions. Thinking the same, we both turned to get a better grip—

Boom!

We jumped like cats stepping on a hot tin roof as buckshot punched through our butts and upper back legs.

We banged shoulders a couple of times but somehow managed to get out the small door, then kept our wits about us enough to run in opposite directions down the street. We met at the garage, jumped in the Pacer, which made us cry out in perfect harmony because of our shot asses. Then we had a moment of consternation when the starter wouldn't turn over. It finally did, and we hauled our bleeding selves down the alley and caught the freeway to Hood River up the Columbia River.

‹0›

"I'm sorry," Grant managed after he stopped laughing. "I mean, that's awful. It could have been worse. I know a little about shotguns, and if it had been loaded with slugs, you guys might have been wearing a pee bag afterward along with that kid in your first robbery."

"I know."

"Who was the shooter?"

"A priest. A crazy son-of-a-bitch who had been sent to that church from Los Angeles County after he beat the crap out of a Catholic who had been saving the big bills out of the offering bowl for himself. The newspaper story on our botched robbery played up how the man had been a purple heart recipient in the Korean War."

"You guys got away with it?"

"We did. I think the bandages on our faces helped," Leo said with a chuckle. "That's all they remembered, see. We didn't stop until we got to Hood River. My dad used to be friends with a veterinarian there, old Doctor Philips, long dead now. Sensei caught three pellets in his right butt cheek, and I caught two in my lower left butt and upper back leg. Those things hurt going in, and they hurt coming out. Worse coming out, I think. Sensei claimed they weren't serious wounds, but I argued that anytime a chunk of metal punched through your flesh, it should be considered serious."

"How did the rest of it play out?"

"My vet friend had a cabin on his hundred acres of farmland, and he let us lay low there for a couple of weeks. We sunk the car in the Columbia River." Leo laughed. "Can you believe that?"

Grant leaned back in his chair and shook his head. "Were you guys featured in one of those crazy crook TV shows?"

"You mean stupid crooks. No, but we should have been."

"How was Sensei doing?"

"He got quieter every passing day."

"You know why?" Grant asked, jotting on his pad.

"I think he felt guilty. That's what I was thinking at the time, and later, I learned I was right; he was racked with remorse. He told me he felt terrible about creating fear in the victims: the store clerk, the porno theater guy, the kids working the Dairy Queen, and the sweet old ladies, nuns I guess they were, working in what turned out to be the office of the Catholic church. It had nothing to do with the city. The bags of money I saw that day were the offerings from the previous Sunday."

"Oh man, you almost robbed a church."

Leo nodded. "You can be forgiven for about anything in the Catholic faith but not for stealing money from them."

Grant nodded, not admitting he was a backsliding Catholic. "Can you tell me more about Sensei's guilt?"

"Guilt. Depression. Vietnam memories. All of it. Of course, I didn't know or understand all that then, but I would later when we got back together."

"Got back together?"

"Yeah. But I don't want to get ahead of myself. Anyway, we returned to Portland a couple of weeks later when we could walk and sit without limping or groaning and drawing attention to ourselves. On the bus ride back, Sensei told me he was done with the robberies. He said he meditated on it a lot during our days and nights at the cabin and sitting by a creek. He concluded it was definitely the adrenaline rush he was chasing after. Coming back to the states was like an energy drain—boredom, restlessness, and a sense of feeling out of place, so much it made him anxious. The idea of doing robberies excited him. He liked the danger of the close calls, the risk, especially the two times there was gunfire: the store and the church office. Can you believe that? He liked the gunshots.

"Even years later, when we talked about it, Sensei said he still believed he needed that rush at the time. But he also realized he had been afraid of what he was doing. Not for himself, but he was scared he would hurt someone during the robbery or when trying not to get caught."

"You think he had seen a shrink?"

Leo shook his head. "I asked, and he said he didn't need one to understand his simple philosophy."

Leo watched two crows fly into the corn and disappear. "Here is an example of the kind of guy he was: He told me he paid everyone back."

"Really? How so?" Grant asked, jotting in his notebook.

"He got a small inheritance from someone; I don't remember now who it was. So a few years later, he spent several months tracking down all of our victims. He learned that the elderly clerk at the Plaid Pantry who passed out when our attempted robbery got aborted by other robbers had died of lung cancer. Sensei said he would have given money to his relatives, but he learned the man had never married, had no children, and no living relatives. So he donated five thousand dollars to a charity that the store sponsored. Dog rescue, I think. This despite that someone there had lied about the amount stolen.

"The three teens who worked at Dairy Queen were all married and were spread around the country. But he tracked each one down, apologized, and offered them money. The two females refused it and hugged him. When he asked them if they had a charity, they both said the Red Cross, so he gave the money to the organization. The male who passed out threatened to call the police when Sensei appeared. My friend quickly left, but later sent the man five thousand dollars in cash with a note of apology and said to keep the money or donate it."

"That was close," Grant said.

"Sensei knew tracking the victims down was a risk, but he intensely felt that it was the right thing to do. He told me a couple of times that when you realize you've hurt someone, make amends as fast as you can. 'Eat crow while it's still warm,' he said. He also said to never be a prisoner of your past. Whatever you did was just a lesson, not a life sentence."

Grant jotted that down and circled it.

Leo said, "On the other hand, Sensei didn't want to go to jail for something that was a product of his messed-up mind at the time, nor did he want to get me in trouble. He said if taking off when the Dairy Queen guy said he was going to call the cops made him a coward in some people's eyes, so be it, although I was the only person he told. His thinking was that if he could stay out of prison, he would have more opportunities to do good for people."

"Like building up good karma to make up for the crimes?"

Leo shook his head. "I asked him the same thing. He said he didn't believe in that. In his mind, building up good karma points was self-serving. It was all about the person trying to gather merits for himself instead of really helping people out of compassion for them. In fact, later, when he had children's martial arts classes, he had a thing where every Friday he'd tell the kids they had to do something for their parents over the weekend but not tell their mother or father they did it. It could be anything, like cleaning their room or sweeping the patio. He was teaching them to do things for others without expecting anything in return, you see."

Grant smiled. "I like that. Was he getting into Eastern religion? That's what it sounds like."

"I asked him that, and he said religion is a personal thing. That's all he said."

"What happened with the other two robbery victims?"

"The porn theater owner was in prison for sex trafficking. Sensei sent him an apology letter and donated five thousand dollars to a charity supporting victims of sex trafficking.

"The priest who shot us had died a year earlier from a heart attack. Apparently, he passed away three days after his attorney told him he was being indicted for child molestation." Leo shook his head. "Imagine a religious guy shooting us, though we hadn't displayed a weapon. But then he messed up little kids for the rest of their lives. Both of the nuns were in a rest home by then, and they refused Sensei's money too. Said they had no use for it. One of them suggested he donate it to an organization that worked with survivors of abuse by priests. I don't remember the name of it."

Grant shook his head with disgust. "Hopefully, those priests will get an extra hot fire in Hell."

"Agreed. Okay, so Sensei and I went our separate ways after the last robbery, our failed robbery. I ended up in San Francisco, where I joined a kenpo martial arts school and went to college. I trained for a couple of years and earned a black belt with them. I got it fast because I already had a black belt, and their system was close to what I studied over in Portland.

Every three months or so, I visited up here to see my sister, but I never looked up Sensei. I figured I was bad news from his past, and it was best left there."

"What did you do for a living?"

"I was a nurse, an LPN. I went to college at night and got a degree. The job market was hurting for nurses when I graduated, so I got a job in the blink of an eye. I'm smarter than I look, you see. Anyway, I worked in it for a year in California until my sister got diagnosed with dementia at thirty-eight. She was divorced with no other family. So I moved up to Portland and jumped through the necessary hoops, and subsequently got hired here. I retired nine years ago.

"As it turned out, another nurse where I worked when I got up here studied with Sensei and talked about what a great teacher and person he was. So I took a deep breath and paid him a visit. My nervousness and worries were for nothing because he greeted me with open arms. He was a totally different man, and he said I was too. He praised me about my nursing career and how I was giving to others."

"Did you begin training with him right away?"

"I did. My kenpo fit well with what he had been modifying into what he called American Free Style, an eclectic system that included all kinds of fighting arts. Sensei's slant was street self-defense, so there were no, what he called, 'fancy-schmancy techniques designed to be pretty and draw oohs and aahhs from onlookers.' It was all about surviving in the mean streets. I worked my way up through the ranks, and helped him open branch schools, teach the elderly, work with troubled kids, all kinds of positive things. I'm still there thirty-some years later. Oh, and he never charged military veterans and cops."

"That's cool," Grant said, making a note. "How much longer are you going to teach?"

"Sensei put it in writing that the school would be mine should he pass first. He and his wife never had kids. We've got lots of highly qualified teachers, so I plan to visit the schools two or three times a month and sit on promotion boards. By the way, twenty-five percent of the net profit from the four schools goes to different programs the city has for kids. All but four of the teachers waive their salary and teach for free."

"Really," Grant said, looking surprised.

"It's the kind of atmosphere Sensei established. He was the most giving man I've ever met."

Grant reached into his bag and retrieved a folder. He extracted an envelope. "Sensei sent me a letter that I got two days after he died. I've made a copy of the page that expresses his wishes for the royalties of this book. I'll take care of it on my end with the publisher and send you copies of the contract.

Grant waited for him to read it, which provoked a tear and a sniff. Then, "You've seen his life travel quite an arc over the years. You saw him when he was stealing—"

"Yes, he stole," Leo said sharply. "But it wasn't for the money. It was for, in his words, 'to try to duplicate the intoxicating thrill I got creeping through the jungle, getting shot at, and getting rained on with rockets and mortars.' He was only twenty-three when he was over there. Who knows themself at that age? Then mix in the confusion of war."

Grant said, "We didn't know back then what we know now about

PTSD and all that happens to men and women who experience it."

"Correct. Sensei told me once about a buddy of his. His friend said that on a Monday at the end of his year in Vietnam, his basecamp got hit hard by a mortar attack followed by a wave of VC that killed twenty-two of the fifty men entrenched there. That afternoon, a chopper whisked him away to Bien Hoa where he flew out of Vietnam in what they called 'the Freedom Bird,' a passenger plane, to Oakland. There, he spent twenty-four hours processing out of the Army and was home sitting in his parent's house on Thursday. He had trouble talking with his mom and dad because his hearing was still in bad shape from the mortars and firefight less than four days earlier."

"Jesus."

"Yes." Leo sighed and looked out the window for a moment. "I'd like to stop now, Grant. I'm tired, and quite frankly, my heart hurts. Let's have a bite to eat and, if I may, invite you to call me on another day should you have follow-up questions."

<0>

Grant slowed to let a semi-truck move into his lane. He had two reasons to be flying high on adrenaline. Leo's interview was incredible and provided a fantastic look at Sensei, his low points, and his high. Coupled with Ben Walters's story about his heroic actions in Vietnam and their trek around the country, the book was shaping up nicely.

The second reason for the buzz was because Brooklyn said yes when he asked her to dinner. He smiled, thinking how he had waited until Leo left the kitchen for a few minutes before he popped the question.

He had cleared his throat and played with his napkin. "I was, uh, …" He cleared his throat again. "I was thinking…"

"You trying to ask me out?" Brooklyn said, her amber eyes teasing him.

He sputtered an embarrassed laugh. "I guess I am. Yes. You want to? Go out for dinner, I mean?"

Brooklyn's mouth struggled not to smile. "You too scared to ask in front of my dad? Is it because he's a seventh-dan and for an old man can move like lightning?"

"Me?" Grant said, feigning indignation. "Me, afraid of him? Well, yeeeesss!" Brooklyn laughed at that. He raised his eyebrows. "So…?"

"You have to help me in and out of your car, and when you make a reservation, you should tell them I'm bringing my own chair."

"I can do that."

"And no sex on the first date." She laughed when his mouth dropped open and his face flushed. She squinted her eyes, pretending to study him. "You suuuure you can handle me, Grant?"

They held each other's gaze for a moment. "I'd like to give it a try," he said softly.

Brooklyn's ear-to-ear smile brightened the already bright kitchen.

"Good answer," she said. "Then, yes, I'd love to go out with you."

He replayed that moment several times in his mind as he crossed over the Glenn Jackson Bridge back into Oregon.

A few blocks from his home, something began to gnaw at him. Leo had revealed a lot about their early years. But while there wasn't anything Grant could put his finger on, he couldn't help but think there was something else. Why am I thinking that? Was it something he said? Or something not said? If he was willing to talk about his felonies, although telling them in such a way to be funny, though not to the victims, why am I thinking there might be something else?

He flashed on a quote he saw somewhere: Three things cannot be hidden: the sun, the moon, and the truth.

Might he have something else to tell me that's right there wanting to come out but not quite yet? Some people think the truth can be hidden with less significant truth. But the real truth is always laying there, gnawing its way out. Is that what I'm sensing? Grant pondered. Is there something gnawing at Leo?

Grant shook his head as he pulled into his driveway. What am I trying to do? The guy revealed a lot about Sensei and himself. So why do I think there is something more?

Grant thought of Doctor Steward Kane, a writing prof he had at PSU. He used to say around his unlit pipe, his gigantic white mustache bobbing on every word, "Your sixth sense should be your first."

CHAPTER FOUR

CARL HANES

Grant was about to get out of his car when his phone rang. He didn't recognize the number and was about to decline it when he remembered that some of those at the funeral said they would call him.

"Grant," he said.

"Hello?" Older male's voice.

"Hello."

"I'm callin' for Mister Grant Perry."

"I'm Grant. How can I help you?"

"My friend Sensei called me a few days ago…before he passed, and he said I should call you. He said he wanted me to tell you of our time together. I was at the funeral, but I didn't know if you were there. I didn't know what you looked like, plus I don't see worth shit anyway."

"Sorry to hear that, Mister…"

"Oh, forgot. Carl Hanes. H A N E S, like the underwear."

"Nice to meet you, Mister Hanes. Do you live near Portland, by chance? I prefer to do it in person. Just not today. I just finished a long interview, and I'm tired."

"Sure, no problem. Have you talked to Leo Ichiro yet? Or plan to?"

"I have."

"Good. I know the man. I don't know much about writin', but I think it's best you heard his story before mine. Sensei and I met after his time with Leo. He called our time together his 'dark period.' I told him I didn't know if I should feel insulted or not. That made him laugh. I'm black, you see?" Carl paused for a long moment, then, "He had an easy laugh these last few years. He didn't always."

Intriguing, Grant thought. They made arrangements to meet the following day at noon in Couch Park in Northwest Portland.

Grant spent the evening listening to Leo's recorded interview and rewriting his sloppy hand notes. A few months earlier, he returned home after interviewing a custom vehicle graphic artist for an article in *Auto Monthly,* to discover his digital recorder hadn't captured a single word. Fortunately, the man's story wasn't complicated, so his hand notes saved the day. But the experience made him paranoid that his recorder—he bought a new one—would fail again.

With Leo's notes rewritten and organized and his digital notes filed, he made a sandwich and watched some martial arts videos on YouTube, noting descriptive phrases and catchy colloquialisms. He thought about texting Brooklyn as he prepared for bed but decided that would be pushy. Or would it be? Yeah, it would. Maybe she'd call or text him. No, she would think that would be pushy. What if she were hoping he would?

Damn.

He washed some laundry and went to bed.

He woke up to a clear blue sky with the temperature in the upper 30s. By noon, it hadn't warmed up more than a couple of degrees.

"Thanks for meetin' me in the park," Carl said from where he sat on one side of a picnic bench. "My wife is quite ill, and she needs her rest. Us gabbin' at the kitchen table would keep her awake. At least that's what she said." He chuckled. "I think she just wanted me out of the house."

Carl looked to be well over 70, maybe approaching 80, with snow-white hair, a deeply lined face with dark bags under his eyes. His chest was sunken, his shoulders sloped, and the gnarled hands he clasped atop the table revealed a working life. He was wearing blue work pants, and a blue shirt under a black work jacket. Grant figured he was one of those men who retired twenty years ago but still wore his work clothes every day.

Carl said, "You look like a writer, kid, and you're lookin' at me like I would imagine a writer looks at everyone. Well, I hope that you come to the conclusion that old age and wrinkles on my face haven't wrinkled my spirit."

"Yes, sir," Grant said.

"You don't look old enough to have read many books, let alone written any." He chuckled. "Just bustin' your balls a little to break the ice."

Grant stepped over the picnic bench seat and sat across from Carl. "Well, my grandfather says at his age there are three rules: 'Never pass a bathroom, don't waste a hard-on, and never trust a fart.'" Grant smiled. "You agree, Mister Hanes?"

Carl slapped a hand on the table, threw his head back, and guffawed. "That's a good one, Grant, and I consider my balls busted right back. We're even. Let's start chattin'. And call me Carl."

Grant retrieved his notebook and recorder and set both on the table. Carl pulled out a small silver flask from his overalls' pocket, unscrewed the cap, and offered Grant a pull.

"No thanks, sir. Long story, but my body can't tolerate alcohol." There wasn't a story at all, but Grant's quick assessment was that Carl would take his refusal as an insult. Plus, Grant didn't like hard liquor.

"Probably best," Carl said after knocking back a gulp. "Made it myself. It keeps me even all day long. And if I need to, I can strip the varnish off a table with it."

Grant laughed. "Please tell me how you met Sensei."

"Met him in Chiefs Tavern. It's not there anymore, but it was a kick-ass place in the seventies, and for forty years before that, I heard. It was at the corner of Third and Burnside in Skid Row. Now the area's called Old Town; ain't that cute?"

"Was he drinking there?"

"Well, he sure as hell wasn't perusing their library."

THE BEGINNING OF A FRIENDSHIP

The joint was hoppin' as usual, and the cigarette smoke was so thick someone shoulda called the fire department. Country music blared from large speakers mounted near the ceiling in every dark corner, some cowboy croonin' about his wife leaving him and taking his dog, and he sure did miss his dog. A few couples clung on to each other swayin' in the little dance spot. I had to nudge my way through the folks to take the only free barstool.

To my right, a woman slumped against a man's shoulder. He was sippin' his beer; she looked passed out. On my left, sat a man a half dozen years younger than me, which woulda made him about twenty-five, give or take. He was just starin' in the little hole atop his can of Budweiser; there were four other crumpled empties in front of him. My first thought was he looked beat down like he'd been through somethin', and like he was packin' somethin' heavy on his back.

I was halfway through my Bud before the man glanced over at me and nodded, pleasant-like. I returned it. He looked down at my forearm tattoo, a hula dancer in a grass skirt dancing on top of the letters "USN" in all caps. The man took a swig and looked back at me. "Navy. When did you get out?"

"Three and a half years ago. Served four. Went to so many ports I couldn't count 'em all."

"Vietnam?" the man asked, turning back to his can. He lifted it and swished it around a little before taking a chug.

"Yes, sir. But just for a few months. I worked on the Navy's computer. Didn't see no action, unless you count bar fights. Three of them. Won two of them handily, but I had to cheat on the third. He was a tough one."

The man lifted his can again, started to put it down, changed his mind, and took a swig, makin' a face like he was tired of the taste. "If you don't cheat at fighting, you're not doing it right."

Carl chucked. "Guess I did it right. I pulled his shirt over his head and nearly beat the black off the brother.

The man smiled at that. I told him my name was Carl and extended my hand. He shook it with an honest grip.

"They call me Sensei," the man said. "I was there in sixty-nine and seventy. Infantry."

"I had it harder, man," I said. "Computers can be a challenge." I laughed at the look Sensei gave me. "I'm playin,'" I told him. "Bet you were in the shit." When Sensei didn't answer, I asked, "When you get home?"

"About ten months ago. Did you have any problems finding work?

I laughed at that and said, "Well, I'm black, so there's that. I ain't cryin' pity. It is what it is, you know? I had about four bosses say they didn't want anybody who'd been in Vietnam. I told them I had an office job for four months and didn't hear no gunshot once. They didn't care. So I went back to school on the GI Bill, you know. Now I'm an electrician's apprentice. Gettin' that wasn't easy too. Got turned down some, even from the places posting help wanted in the papers. But I finally got a job working for the City of Portland. Been there four years, and so far, so good. How 'bout you?"

"Some carpentry work. Pays good but irregular, two or three days a week. A Nam vet hired me. No one else would even consider me. One guy said Nam vets were screwed up in the head, and he didn't want anything to do with them. I wanted to kick his face to prove him right."

"I woulda lent you a hand doin' it too. The son-of-a-bitch."

Suddenly there was a bunch of shoutin' behind us to our left. I twisted around to look, but Sensei didn't. He just took another swig of his Bud.

"Couple of dudes actin' like banty roosters," I told him. "Bumpin' chests with their hands down at their sides and cluckin' practically chin-to-chin."

Sensei nodded slightly without turning to look. "The first guy to look away then look back will throw a punch. And he'll land it."

"Now they're bumping chests harder and shuffling their feet to keep standing. They look damn silly."

"One will step back a half step. He's the puncher." Sensei took another pull on his beer and looked down at his can. Apparently, not interested enough to turn around.

I watched the dudes 'cause I like a good fight. A second or two later, the smaller of the two men did exactly as Sensei called it. He took a step back, lookin' away, then he looked back and threw a big overhead right punch into the big guy's kisser. Women screamed and chairs were scrapin'.

"He did what you said," I told Sensei, who still had turned around on his stool. "The big guy didn't even try to block it. He's down and not moving."

"When two knuckleheads are nose-to-nose, the first one to swing will succeed because his action is faster than the other man's reaction to it. It happens when you're too close."

I watched the unconscious man's friends carry him out and then turned back to the bar. "How you know that stuff? You used to box or somethin'?"

"Something like that."

I didn't push it. I took a swig and eyed Sensei out of the corner of my eye. Hard face, thick neck, fit physique, and callouses on the knuckles of his hand curled around the beer can. Calluses on his palms from wielding a hammer, I understood. But on his knuckles?

"You favor men, Carl?"

I about sprayed out my beer when he asked that. He asked it without lookin' my way, but I could see he was smilin' a little.

"Sorry. Guess I wasn't as subtle as I thought I was bein'. You said your name is Sensei. What's that?" This was around nineteen seventy-four or so. Not too many people knew about judo and kung fu then.

"Long story. Listen, it's been nice chatting with you, Carl. But I got a job tomorrow. I need to quit drinking while I'm behind." He signaled the bartender. "Include my friend's beer too." He slipped off his stool and plopped some bills on the bar.

I extended my hand. "Thank you, sir. I hope we can chat again." He reached out to take my hand, but before we could shake, he real quick-like stepped to the side.

Right then a fat slob of a man crashed against the bar where Sensei had been standing, sending my new friend's empty beer cans over the far edge. Sensei wasn't even lookin' that way, so he sensed it or somethin'. He reached out to guide the man onto his stool, but a hand grabbed my new friend's arm. I recognized the grabber as the same one who had decked the other big man minutes earlier.

I didn't know what Sensei was doin' because he didn't struggle against the grab. Instead, it seemed like he allowed the dude to pull his arm toward him. A second later, probably a half a second, Sensei jabbed the thumb of his other hand into the man's throat. He did it pretty damn hard, and the dude bent forward, gagging and wheezin'. Sensei retrieved his grabbed arm back, slapped both of his palms on the back of the man's head, and drove him down flat on the wet floor. It wasn't fancy like you see in the movies these days. But man, was it ever sweet.

Sensei looked back at me—my mouth must have been open in all kinds of amazement—and he winked and nodded goodbye again. It was all so damn casual like he was havin' a nice stroll in the park.

But a second after he left out the door, the people who helped the dude up Sensei put down streamed out after him. So I followed behind them. Outside, I spotted him on the sidewalk, headin' toward the corner. I sensed things were going to get even crazier, so I hurried over to my Chrysler, it was powder blue, painted it myself with a house paintin' brush. A few seconds later, I bounced over the curb and headed for my new acquaintance, who was maneuvering himself for an advantageous position as the mob of drinkers were surroundin' him. I nudged three or four of the men aside with my big ol' Chrysler's grill and pulled up next to Sensei.

"Better get in," I yelled to him through the closed passenger window. He didn't argue and bailed inside. My seat covers were powder blue too. I was real proud of that car.

Anyway, as I goosed us away from the mob, and that's what they were because they were hollerin' and beatin' on my roof, I said to Sensei, "I'm thinking you might have to find a new waterin' hole." A bottle bounced off the side of my Chrysler then, and another shattered on the street outside my door. I got to tell yuh, if they'd hit my car with one more bottle, I'd a run them down.

Sensei says, "I live on Sixth if you don't mind dropping me off." I mean, he was as calm as if I were giving him a lift to get a haircut. Then he says, "I'll pay for that dent or scratch." That was the first of many examples of how generous the man was. I told him it was no problem.

Third Avenue, where we'd been drinkin', was in the heart of skid row. Sixth Avenue was mostly low-income rooms and apartments. There were a few bars there, mainly in the Chinese restaurants that made up a feeble China Town.

I said to him, "I been thinkin' where I'd heard that 'sensei' word before. It means teacher in Asian, right? I was stationed in Japan twice, and I remember hearing that word. Some of the guys took judo in the port, and they talked about their sensei."

"Yes. It's Japanese."

When he didn't explain further, I asked, "Sorry for being nosey, but why are you called that?"

"My friends called me that. It just stuck so much that I even call myself that now sometimes without thinking, like with you earlier. It probably sounds like an ego, but it isn't." He looked like he was thinking for a second. "Well, maybe it is a little. Lots of people want to be different. Maybe that's my way. I haven't analyzed it. I just go with it."

"But why did your friends call you that? Sorry. Tell me to mind my own business if you want."

He turned toward me and gave me a long look. I returned the look for a couple of seconds, but I had to look back because two ambulances were parked partly in the street, and I needed to focus on jockeying around them. I remember thinkin' how intense the man's eyes were.

But I had seen somethin' else there before I turned away—trust. Crazy, huh? But that's what I saw looking back at me, trust. When I've thought of that moment over the years, I think it was then when we started to become friends. I know that's crazy too. We just met and all, and I wasn't desperate for friends or anything. But I still remember thinkin' that. Some things like that happen fast.

Then Sensei started talkin'. "I began studying the martial arts at a young age," he said, pointing at where I should pull over. It was a six-story building on the corner. "I took to it like a duck to water, and by the time I was seventeen, I was a brown belt and teaching the kid's class. The 'Mighty Ninjas' liked me, I guess, and they called me Sensei, the same name as the headteacher at the school. I continued training until I went into the Army. Then in the hand-to-hand course, they made me an assistant to the sergeant leading the training. Although I hadn't told anyone about my nickname in civilian life, my buddies started calling me Sensei. But later when I was a sergeant in Nam around new people, they called me Sarge. Well, I did run into two guys over there I knew stateside, and they called me Sensei."

He smiled a little for the first time. "For a while, I didn't know what to answer to. When I got out, the Sensei tag continued. Now when someone asks my name, I just answer 'Sensei' without thinking."

"Cool," I said. "My mama used to say, 'You can call me anything, so long as you don't call me late for supper.' You trainin' again, Sensei?"

"Twice a week at the old school. The real Sensei lets me workout for free until I can get on my feet."

"You workin' out tomorrow night?"

"In the afternoon."

"I get off at five-thirty," I said. "You wanna get some chow mein at Rickshaws? We passed it two blocks back. My treat."

"Well then, let's do it," he said. And for the second time since we'd met, Sensei smiled.

<0>

As Grant checked his small recorder, Carl reached into his pocket and pulled out a clear plastic grocery bag, the kind found in a grocery store's fruit and vegetable section. It held about a cup of M&Ms. "Help yourself."

"Thank you," Grant said and shook out a few into his palm. "You said you saw what you thought was a look of trust in his eyes. Can you tell me more about that?"

Carl tossed back a few M&Ms and looked thoughtfully off across the park. "It was the damnedest thing. I read once where the writer was talkin' about his life-long buddy. He called it 'the magic of friendship.' We all meet and interact with a lot of people in our lives, but most of us only have one or two true friends. With Sensei, our connection was fast, and it lasted nearly fifty years."

Carl looked away, but before he did, Grant saw his eyes tear up. "I'm sorry for your loss, Carl. I wish I'd known him longer than I did."

"He was special, yes, sir. Don't get me wrong. I like women, brown, big booty, big titties. But Sensei and I had something special." He shook his head as he poured more M&Ms into his palm. "We got together two or three times that first month for beers, but the following two months were rough. Rough, and some."

"What do you mean

"The last time we met up that first month, he seemed down, real down. We know a lot about PTSD now, but we didn't know nothin' those early years after the war. But I could tell he was in a funk, frownin', his face tight. He drank a lot too. That first night we met, I guess he'd been down then too because he had been drinking hard. But the next two times we went out, he limited himself to two or three beers."

Carl offered Grant the last few M&Ms. The writer gestured for Carl to take them.

"We always went to that shithole where I first saw him. I wanted to go to Rickshaws, where we had been going for dinner, but he was insistent. When I looked back on it later, I think he knew his odds of getting' into a fight were almost guaranteed there, and he needed to punch people."

FIGHTING

Sensei was chuggin' his sixth can of Budweiser. I had been watchin' two guys sitting on the stools on the other side of him checkin' him out, and not in a good way. Maybe it was because Sensei looked out of place in Chiefs with his short hair, fit physique, hard look. Everyone else in the joint looked like they had one foot in the grave and the other on a banana peel.

Sensei turned to me and said loud enough to be heard over the big speakers where a dying cowboy was singin' about his sorrows, "I'm aware of them, Carl." Then he turned back to lookin' at his can restin' on the bar.

"You wanna leave?" I asked.

"Not yet."

I could tell by his tone that the two words weren't negotiable. A couple of minutes later, the man closest to Sensei got up and headed toward the pisser. I glanced at Sensei, thinkin' I hadn't seen my new friend take a drink for the last ten minutes or so.

The remainin' man leaned toward Sensei and said somethin', but it was lost on me due to that goddamn hick music. Sensei ignored him and ignored him again when the man leaned in again to say somethin'. That's when I noticed that Sensei had switched from holdin' his beer with his left hand to his right hand. Like I said, the asshole was on Sensei's left.

The man leaned in again, but this time when he spoke in Sensei's ear, he underscored his words with several finger jabs to my man's shoulder. Now, that wasn't a good thing to do because Sensei turned slowly toward the man and said somethin'. I couldn't hear that either, but I'm guessin' he said somethin' like, 'Don't poke me again.'

The dummy took that as a challenge because he poked again, I mean, he tried to, and that time toward the side of Sensei's face.

When that happened, I'm thinkin' two things: Uh oh and oh shit.

Sensei snapped up his left open hand and backhanded the dude's hand away. The knucklehead followed with a hard-straight punch with his other, and Sensei just casually slapped that one aside. Both blocks were mighty fast, easy-going, and with hardly no movement at all.

When the frustrated man drew his right fist back to try again, Sensei, for the first time, turned slightly toward him, cupped the back of the man's head as fast as can be, and slammed his face into the top of the bar.

Cans went flying, the bartender shouted, a man somewhere laughed, and that damn country song finally stopped. The man draped over the bar for a moment, then slid off onto the beer-splattered floor next to his stool. Now, that's a hell of a bad place to fall because, on more than one occasion, I seen lazy-ass winos drunker than shit just whip out their ding-dongs and piss right there where they were sittin'. So there was probably a pool or two of that on that skanky floor.

Then Sensei jerked his head toward me. That's what I thought, anyway, but it turned out he was really lookin' at the other guy comin' back from relievin' his water. Apparently, he seen his friend lyin' there on the floor and decided to launch a haymaker at the back of my head.

My damn head! What'd I do?

Sensei was off that stool in the bat of an eye, whippin' his arm out to protect what few brain cells I got. He stopped the punch in flight, then clasped his hands behind the man's neck and rammed his knee up into his crotch. I knew that hurt like a bitch. But I guess Sensei wanted to leave him with a night to remember because he sorta bounced his foot off the floor and slammed his same knee into the dude's liver in his right side.

I've seen enough boxing matches to know that a hit to the liver is a showstopper. It for sure did that because my personal assassin fell to the floor and puked up his beer and chips on his friend's face. It was really somethin' to see, and I 'bout laughed my skinny ass off right then and there.

Then I stopped cacklin' and got insistent with Sensei, and said, "It's time to leave. Not an hour from now, but right now."

He didn't argue. He dropped some bills on the bar, nodded an apology to the bartender, and followed me to the door.

I went out the door first, but when Sensei began to follow, a woman ran toward him, screeching like a drunken banshee, her arms flailing the air. Sensei palmed her face like it was an old basketball, stoppin' her in mid-stride. Then he thrust her back into the arms of her friends who were comin' up behind her.

Some men might not have done that to a woman, but Sensei told me he prides himself in treating all genders the same. He was ahead of the times, see?

By now, someone was holding that woman back as she flailed with her arms and legs wantin' to hit Sensei though he was about a dozen feet away. It looked funny, except the crowd was gettin' larger and lookin' like they wanted a piece of us. Over his shoulder,

Sensei says conversationally, "Carl, we probably ought to get to your car."

He was always so damn calm like that.

The next two months were rough for Sensei, and it was rough for me because of what was goin' on with him. I have to be honest and say that at one point I considered ending the friendship. But I couldn't. I figured the good Lord put him in my life or me in his for some damn reason. And as usual, the Lord was making my burden a hard one.

Four days after the tavern scuffle at Chiefs, my phone rang at two-damn a.m.

"Carl. It's me," Sensei says, soundin' like he had been drinkin'.

"Sensei?" I said, my head still half asleep. "Where are you? It's noisy."

"I'm at Chiefs. I know, I know. But I'm here, and I'm about to kick some asses. Can you come and get me?"

I probably sighed in his ear. "I'll be there in under ten. If it gets too hairy, meet me at the intersection of Sixth and Everett."

I didn't change out of my pajamas. I just slipped on my shoes and a jacket and headed out. About seven minutes later, I saw Sensei in the intersection of Sixth and Everett duking it out with four men. Actually, two were already down, moving a little but not getting' up. Sensei was holding his own with the last two, but for the first time since I knew him, he was takin' some licks too.

So I got out with my Louisville Slugger.

I whipped a homerun across the back of the closest man's knees, droppin' him onto his ass and makin' him scream like a child. Then I belted a triple-base run across his shins. That curled him into a ball. I gotta tell you, his hootin' and holler' were echoin' down the dark streets somethin' good. I looked over and saw Sensei holding the last man by his throat and punchin' the piss and vinegar out of him.

I set my bat on my shoulder and waited for him to take a breath. When his man joined the others layin' on the sidewalk, I said, "If you're done, let's go."

He wiped the back of his hand across his bleedin' lips and said in that calm way he had about him, "I am. Thanks for the lift."

He didn't say anythin' as I drove. When he pulled to the curb in front of the apartment buildin', I asked, "Want to talk about it, buddy?"

He didn't answer for a good 30 seconds. Then, in a voice that I could barely hear, "I don't think so."

I couldn't tell if he was ashamed, embarrassed, or depressed. Maybe all three.

Three nights later, he called me again. "They're coming over the wire!" he greeted me on the phone. "About ten of them! I put three down, but there's more coming!" Then the phone went dead.

I had a hunch earlier in the evening to lay my clothes out in a row so I could put them on real fast-like. So I was dressed, out the door, and in my car in six minutes, shavin' nearly two minutes from the last time he called. But he never said where he was. So I followed another hunch and went to Chiefs first. Sure enough, he was out front fightin' a group of men as if possessed. Before I could get out, two police cars slid to a stop in the middle of the street. If I'd been a minute earlier, I would have had my bat in my hand. A black man in those days holding a big-ass bat didn't have much of a survival rate.

Sensei saw them and stepped over to the brick wall, his hands in his pocket, affecting casual innocence. Two of the men who Sensei had been fightin' tried to take on the cops, but they quickly joined the four my friend had beaten down onto the sidewalk.

What I could put together from the bits and pieces I overheard as the cops sorted things out was that Sensei was the victim. It was never clear what occurred inside Chiefs, but what was obvious was that about ten men followed him out, and the fight was on.

Sensei told one of the officers, his earnest face and voice spreadin' it on thick, "If it hadn't been for the self-defense that I learned in boot camp before fighting for my country and getting wounded, the bullies might have killed me." The youngest of the two officers had served in the war too. He patted Sensei on the back and asked if he was okay. Sensei said, puttin' on a pitiful soundin' voice, "That angry man there punched me in my shrapnel scar, and it really hurts. But I'll be fine… I think."

A moment later, the man he indicated, though semiconscious, was thrown head-first into the back seat of the patrol car. When they told Sensei he could go, I got him out of there posthaste.

After I took him home this time, we sat in my car in front of his place without speakin' for nearly a half-hour. I had already said all I had to say on other nights, so I just waited for him this time. Finally, he said, "I used only my hands. My kicks got rusty while I was in Nam, and I need to bring them up to speed."

I looked at him like he was crazy, which he kinda was. "That ain't the damn issue, Sensei," I told him. "You shouldn't be fightin' at all. You're either goin' to hurt someone bad, kill someone, or get hurt or killed your own self."

I thought about tellin' Sensei that the drunk who was staggerin' and stumblin' past us out on the sidewalk right then could be him in a short while, but I held it back. After five minutes of silence, I asked, "You said 'They're coming over the wire,' when you called. You meant concertina wire, that badass barbed wire they put up around bases and buildin's over there in Vietnam?"

Sensei's eyebrows bunched in confusion. "I said that?"

"Screamed it all hysterical like, if you want to know the truth. That's hard on a guy who ain't fully awake yet."

Even in the dark car, I could see my friend's already flushed face deepen to a darker shade of red.

"This is all about Vietnam, isn't it?" I asked him. But he just looked out the window. "You ready to talk about it yet?"

He sighed as if exhausted, and I think he was. Mentally exhausted especially. Then he opened the door and swung one leg out. He twisted back toward me without making eye contact and said, "You're a good man, Carl. I'm very sorry. I won't bother you again."

I grabbed his jacket sleeve and wadded the material in my fist. "I'm your friend, you son-of-a-bitch. I'm here for you, and I hope you're here for me. Call me anytime. And remember, I got an ear when you're ready."

The streetlight was picking up the tears in his eyes. He got out, and I waited until he got in the front door before I pulled away. I was tearing up too.

Two nights later, at 3:30 a.m., Sensei called from the Multnomah County Jail. He had been arrested for assault.

"I can't come and get you, Sensei," I told him, which was true. "I'm catchin' a cab to the airport. My father called a couple of hours ago from Atlanta and said my mama had a stroke. The doctors said they don't think she was goin' to come out of it. So I gotta get there. I'm sorry. I got some money. How much is the bail?"

"No, no, no," he said real fast. "Don't worry about me. Sorry about your mama. You take care of your business; I'll be fine."

After my mother's funeral, I returned to Portland a couple of weeks later, but I didn't see Sensei again for almost three months. He had moved from the Sixth Avenue apartments but didn't leave the manager a new address. I remembered he had a sister somewhere in southeast Portland, but I didn't know her name.

‹0›

"Where did he go?" Grant asked.

"To his sister's. She had a different last name, so I would have never found him. I guess he had been drinking a lot more than I knew about. He could hold it, you see. He could knock back ten beers and still walk a straight line and talk without much of a slur. Good thing because he would have gotten his ass kicked a few times, karate or no karate. In fact, he did at least once."

"What happened?"

"He told me about it about a year later. He said, 'You can't block what you can't see.' He was holdin' his own against some dudes at the intersection of Third and Burnside. He didn't say, but I'm guessin' it started in Chiefs joint one block away. Anyway, he had knocked one guy dead out. He punched a second guy, who staggered out into the busy street before he collapsed and came real close to gettin' run over by a Jeep. As it was, the Jeep swerved and sideswiped a truck, which hit a Volkswagen Bug.

"While traffic was all jammed up and the drivers of the three vehicles were pushin' each other back and forth arguin' over who was at fault, Sensei was busy fightin' the remainin' two guys, one of which was a good boxer. He said a couple of hard kicks to the boxer's kidneys weakened him, and he was about to put the coup de grace on him when the fourth guy came up behind him and hit him with a chunk of a bumper that had broken loose during the three-car crash. The head blow knocked Sensei to his knees, but the rib kicks sent him down to the cement. I think that was the fight that led him to his sister's."

"Wow. It's hard to imagine him knocked down. There were more fights you didn't know about?"

"Yup. He always had new welts, scratches, and bruises on him when I hadn't seen him for a few days. This was back during the time he'd call me at night to come and get him." Carl shook his head and flicked a loose M&M off the table. "The guy was troubled, and it hurt me that I couldn't help him. I'm no shrink, but I've often thought that maybe he was hittin' himself in all these fights. You know, tryin' to punch away the pain he felt. Maybe he was so depressed or guilty over what he had to do over there in Vietnam that he wanted guys to hurt him. Or maybe he needed the rush. I don't know. But like the warrior he always was, he dug himself out."

"His sister help him slow down?"

"It took more than that. What I didn't know is that at the time I came into Sensei's life, he had already been drinking hard for a long time. He told me later that arrest that night when he called me was the sixth time the cops had picked him up. Not arrested but taken to The Detox Center where they let street drunks sober up. He said the detox place was just a big cell where the floor was mostly covered with piss and puke. They'd hold guys for four hours and then let them out to do it again. Sensei wasn't a wino, but he was movin' toward the lifestyle.

"He said, getting' tossed in the hoosegow after we became friends embarrassed the hell out of him. Thing is, when I thought about it, I don't think it was us being friends that bothered him. I think Sensei had finally reached a place where he knew if he didn't do somethin', he would go to prison or someone would kill him. And my gut was tellin' me he would rather be killed than hurt someone during one of his drunks. That's the way he thought about things."

"Did he dry out?"

"He did. His sister's standalone garage had a small apartment above it, and he stayed there and went cold turkey on the booze. Took him six weeks, which is a record, I think. I didn't know any of this was goin' on until a month or so after he got sober. I ran into him by accident in a restaurant, a nice one in southeast not far from his sister's place. He looked healthy, fit, just great. He told me about kickin' the booze and trainin' four or five days a week.

"That was the beginnin' of his karate success." Carl shook his head and chuckled. "He was pretty damn successful on the street, but I'm talkin' about his professional life. He would eventually teach classes at the school, then become an assistant instructor or sensei to match his nickname. A few years later, he would be half owner and eventually full owner. By about two thousand three or four, he had three other school locations, all very successful."

"I don't think I know what he did for a living. I can't believe I haven't asked. Or was that his living?"

Carl chucked and tossed an M&M into his mouth. "Sensei wasn't makin' much of a living off his teachin', so he definitely needed a job. He started out as a plumber's apprentice and stayed with it until he got his license or whatever they get. He did that for about twenty-five years. One of his students was a trainer in Portland's police academy. He invited Sensei to teach a couple of classes, which led him to teachin' there part-time for about ten years. He was very well-liked by the officers, and they thought it was funny that he had been in jail and detox. He retired from plumbing when he was sixty-two, about ten years ago or so."

"I love it," Grant said, making notes. "He never wanted to become an officer?"

"I asked him that once. He said officers worked too much overtime, and they could never count on getting off shift on time. You know, late calls and the like. You see, his martial arts and his schools were all important to him. They saved him not only physically—you know, self-defense-wise—but saved his thinkin' too. He respected the police, but he thought he could also do good work in the dojo by helpin' people with what he called 'their internal battles,' getting' fit, developin' discipline, all that."

"I'm glad you remained friends after his rough period."

Carl nodded, his eyes revealing the affection he felt for the man. "Oh, yes. We shared each other's' journey, as he called it. He came to my weddin', and I went to his. God rest Roni's soul. We had dinners together as couples, and Sensei and I met once a month or so for chow mein, you know, to remember the past, and to be glad it was in the past. I went to several of his local competitions, too, in the 80s. Holy shit, he could fight. Scary, but always with respect for his opponents. Some of them tried to hurt him bad, but he never let it rattle him, and he never tried to hurt them back.

"One time, I had a poster made up for him from a picture I took at a match. He was squaring off with his opponent, his front toward the camera, his opponent's back in the foreground. The expression on Sensei's face, the focus in his eyes, was chilling. I mean, damn focused. I had a printer put this on the poster: *Fast as the wind, quiet as a forest, aggressive as fire, and immovable as a mountain.* That was him."

The old man looked away and chuckled. "About three years ago, I started having trouble with my balance. I fell a bunch of times and cracked my pelvis on the last one. I finally listened to my wife and went to the doctor. He did a shit-load of tests and gave me these pills to take. A couple of weeks later, I got a package from Sensei, a cardboard tube. Inside was a poster that read, 'We are best friends. Always remember that if you fall, I will pick you up…after I finish laughing.'"

Grant started to ask a question but stopped when he saw Carl looking down at the picnic table's surface, lost in thought. After a moment, he looked up at Grant, his eyes wet.

"Here's a story for your book. My wife, Shantell, and me liked the outdoors. We hiked and camped and climbed when we were younger. Me and her were mountain goats in our prime. One time, we were climbing up the side of a waterfall. Crazy, right? It was a small one, about thirty feet high, with lots of moss-covered boulders on each side of it. I was in the lead findin' the right place to tell Shantell to step. Five feet from the top, I found the wrong place, and I went ass-over-teakettle all the way to the bottom, hittin' every big rock on the way, breaking twelve bones." He laughed. "They had to stretcher my ass out of the woods.

“But there was more bad news. We discover at the hospital that there had been an eff-up, pardon my French, somewhere, and our insurance had expired. It wasn’t our fault, but the company had no mercy. The hospital did and fixed me up and sent me home three days later. Three weeks after that, I got a bill from the hospital and another from my doctor.

“The bills were stamped paid in full. We didn’t owe nuthin.’”

“Sensei?” Grant asked.

“Yup. He never said as much, but I could tell by the way he looked down when I told him about it. When I came right out and asked him, he just said, ‘You’re my friend.’ He knew we were hurtin’ because I’d been payin’ on my mama’s rest home on top of all of our other bills. I sent him a check once to pay him back, but he gave it back to me. It seemed like I hurt his feelin’s, so I never did it again.”

“That’s pretty incredible,” Grant said.

“That’s the way he was. Never wanted thanks, and most of the time, people didn’t know it was him helpin’ them.”

Grant remembered what Leo said about Sensei telling his kids’ class to do something for their parents over the weekend without telling them they did it.

Carl’s eyes widened, remembering something. “I almost forgot to tell you this story. It’s the only time I saw him get into a fight, one-sided as it was, after he had cleaned up at his sister’s. We were having chow mein at Rickshaws.”

ONE MORE BULLY

“How long we been comin’ here?” I asked around a mouthful of noodles. There were only a few tables occupied in Rickshaws, and two people sittin’ apart at the counter.

“I was thinking the same thing,” Sensei said smilin’. “It’s scary we’re on the same wavelength. Uh, let’s see. The first time was in nineteen seventy-four, I think. So, at least twelve years.”

“There’s lots of Chinese joints in the city, but we keep comin’ to this one on the edge of skid row.”

Sensei nodded. "Nostalgia, I guess. Next time, though, I'm going to order moo shu pork. I had a plate the other day at Kim's Cantonese Restaurant on Division Street and Fortieth. It was—"

"WELL, YIPPEE KI-YAY!"

The shout made me practically fall out of my chair, but Sensei just looked over at the counter. It was a man sittin' on the end stool. He was holdin' his fork up in the air like the Statue of Liberty, a small chunk of somethin' in the tines. He stood up and faced the room with his fork still held up in the air. He looked close to 40 years, beer belly, a scowl that looked permanent.

"I just found an actual piece of chicken in my chicken chow yuk, or whatever the hell it's called. One damn piece. And here it is." He showed it to everyone. "It's probably dog meat. Damn slopes eat Fido over there where they come from. Betcha this is some right here."

"You sit down, please," Kim said, a fine lady who'd served us since the first day we came in. "Please, no shout in restaurant."

"I'm just showing your customers this piece of dog meat, the one piece of meat in the whole bowl of noodles, so they know what they're getting for their money." He lifted his fork higher. "SEE PEOPLE!"

"You leave now," Kim said, taking his arm. "I call police."

"Get your damn hands off me, gook," he shouted at her, jerkin' his arm away, pullin' her off balance. She caught herself by the counter, sendin' the napkin container and the man's water off onto the floor.

I turned to say somethin' to Sensei, but he wasn't there. I looked back toward the counter and saw him standin' in front of the loudmouth. He had his palms up in front of him like he was tryin' to calm the dude. The loudmouth was pointin' his fork at him, the tines toward Sensei's chest. Sensei was sayin' something to the man so low that I couldn't hear him, and slowly anglin' himself—'bladin' the body,' he called it one time—to make his torso smaller and harder to hit.

"You trying to get into the dragon lady's skivvies, or something?" the asshole shouted.

Sensei stepped aside to give him room and pointed at the door. He was talkin' low in order to mellow out the man so he could save face and leave.

"What if I just kick your ass, hee-ro? Huh?" His agitation doubled real quick-like. "Kick your—"

He jabbed the fork at Sensei's middle. It was a move he would live to regret.

Real slick, Sensei caught the man's wrist, twisted the damn thing farther than it was meant to go, which made the man curse and cry somethin' terrible. Then my buddy punched the back of the guy's hand. Sensei said when you slug a hand that's already twisted as far as it will ever go, the end result is a broken wrist. I got to tell you, that dude's bone cracked like a tree branch.

Too stupid for his own good, the red-faced man swung his other fist. Sensei snapped his arm out and smashed it into the nerves of the man's forearm; then he whipped his open hand into the side of his fat face, the slap louder than you'd think was possible. The hit knocked the man's head toward his shoulder. But his noggin never got that far because Sensei stopped it with another slap against the other side of the man's fat face. That one was as loud as the first, maybe more so.

Sensei told me later that when you interrupt the head's reaction to the first slap with a second one to the other side of the face, it makes the dude's brain bang into his skull, making for a knockout. A concussion.

I never before knew any of this Asian fightin' stuff, but I always got Sensei to tell me after his fight what he did and why. I found it kinda fascinatin' and scary that he knew how to do this stuff.

Anyway, the bully fell to the floor and stayed sleepin' there until the police came.

After that, Kim never gave us a bill when we ate in the place. Of course, we always left a tip more considerable than the bill would have been.

There happened to be a newspaper reporter eating in the place who wrote a little article about it in *The Oregonian.* He called it "Good Samaritan Karate Expert Saves the Day." After the story appeared, Sensei got about 40 challenges to fight, all by phone and letter. No one had the *cajones* or was stupid enough to challenge him in person. His teacher's school enrollment went up 40 percent. It eventually all blew over, and Sensei returned to the quiet private life he preferred.

‹0›

"This has been great," Grant said, bent over his notepad scribbling. He looked up at Carl. "He didn't get into trouble with the police for hitting the guy the way he did? The double whammy on his head."

"Nah. This was in the seventies, about nineteen seventy-seven, I think. At any rate, it was when people weren't so namby-pamby the way they are now. Did I mention the guy was black? Today, there would have been riots, people lootin' and burnin'. Never mind that the black dude was the racist that day."

Grant would have loved to discuss that, but he decided to stay on track. "So you never got into the martial arts?"

Carl shook his head. About a year after I got out of the Navy, I started experiencing extreme fatigue. Man, it was somethin'. Long story short, the doc gave me pills—let me tell you, I take a shit-load of pills every day—and said I shouldn't ever do nothin' strenuous. This was also in the nineteen seventies, and the doctors didn't know shit about exercise like they do now. But for a short while in the eighties, I defied them, and my bride and me did some climbing like I told you. It was hard on me, but I forced myself. That damn fall was hard on me too and ended my climbin' days.

"I wish I had ignored the doctors and done karate too back then." He shrugged. "Wasn't meant to be, I guess. Besides, I would never have been able to do half the things I saw Sensei do. He moved like a dream. Or nightmare, depending on whether you were watchin' him or receivin'."

Grant straightened his back and stretched. "This has been very insightful, Carl. I think I won't take up any more of your time right now, but I hope I can call you should I have a question or two more."

"And vice versa if I remember something you might find useful." He feigned looking thoughtful, then, "There are two things you lose at my age, one is your memory, and the other is…uh… Oh, yes, the other is your memory."

Carl laughed along with Grant. The senior tried to twist around on the seat to get his leg out from under the table but failed.

"Help me unwind from this thing, will you, son."

CHAPTER FIVE

GRANT AND BROOKLYN

"So why did you ask me out?" Brooklyn said after the waiter left with their order. The upscale Thai restaurant, complete with mood lighting, soft music, every table occupied, and sans screaming kids, was called Thai Fabulous. Grant had eaten here twice before, and the writer in him always wondered if the Thai language put the adjective after the noun, or it was just a cute title.

For the last three days, Grant had worried about how he would get Brooklyn into the car, out of the car at the restaurant, and how they would sit at a table. As it turned out, it wasn't an issue. When he picked her up at the house—thankfully, her father wasn't there—she rolled alongside him from the front door to the passenger side of his Toyota. When he asked how he could help, she said, "Time me. If I take longer than a minute to get in, dismantle my chair, and load it in the back, there's no split bill. You buy."

"No, no, it's fine. I can help you—"

"Get your phone and time me. Starting…now."

Brooklyn pushed down the chair arm closest to the car seat, grabbed the door frame, and swung herself onto the seat. Leaning out, she snatched her chair cushion and laid it on the driver's seat. She pulled off the closest wheel, slipped it between the front seatbacks, and set it on the backseat. Then Brooklyn did the same with the other wheel and laid the seat cushion on top of them. "So my seat doesn't get squished," she said. She then slipped off two 15-inch bars—Grant hadn't a clue what they were—and inserted them through the seat openings to the back. Then she lifted the rest of the light-weight frame, folded it as far as it would go, and maneuvered it into the back.

"Time," she said, looking at him.

"That was impressive," he said earnestly. He looked at his phone. "But I'm afraid it's Dutch."

"Bullshit," she said, her mouth fighting a smile, her laughing eyes accelerating his heartbeat. "Fifty-seven seconds, right?"

Grant stuffed his phone in his pocket. "Exactly, and that was amazing," he said.

It had been 72 seconds.

At the restaurant, she put the chair back together in about two minutes, then swung smoothly out the door opening and into her seat. When Brooklyn saw Grant's astonished look, she said as she pushed the door shut, "My dad says I'm half chimpanzee."

"But much cuter," Grant said, grinning.

"Ahh, I'm a cuter than a chimp, thanks," she said, leading the way to the door. "Since you're buying, I'm ordering big and food to go too."

Someone had already removed the second chair from their reserved table, so Brooklyn simply rolled hers up to it. All the worrying for naught, Grant thought, plus they had a fantastic view of the Willamette River and city lights.

"How's the book coming?" she asked after their wine came.

He shrugged. "It's coming is all I can say at this point. I see some structure, but it's still early in the process. Your dad was a great interview."

"I heard it. Dad forgot that we discovered a long time ago that the heat vent out in the sunroom acts as a conduit sending voices through to the kitchen."

"On no. Your dad said you didn't know any of that stuff."

She took a sip of her sauvignon blanc. "I didn't. It was a bit of a shock, but kind of funny too. The blind leading the blind. Pretty amazing that Sensei paid the money back and some."

"Did you know him well?"

"He came to the house a lot. I called him Uncle…for a while." Grant saw something pass across her face when she said those last three words. She continued her voice slightly lower. "He and dad trained out in the yard when I was a kid. Dad was good, but Sensei should have been in the movies…" Her eyes slightly narrowed as they searched Grant's face.

"What?" he asked. "You stopped like you had a 'but.'"

She shook her head and took another sip, her eyes on her wine. She set the glass down and looked up at him.

"You can't do that," Grant said.

"Did you ask me out to get more story?"

Grant shook his head quickly. "Absolutely not. I asked you out because I thought your eyes were amazing, I liked how you looked at me as if you were sizing me up, and I thought you were fun when we all ate after my interview with your father."

Her face didn't give away anything as she studied him for a long moment. Then, a smile lit her face and sent Grant's heart racing. "Great answer. I just might put out for you."

Grant's eyes widened, and his hand froze as he went to lift his wine glass. That made Brooklyn laugh.

"And there's one other reason," she said, watching him try to collect himself after what she said. "You fibbed about my time loading my chair. I have a very good sense of time. It takes fifty-seven seconds to get into my Ford. But your car's front seats are closer together, and your console is bigger, which slowed me down. Anyway, I liked that you fibbed so as not to make me feel bad."

He flushed a little, collected himself, and said, "I do lots of cool things like that. I'm just basically a cool guy."

Brooklyn laughed. "So let's do the getting-to-know-you talk. And you can forget the 'I just might put out for you' comment. I was just busting your… I was just teasing."

They dined on Thai barbecue chicken, spring rolls, pad Thai, as they talked and laughed for the next hour. There wasn't the usual "the wonder of me" where first dates try to impress one another. Instead, they shared weaknesses, mess-ups, as well as their successes.

When their dessert of Thai fried bananas and ice cream arrived, Brooklyn said, "You're a wonderful writer." Grant looked at her, puzzled. "I read Surviving the Second Tower after you asked me out. I got it on Kindle and read three-quarters of it the first night and finished it before lunch the next day. It was amazing. I felt like I knew her."

"Thank you. I can't believe you ordered it the same day."

"Of course. You think I would go out with a guy who used weak metaphors and misplaced modifiers?"

Grant smiled again. "I'm glad I passed. Sensei asked me to write this book about him. I was surprised when he did, shocked, actually. At first, I didn't know why he wanted me to, a relative newbie at bio writing, or why he wanted a biography at all. But later, he said he had had a lot of challenges, made a lot of mistakes, and he wanted the book to show that we aren't locked into past missteps, that we can all rise above them."

"To show that he was human," Brooklyn said, a noticeable coolness in her tone that Grant noticed. Curious, but he decided not to ask about it. Not yet anyway.

"Yes. And Sensei's request came at a time when I'd been observing how the students literally worshipped him. He was like a king, a benevolent one, and when he spoke, people bowed and scurried about to do what he said. I get that he was a karate master and a tenth-degree black belt and all that, but I had never been in a place where a person was so esteemed. And I did two years at Yale, where there are some amazing professors with multiple doctorates. The students respected them, but they didn't treat them like holy figures."

"I saw that too," Brooklyn said. She gestured toward her legs. "Before this happened, I took classes in the dojo where my father taught. The students sort of idolized him, but when Sensei dropped in to watch or teach, I thought how they carried on was over the top." She took a sip of water. "But what I liked was that my father and Sensei treated everyone the same, from the beginners who were trying to figure out how to tie their white belts to veteran black belts who had won big tournaments."

"Yes!" Grant said enthusiastically. "That's what I saw too. I worked on a movie set one summer as a gopher. The egos there were laugh out loud funny. The young actors and the veterans all thought they were hot shits. Wait, that's not true. The lead, Aaron Hudson, wasn't that way. He was so nice to everyone, even to me.

One time, I brought a glass of ice water to this producer without being asked because it was so hot on the set, and he was really pitting out. He tossed it aside and cursed me out because I should have known that he only drank chilled orange juice, the kind without pulp. A minute later, Aaron Hudson came up behind me and handed me an iced tea. He smiled at me, nodded toward the producer, and said, 'The smaller the mind, the greater the conceit.'"

"Good one," Brooklyn said. "And it's so cool you met Aaron Hudson. When I was in high school, all the girls thought he was so dreamy." She laughed at that.

"Sensei and I only talked about the project twice. He did say he didn't care for the excessive bowing and carrying on whenever he was in one of his schools. It was important to him that the book showed his students that he was just a man, one with a history, one who overcame a lot to establish himself as a contributor to the community." Grant shrugged. "He didn't say it exactly that way, but that was what I picked up from our conversation."

Brooklyn's eyes narrowed for a moment. She looked toward the window as if to hide it, but Grant had already noticed. It was the second time she had responded oddly when talking about Sensei. Why? Grant wondered. When she looked back at him, the look was gone.

"He was quite a man," she said, stiffly, then sipped from her wine glass. Grant filed it away for now.

"So," he said, after remembering where he had left off, "your dad and others said Sensei didn't want his story sugarcoated. Sensei did say that the larger-than-life character he had become to his students over the years was not of his making. In fact, he even wanted the students to stop calling him Sensei and just use his first name. But his senior students voted that down. They insisted there be that hierarchy in the schools. Sensei didn't like it but eventually gave in to their desires."

"I remember when there was a thing about not calling him Sensei," Brooklyn said. "My dad didn't care what the students called him, but he agreed with the seniors that everyone should call Sensei by the title, 'Sensei.' Dad thought his friend's reluctance was something he was going through at the time, maybe with his

Vietnam experience. Dad said he had a lot of issues with the war. Not all the time, but like every year or two, it would raise its ugly head. My dad said it had to do with when he got wounded."

"Interesting. I'll call my first interviewee again and ask about that. He served with him over there."

Brooklyn nodded. "I think a book that shows the human element and all that that means is a fantastic slant too." She looked out the window and watched a tugboat work its way up the river. It was a full moon, and the reflection on the river was breathtaking.

Grant detected something change in her again. When she said to 'show the human element and all that means,' her volume dropped a little, and the skin around her eyes and mouth tightened.

"Is there something else, Brooklyn?"

She looked at him for a long moment, then, "I don't know."

"I don't understand."

"It's our first date and everything."

Grant nodded. "Okay, whatever you're comfortable with. Just know I'm a good listener."

"I bet you are," she said softly, studying him for a long moment. Then, "Okay, there is something, but it can't go in the book. If I tell you, it would be for your info in the event something else you learn hints at it."

"Okay, I think."

"Okay, never mind."

Grant reached across the table and rested his fingers on the back of her hand. "If you don't want to tell me, that's fine. But know that if you tell me it's off the record, then it is. It won't go into the book."

Brooklyn moved her thumb over the back of his hand and gently stroked it. She turned her hand over and moved it so that they were clasping hands. She closed her eyes.

"One day, when I was in my senior year going to PSU and living at the farm, my building got a bomb threat. Everyone had to leave, and since it was my last class anyway, I went home early. I walked into the back door as always and called out to my mom. I heard voices and sounds like someone was scrambling around. I got scared because I thought there was a burglar or something.

"Dad has always taught me that I should look for a weapon when something doesn't feel right. So I grabbed a kitchen knife. I kind of froze there in the kitchen, and a couple of seconds later, I heard movement coming from around the corner where the hall is. I was more pissed than scared, and I lifted the big knife up to my shoulder, ready to stab. I saw a foot and leg appear at the corner, followed by Sensei. I just stood there with my knife ready to plunge, and he kind of froze, looking at me.

"I heard my mom say, 'What is it?' then she came around the corner. She says, "Brooklyn? What are you doing home?' I mean, they were both standing there acting all guilty like."

Grant squeezed her hand lightly and waited for her to continue.

She took a deep breath. "They had been in the bedroom."

The waiter came with a water pitcher and the check and told them how wonderful it had been to serve them.

Twenty minutes later, they were outside, Grant sitting on a park bench on the restaurant's lawn and Brooklyn sitting next to him in her chair. He had retrieved a blanket from his car and draped it around the two of them. They held hands underneath it.

"I'm sorry," he said. "Did you have any clue?"

"A little, but I kept denying it. Mostly, mom and Sensei would exchange these looks, you know. Like when my dad would get up to go to the bathroom or get a beer, Sensei and my mom would glance at each other. He..." Brooklyn took a deep breath and looked out over the river. "The bastard was supposed to be my dad's friend. And I thought he loved me like I did him. I called him uncle up until then. He and I even went fishing a couple of times. There's a pond on the south end of our property."

Grant could feel her hand trembling in his. He let her ride her emotion out without saying anything. A few minutes later, she coughed and stirred in her chair.

"Sorry. It still brings back some tough feelings."

"How was it between you and your mother?"

"No one in my family hems and haws, and we're never vague or speak in a roundabout way. So after Sensei left, I got in her face. I shouted, 'What the hell are you doing? What are you doing to our family?'" Brooklyn took a breath and continued. "My mom fell apart. It was like she had been holding in this guilt, and when caught, it just spilled out of her. She didn't lie and deny it, and she didn't give me any details, thank God. She said when I came home early, they were breaking it off. I know, b.s., right? But I believed her."

Brooklyn let a minute pass to get control of herself again. Then, "Sensei didn't come around much after that. He and my dad saw each other at the schools, but he didn't come out to the house to train or help with the corn. Of course, it was winter then, so my dad and I did the work in the barn."

"You think your dad knew something?"

"With him, it's hard to tell. He holds stuff in a lot longer before he lets it out. And for a martial artist, he isn't confrontational at all. I never heard my mom and him fight. She'd get on him about something, but he said little back; he'd just wait for her to get out of her mood. If he knew about the affair, maybe that's how he was handling it: just waiting for her to get over it. I never went back to karate classes after that. I told my dad my homework was too much, plus I wanted to try out for tennis, which I ended up playing all through college."

"If it's not too personal, Brooklyn, I hope you and your mother were okay, uh, you know, by the time…"

"By the time she and my husband died in the accident? Yes. We hadn't talked about it in years. Nothing left to talk about, really. Besides, she always had this philosophy that we can't change our past mistakes, but we can promise to ourselves to do better from the present forward. I think Sensei shared that philosophy, at least as far as my parents were concerned. It was a while before he came around again, but not as often, and it was never again like it was before. By that, I mean, he didn't feel like part of the family anymore. Mostly he helped my dad in the barn. And when he saw me, he was very respectful, formal almost. Same when he and my mother crossed paths. But…"

Grant lifted his eyebrows. "But?"

"Still off the record. By that I mean you didn't hear what I'm going to tell you from me, okay?"

"Of course."

"I heard he was quite the womanizer. Have you talked with his wife's caretaker?"

"Not yet, other than to introduce myself at the gravesite."

"Well, if Sensei wanted all his warts on display like you and my dad said, you might bring up the subject with her to see what she has to offer."

‹0›

So this is what floating on a cloud feels like, Grant thought as he slipped into bed. What a date it was. He picked up Brooklyn at 6:30 and had dinner. Then they sat outside and looked at the Willamette River and Portland's skyline as they held hands and talked and talked. They ended the night with beers at Loggers Pub.

They didn't say a word about Sensei when they were at the pub. They shared each other's early years and their hopes for the future. But it was the silent moments that sent Grant's head spinning—their hands touching, looking into each other's eyes, smiling dumbly, giggling at everything, and just being close to one another. The last thing she whispered in his ear as he bent down to hug her goodnight at her door was, "That was the most wonderful evening I've ever had."

He whispered back, "It was the best evening and morning. It's two twenty a.m."

What a difference a single night can make, he pondered as he lay wide awake. He reflected on the first time he saw her wheelchair at the gravesite, and those mysterious eyes looking at him out the darkened SUV window. Then at her home when he talked with her father and how he couldn't take his eyes off her every time she came into the sunroom. And the way she looked right back at him.

Nayyirah Waheed, a young poet he had been following, wrote, "Chemistry is you touching my arm and it setting fire to my mind."

Yeah, like that.

He thought about their conversation at the table, and how Brooklyn's disposition had changed when they were first talking about Sensei. He hadn't said anything the first time it happened, but the last time her mood altered, he asked her what was wrong. Like most women, she said nothing. But after a moment, she made him promise it was off the record. When he agreed, she told him about her mother's affair with Sensei.

He would certainly respect Brooklyn's request not to write about the affair, but she said she had heard there were others. He would have to do some digging on that. Hopefully, Sensei's wife's caretaker knew something.

What had they been talking about the first time her mood changed? Oh yes, he had said something about what an amazing man Sensei was. That's when it changed. It was like a shadow fell across her face. It only lasted a moment, but it was definitely there. Was that when she started thinking about her mother's affair? Anything was possible, but his gut was telling him her abrupt change the first time wasn't about that. Okay, so what was it? It seemed to have been triggered by the word 'amazing?'

Grant yawned. Maybe it was just his writer's imagination at work.

Maybe it wasn't.

He managed to get a little sleep but woke when the early morning daylight slipped through his window blinds. He stumbled into the bathroom then after looked around his bedroom for his phone. He found it in his pants draped over the chair. He hadn't turned his phone back on after their date. He impatiently waited for it to come alive. Would there be a message from Brooklyn?

There was! Her father called her Brookie. Grant wondered if he would eventually do that.

Brooklyn's voice. "Best night ever. Have a good day."

Grant nodded and nodded some more, his smile impossibly wide.

There was another phone message: Unknown. He read the first part of the transcription: "Grant Perry, this is Miss Lindsay Graham."

The ice queen, he thought. AKA, the home nurse who took care of Sensei's wife during her terminal illness. He poked the audio transcription.

Grant Perry, this is Miss Lindsay Graham. I'm available today. Call me.

Terse, to the point, no frills, no warmth.

CHAPTER SIX

LINDSAY GRAHAM

Grant's first impression of the woman as she walked up to the outside table at Drako's Deli was that she had a yardstick up her butt. Everything from the way she carried herself like a queen to her expensive-looking attire—burgundy lambskin leather jacket, black slacks, and burgundy heels.

She said she would meet him outside at 10 a.m. sharp and to order her an Earl Grey tea, two bags, and a water. It was ten on the nose as she approached, and her tea was waiting across from him. He stood as she pulled out her chair and sat.

"Thank you for getting my tea." She pulled off the lid and blew across it, not looking at him. "How is the book coming?"

Her tone was less rigid than she sounded on the phone, Grant thought. Maybe she wasn't as brave in his presence.

He wondered what Brooklyn was doing.

"Pretty good, thank you. I've interviewed a few people and learned some amazing things. He was quite a man."

"He told me about the book."

Interesting, Grant thought. He was still in contact with her two years after his wife's death. Friends? More than friends? He decided it was too soon to open with that question.

"May I ask what he told you about it?" Grant asked.

"What did he tell you he wanted?"

She's going to make me work for this, he thought. "Well, he wanted a bio, an honest one. He wanted the book to show him as a man with strengths as well as weaknesses." Grant smiled. "He didn't say it exactly that way, but when I paraphrased back to him, he nodded and said, 'Nailed it.'"

"I see. Here is how this will proceed." Uh-oh, the tone she used on the phone was back. "I'll tell you my story, but you do not have permission to use my name in the book. Use an alias. If you use my name, I'll sue you for everything you have and some."

Bitch! he thought, straining to keep the judgment off his face.

"I can do that. Though people who know about your job taking care of his wife will know."

"My friends wouldn't read such a book as this. His friends had never seen me, so they wouldn't know me. He kept his private life very private. He didn't socialize with his students, but he visited some of his old friends at their place or in coffee shops and restaurants. The few people who called to check on Roni, his wife's name if you didn't know, were her friends, and they knew me only as Liz, no last name."

"Okay, if you're comfortable with that, I am."

"Thank you." She extracted a large envelope from her shoulder bag. "So we're both on the same page, my attorney has drafted this agreement regarding my anonymity. It also states that you understand that I have the right to approve my section before it goes to press." She set it on the table. "Sign it right here where I've put the little x."

In one of his writing classes, Grant learned never to let an interviewee read his or her section because it can turn into a nightmare of adding and subtracting to put them in the best light. But in his short writing career, he had let people approve their piece, and it had yet to be a problem. Then again, none of them had the personality of a Russian prison guard like this woman.

He scanned the document and didn't see anything that would be an issue. "I'll sign it, Miss Graham," he said, doing so, "but let's be clear that this is my book with my slant and my tone. I won't write anything that I disagree with. But I'm sure we can work together smoothly and get a fine product." He couldn't tell if she widened her eyes out of anger or surprise.

"Excellent, Mister Grant," she said with a small laugh. "You've got balls. Maybe there's hope for your generation after all."

Grant smiled weakly. "Uh, thanks?"

"Yes, you may take that as a compliment." She folded the form and put it back into her bag. "I came into Roni's life when her illness became extreme."

Grant quickly retrieved his recorder and placed it on the table. She was already controlling the interview, he thought, but it's better than having to pry out information. He saw her frown. "No one will hear this but me. I use a recorder, and I take notes. It saves me from having to call and bother you to double-check on something."

"I see," she said, not happy about it. Maybe she's afraid of me showing my balls again, Grant thought. She tapped a finger on the table while he set it up. "Done?" she asked pointedly.

"Yes, ma'am," he smiled sweetly.

She glared at him for a moment, then, "At first, I worked eight-hour days, but I was a live-in for the last few weeks. Nathaniel—I understand everyone called him Sensei, which seems silly to me—was as helpless as a child when it came to helping his wife. When Roni coughed or had difficulty breathing, he would just stand there, his feet together, his hands clasped under his chin.

"I understand he was a karate expert, a champion at one time. And a soldier overseas. But I didn't see that side of him at all." She paused as if suddenly remembering something. She frowned. "There is one exception when I saw that side. Understand, I abhor violence, so I've shoved the terrible incident far back in my mind."

"Please tell me what happened," Grant said, gently so as not to scare her off since whatever it was seemed to bother her.

She frowned again, and for a moment, Grant thought she was going to refuse. Then, "Nathaniel and I went to a small outdoor café a few blocks from his home. It's called Mediterranean Best, on Southwest Knight and Eighth. There are many little shops on Eighth, so a lot of people were walking by. It was early evening, warm, and the sidewalk tables, about a dozen, were all occupied.

"We had just been given our salads when we heard some chanting coming from the street. It was a group of protestors, maybe fifteen or twenty, marching down the street carrying signs about police brutality. They were all dressed in black clothing, mixed races, many of them wearing bandannas to shroud their faces. There was something about the protests in the news, but it was the first I'd seen. It was quite frightening to me.

"When they got even with our outdoor café, they stopped and chanted loud, obnoxious things. Someone, actually more than one person, was blowing whistles, and at least two people were beating on drums. I didn't understand any of it; I mean, what did the ruckus and the intimidating glares at us have to do with what they were protesting? To me, they were just stupid people wanting to terrorize.

"There was a low, decorative fence that separated the diners from the passersby on the sidewalk. Suddenly, the protestors, I don't know how many, stepped over the fence into the dining area. They shouted at us to donate to their cause and demanded that we say aloud that we support it. When a protestor pushed a woman at a table next to us, her husband quickly jumped up. Well, two of the protestors knocked him down and then screamed at the woman for money. It was all very horrific."

Grant nodded, hoping it came across as compassion. "It must have been terrible, Miss Graham. I can see the memory still bothers you. Did they harass you and Sensei?"

"Harass?" she snarled. "No, it was much worse. What they did to me is called assault and sexual molest."

"I'm so sorry. Did Sensei stop it?"

"I had never seen anything like what he did that night. To say it frightened the hell out of me is an understatement. I mean, he was in his late sixties then." She opened her hand and chopped the table lightly. "I knew he did something like this in his schools, his karate schools, but I never…" She shook her head as if the memory bothered her.

For Christ's sake, just tell me, Grant thought. He nodded his understanding of her trepidation. "Please tell me what happened, Miss Graham," he asked gently.

"Two men, maybe early twenties, came up behind us. Nathaniel saw the one behind me, but I don't think he knew there was one behind him until he saw me look over the top of his head. It was so noisy, and there was so much going on. Nathaniel told me later that he didn't react faster because he thought the man was just going to ask us for money."

She again stopped to take a deep breath. "But the terrible person who came up behind me pressed his palm into my plate of food. Then he wiped it across my chest. I mean, I screamed because the filthy man smeared it on my chest, my breasts. I looked at Nathaniel, but he was busy with the other man. He told me later that the man behind him had started to slap the side of his face.

"Nathaniel somehow grabbed the man's hand before it contacted his face, and he pulled his arm down across his own chest. What I saw next, I didn't understand until I thought about it much later. But Nathaniel moved his shoulder sharply forward against the man's straightened arm, against his elbow. My God, I heard it break. I mean, I could hear his joint crack over all the other noise going on.

"But what was so chilling was how Nathaniel was sitting so calmly when he did it. Then he jumped up while the man with the broken arm was screaming something awful." Miss Graham shivered. "I'm sure what Nathaniel did to him crippled his arm for the rest of his life."

She took a deep breath, then continued. "Nathaniel grabbed a handful of the hurt man's long hair and spun him around like a top." Miss Graham circled her hand in the air to mimic Sensei's action. "Then he used his hair to fling him over the low fence, knocking the entire thing over onto the sidewalk, as well as knocking down two of the other protestors."

"When the man who smeared my dinner on my breasts"—Miss Graham patted her chest with her palm—"saw what happened to his friend, he moved around the table and headed toward Nathaniel. For what reason, I never knew because Nathaniel hit him so many times… My God, I mean, I couldn't comprehend what I was witnessing. He was hitting the man's face, neck, chest, and he kicked him between his legs. I almost felt sorry for him as he collapsed into an ugly writhing heap next to my chair.

"I was so frightened then because the demonstrators started screaming at us and coming our way. But thank God, the police arrived, at least a dozen of them. As they went about beating people with their clubs, Nathaniel wrapped his arm around my back and whisked me out of there."

Miss Graham leaned back in her chair as if exhausted, her chest heaving. She gulped from her water glass, once, twice.

"Would you like me to order some wine?" Grant asked though it was before noon.

She shook her head. "It's just that I haven't thought about that night in a while. Violence like that isn't part of my life. I see it on the news, but I didn't know what it felt like to experience it. Or to be a victim of it."

"I'm sorry you had to go through that. It must have been awful." Miss Graham's eyes were focused on her salad, although it looked to Grant that she was still remembering that night.

He took a moment to check his recorder and then jotted in his notebook. There was something about how she told the story that he couldn't quite put his finger on. Miss Graham got herself worked up relating the incident, talking faster and faster as her story unfolded. In the end, she was breathy, and her face flushed.

Yes, the event was traumatic, and yes, the asshole protestor did violate her body, but he couldn't stop thinking there was something else going on.

"You said you were shocked at Sensei's actions."

She nodded. "I didn't expect that from a man his age. I had never thought about it before, but every man I knew up to then who was in his sixties, close to seventy, even those fifty years old, wouldn't have been able to do those things. And the speed and almost nonchalance he displayed made it even more incomprehensible."

Miss Graham reflected for a moment, and the flush returned to her face. She wrapped her fingers around the long handle of her butter knife as she continued, her thumb gently rubbing the rounded end of it.

"I mean, the physicality of it, the blur-like motion, the *urgent grunting* from the men he was doing things to."

Interesting how she emphasized the words 'urgent grunting,' Grant noted, and how her thumb continues to caress the nob on the knife.

"And the terrible sound of the breaking elbow bone and the thumps on the other man's face and body… It was terrible, terrifying, a-a-nd excit—" She let the knife drop from her fingers and looked up at Grant.

Holy shit! he thought, pretending to check his recorder. She's friggin' turned on. Thinking back on that time has got her "feeling saucy" as a girl from England used to say when they were dating.

"I'm so sorry that happened to you, Miss Graham," he said, pretending he hadn't noticed her fondling the end of her butter knife. "How terrible."

"Yes…yes it was," she breathed.

"What happened then? You said the police came."

She nodded. "Nathaniel took my arm and guided me through the chaos to the maitre d'. They seemed to know each other, and the man let us exit through the kitchen and out into an alley."

Grant had an image in his mind of what happened next, and it was X-rated. "What then?" he asked.

"He apologized profusely all the way back to his home. He said he hadn't kept up on the news, and he didn't know the demonstrations were going on downtown. I was still quite rattled." Grant smiled to himself. So that's what her generation called it, *rattled?* "But he was so cool and unconcerned. It was like he did that sort of thing every day."

Wait until you read about his time in Vietnam, Grant thought.

"I had been working for him for about three months at this point, but I hadn't perceived his overt confidence before. I saw that he was an attractive man. But I'm referring to his machismo, if that's the right word for what he had. I mean, he didn't wear it on his sleeve as some men do, but after that evening, I could see it, his masculinity, so clearly. Suddenly the fact he had been a soldier and was a karate expert was right there. I didn't know what being a karate expert meant, but I think that's what I saw him do at the cafe."

The woman's rigidness she displayed when she first walked up to the table was gone. Grant wasn't sure where it went and what, if anything, had replaced it, but she seemed more defenseless now. He would try to take advantage.

"How was your relationship after that night? I'm fascinated that you saw him differently, beginning on the drive home. This book is about the man beneath the martial arts god as so many of his students perceived him. You said you could suddenly see his machismo. Precisely how did he convey that?"

She watched an overly dressed older woman move carefully by on the sidewalk, a flowered grocery bag looped over her arm, her white poodle leading the way on its jeweled leash.

When Miss Graham didn't continue, Grant said, "I remember breaking up with this girl when I was eighteen… Okay, she dumped me. Anyway, she said before she walked off, 'The world is full of guys—try being a man.' Wow, I mean, I don't know how I'd been acting, but that was like a punch to the gut."

He let his Psychology 101 hang there without commenting further.

Miss Graham was still watching the woman, who was now walking across the street at the signal.

Grant said, "I mean, I was only eighteen, so—"

She slowly turned to look at him, her eyes narrowed. "What exactly are you doing, Mister Perry?"

Shitshitshit. "What? I don't understand."

She picked up her purse from her lap. "Do you think I need prompting to tell my story? Why do you feel a need to encourage me as if I were a child or stupid?"

"I'm so sorry, Miss Graham. I certainly didn't mean it like that. I was doing a poor job of throwing out some, uh, possibilities. In retrospect, I can see it was a dumb thing to do. Again, I'm sorry."

The flash of anger left her eyes. "You're young and still new at this, so I'll let that one go." Then to drive her point home, "But it's the only one you get."

"Yes, ma'am. Again, I apologize."

She set her purse back in her lap and took a sip of her water. Her flash of anger seemed to dissipate as quickly as it had detonated. Might she want to tell the story? Might she need to? He hoped so.

"The violence scared me," she continued, "and intrigued me at the same time. And the way Nathaniel did it, so…so elegantly, was a sight to behold.

"Three weeks later, Roni took a turn for the worse. She needed twenty-four-hour care. We…Nathaniel and I knew it was coming fast, but it happened even faster than we anticipated. I made some arrangements, and two days later, I moved in. I assisted her four days and nights a week, and another nurse took three. This only lasted for five weeks because Roni passed that last week, which happened sooner than anticipated too."

Grant finished a note, then said, "That must have been so hard for Sensei, and I would imagine for you too having spent so much time with her." Whoops. I did it again, Grant thought.

Miss Graham studied him for a moment before answering. "Yes, it was. She wasn't a difficult patient at all, despite her pain. She was always concerned that she was putting me out and that I was working too hard." She thought for a moment, then, "Nathaniel was very attentive to her needs…" She looked at Grant. "How much do you know about their relationship? Did he tell you anything about it?"

"Their relationship?" he said with a shrug. "They were married; I know that. He never said anything specific about his marriage other than something like, 'Roni tolerated my teaching schedule' and, 'My wife never liked that I opened three more schools because it kept me away from home most evenings.' Why do you ask?"

She nodded and sipped from her water glass. "Nathaniel wanted me to be honest with you. So here it is in a nutshell. He and Roni hadn't been living together for several months, about a year, I believe, maybe a little more. When she fell ill, it happened fast, and it debilitated her quickly. So he moved her back in with him so he could take care of her. I came into the picture on the fourth month of her illness, and Nathaniel and I began having a relationship a few weeks after that."

Miss Graham settled back in her chair. Grant looked at her looking at him. Is she waiting for a reaction?

A few months ago, Grant's buddy told him about a recent one-night stand he had with a woman. He said, "She was mental, Grant; I mean mental. Usually, you fall asleep afterward, right? Not me, because I knew if I did, I'd awaken a little while later to find her straddling me, my little nightlight reflecting in her crazy bloodshot eyes and glinting off a twelve-inch kitchen knife descending toward my tender throat."

Grant had been picking up that same psycho vibe from Miss Graham, except she'd be hacking some hapless guy with a big meat cleaver. She seemed to enjoy trying to surprise him about their affair. On top of everything else off-kilter about her, she struck him as someone who got off on shocking people.

"You seem surprised," Miss Graham said, her eyes enjoying the moment.

Yup, I nailed it, Grant thought. "Oh, sorry," he said. "Maybe a little, but I shouldn't be. I mean, I don't know either of you really, but he was an amazing man, and you're an attractive woman, er, I mean…"

She laughed. "Thank you, Grant. Your awkwardness is charming."

Grant smiled to himself. Finally, a gimmick that worked.

"They separated, and she moved into a nice condo. Sensei kept the house until they figured out what was going to happen with the marriage. Then she fell ill, and all their plans went out the window."

Grant slowly shook his head. "We never know where life is going to take us, right?"

"Are you ready for the rest of the story, the sordid details?"

"Of course," he said, wondering what could follow the news of the affair. "That is if you're comfortable with it."

"'Comfortable with it,'" she mimicked. She opened her purse and pulled out a pack of cigarettes. Her eye caught a small No Smoking sign on the table. "Shit," she uttered under her breath. "We're even outside," she grumbled, putting the pack back in her purse. She heaved a sigh. "Okay. I thought we might have something, Nathaniel and me. There was a twenty-three-year difference between us, but I didn't think it mattered much. He was handsome, intelligent, and, well, very, very fit is a good way to put it."

Grant felt his face flush. I thought the Baby Boomers weren't so open about such things, he thought.

Miss Graham scanned his burning hot face, her smile feint, enjoying the shock.

"Anyway," she said, "Nathaniel was a catch. He stole my heart, and from the very beginning, he talked of us having a future together. He wanted to go to Hong Kong with me, go from there up into China, and spend three weeks touring and experiencing it. He had been before, some kind of a martial arts thing. But Nathaniel said he wanted to share it with me and let the wonder of the country cement our relationship even further."

Grant lifted his palms. "Forgive me if this question sounds judgmental, but he talked about all this while his wife was..."

"Dying? Yes, he did. And I'm guilty of eating it up, bad timing and all. My only defense, and I'll admit it's a weak one, is that he had this aura that sucked you in. He hooked me, you see. Right or wrong, he hooked me."

She watched a skateboarder zigzag through traffic for a moment. Grant saw a tear erupt from her closest eye. She knuckled it away and turned back to him. Her face was tight now, and the words came out clipped. "Then he cooled toward me like that," she said, snapping her fingers. "One day, we were making plans for this great life, and the next, it was like we had never talked about it. The love I felt emanating from him was gone. *Ffffft.* Like that."

Grant shook his head. "I don't understand. What—"

"It's easy to understand. Nathaniel's eye never stopped wandering. Oh, I saw him looking at other women when we went to restaurants and walks along the seawall by the river, but... I don't know. I just shrugged it off as a man thing. I was so caught up in him. What I discovered was that sometime during our relationship, and be sure to put quotes around the word, was that his wandering eye landed on the cute and much younger nurse who worked the three days I had off."

That revelation took Grant by surprise.

"That says something about him, right," she said. "Well, the nurse fell for it, just as I did. To say it was uncomfortable for me those last few days before Roni passed is an understatement. But I had to stay because the caretaker business I worked for would have terminated me. I stayed, and I took care of Roni to the end.

"As soon as they removed her body, I hurriedly packed my things and left. We never talked about our so-called relationship after the day he suddenly cooled toward me. When I left, I walked out without saying goodbye." I went to Roni's funeral. I left right afterward without speaking to Nathaniel." She swiped another tear away, the move swift. "I should say that he sent my boss a nice letter of recommendation for me."

"Unbelievable," Grant said. "I'm sorry that caused you pain."

"Thank you."

Then, to test the waters, "Was Sensei what they call a womanizer."

Miss Graham shrugged. "I don't know for sure. I've heard things, but I refuse to pass on what I don't know for sure."

"I agree," he said. "I'm not putting anything in the book that I haven't cross-checked at least twice."

She nodded and sat back in her chair as if exhausted. "Nathaniel phoned me three times after the funeral. The first was about six months after. He called to see how I was doing, but I think he was really feeling me out to get back together. If so, I didn't fall for it. The last time I heard from him was a few days ago when he called to tell me about the book. Three days later, I saw in the paper that he had died. It was strange."

"If I may, knowing now what happened to you, I'm surprised you were at the funeral last week.

She snorted and looked down at her folded hands on the table. "I suppose this says something about me. Although it's been two years since Roni died, and I'm in a lovely relationship now, I just wanted to go to the funeral to see his coffin."

She looked up at him. "And whisper to it, 'fuck you.'"

CHAPTER SEVEN

THOMAS MARTIN

"Mister Martin? Grant Perry here. I'm the guy working on a book about Sensei. We met after his graveside burial." Grant was sitting in a Burger King lot drinking a soda after downing a gut bomb burger, his phone pinned between his ear and his hunched shoulder.

"I remember." Still the cop of a few words, Grant thought. He was hoping for a friendly person after talking with Miss Graham. "You calling for that interview?"

"Yes. I've already talked to a few people, and I'd love to hear about your experience with Sensei."

"Yes, you may. I'm teaching a black belt class at seven tonight, and I'll be free at eight-thirty. You can come and watch if you'd like. It's the Watkins Street Dojo."

"I've trained there. Sounds good. I'll see you then."

It was two days after his interview with Miss Graham. He had spent the break reading his sloppy handwriting, listening to his audio recordings, and jotting down ideas. It was too early to tell, but it looked right now that the book could easily follow the order of his interviews. Sensei's time in Vietnam, his lost months when he first got home, his crime spree, the drinking period, returning to training, and his time with Miss Graham. He guessed that the upcoming Thomas Martin interview would probably fit before Miss Graham's, but he would cross that bridge when he started editing.

He hadn't seen Brooklyn since their date four nights before. But they had talked every day. Twice yesterday, both times for over an hour. He smiled to himself. The connection is strong with this one, he thought, then smiled again because he sounded like Yoda, or was it Vader? When they talked this morning before he was even out of bed, she said, “In case you were wondering...”

“Let me guess,” he said. “You like me a lot.”

She snorted. “Yes, I do, and I can tell the feeling is mutual on your side.”

“Yup.”

“Good,” she said. “But that isn’t what I was referring to. I think you’ve been wondering if I’m able to have sex. I bet you even Googled it, right?”

“Oh. Well, I...”

Brooklyn laughed. “You probably found a lot of ‘it depends,’ right?”

“Uh...”

She laughed. “Well, the answer is...”

Silence.

More silence.

Grant tapped the phone to see if they had been disconnected. “Brooklyn?”

“Yes, Grant?”

“The phone went...I mean, I didn’t hear your answer.”

“I forgot what we were talking about.”

“Are you shitting me! You were answering—”

Brooklyn was laughing hard now. “I’m sorry, Grant. I’m messing with you. The answer is yes. But you have to do most of the work and not until the third date, and after you’ve given me a beautiful bouquet, and let’s see, a nice cashmere sweater would be nice. Black because that color goes with everything.”

<0>

The Watkins Street Dojo, the second oldest of the four Sensei owned, was located in a stand-alone building near the Lloyd Center mall. All Sensei’s schools did a booming business and enjoyed a mix of kids and adult classes. According to Google, Thomas Martin, 3rd dan, had taught at the Watkins school for three years.

The entrance opened into the training room, with a taped off area that served as a foyer. More tape formed a walking lane that led to a few chairs, most of them occupied by observers. An enthralled little boy, maybe seven years old, talked excitedly to his mother about what was going on out on the floor.

Thomas Martin stood in the middle of about a dozen black belts, making a point. He looked over and nodded at Grant as the writer toed off his shoes and sat. There were 20 minutes left in the class.

Thomas was physically impressive, Grant thought. Even in a black gi, his well-developed muscles swelled around the jacket's shoulders and upper arm area. His half rolled-up sleeves revealed thick forearms, and the powerful cords in his neck looked like he could withstand the hardest kick to his jaw.

He stood ramrod straight and made eye contact with each student as he talked about the necessity of snapping the hips with a cross punch. "Like this," he said, assuming a fighting stance. He lunged forward, thrusting a fast punch, the perfectly synchronized rotation of his hips sending the ends of his striped black belt flipping. "You got it?" he asked. Heads nodded. "Now you do it for reps."

While the students' techniques were fast and crisp, not one of them compared to their teacher's.

After executing reps with their right leg forward and then their left, Thomas told them to form two lines and face the front of the classroom. Then for the remaining minutes, he led the students through kick combinations: front kick, roundhouse, sidekick, back kick, groin snap kick, and foot sweep and kick. He then called them to attention, and complimented their progress, and encouraged them to do solo training at home, especially those techniques that needed extra attention. "Unless there is a question," he looked around at his students, "then I order you to have a good weekend."

"Thank you for teaching us," the group chorused as they bowed.

"And thank you for teaching me," Thomas Martin replied with a deep bow. He took a moment to speak to a few students and when the last one headed toward the dressing room, he gestured for Grant to follow him.

The writer bowed to the training floor, crossed the room, and followed Thomas into a small office. The teacher gestured toward a chair in front of his desk. As he was closing the door, the little boy who had been intently watching the class tore across the mat toward the office.

"Sensei Thomas," he said breathlessly at the door.

"What's up, Case?"

"Are you sure you can beat up Bruce Lee?"

Thomas winked at Grant. "Well, Case, the more I think about it, maybe not. He was really good."

Case nodded thoughtfully. "Yeah, he was." Then he brightened. "I'll see you Monday, okay?"

"I'm looking forward to it. I think you're going to be great."

"I know," Case said, again his face serious. "Bye." He tore back across the floor to where his smiling mother was waiting by the door. Thomas waved at her as they left.

"My replacement in about twenty years," Thomas said, scooting his chair up to his desk. "Case's mother is working two jobs while doing an outstanding job raising him. She couldn't afford the dues, so I put Case in charge of sweeping the front of the school on Saturdays and stacking the equipment after the classes. I think he will be a good student."

"How old were you when you began?"

"Fourteen. At this same school. My single mother didn't have the money either, so Sensei put me to work sweeping, mopping the locker rooms, and cleaning the windows. I hated it at first. A lot. Because Sensei was a taskmaster."

"Did your father encourage you?"

Thomas shook his head. "No father. He split to wherever when I was about two. My mother had a few boyfriends. Two of them beat her, and one beat the hell out of me. Cops came that time, and they took me to juvie."

"Took you?"

"Yeah, because I cut the guy with a steak knife."

Grant pulled his attaché case up onto his lap. "I think we should start at the beginning. I really appreciate your time here. Sensei wanted—"

"I talked with Leo Ichiro yesterday. I didn't know anything about the book until you approached me at the cemetery. I'm sorry if I sounded rude or suspicious. My excuse for my rudeness is that I felt bad that day, and my excuse for my suspicion is because, in my work as a police officer, I have to be."

"No problem," Grant said. "Leo told you of Sensei's wishes then?"

He nodded. "He did."

Grant set the recorder on the desk between them and his yellow note pad next to a small figurine of a samurai. "I have learned of some, well, character flaws, but mostly Sensei seems to have been an amazing man." Grant mentioned the flaws hoping it would make Thomas feel comfortable to do the same. "The minister at the gravesite said he interrupted you and some other kids bullying someone?"

"Oh, yes. Beginning around eleven, I started hanging out with a group of guys. It's the classic story of broken homes and alcoholic parents. One kid's mother even prostituted herself out of their apartment, sold dope, the whole shebang. My mother was a good mom when she was sober.

"I grew up fast, physically as well as mentally. By mentally, I mean wise to the fact that the world could be a rough place. At eleven, I was about five feet ten, and at twelve and a half, I was six foot. Within two years, I was running our little gang, breaking into cars, houses, purse snatches, all that. And when other kids didn't give us the respect that we thought we should get, we banged them around."

Grant quick-scanned his notes. "I'm sorry, you said you were fourteen when you met Sensei?"

Thomas smiled. "Yes. Well, if you call knocking me on my butt 'meeting him,' yes."

MEETING SENSEI

My three buddies and I had surrounded a kid on a lawn patch behind the 7-Eleven at 13th and Powell. His name was Shawn, and he was one of the rich kids in school we detested. His kind would look down on us because our clothes weren't as fashionable, because we were bused to school instead of driven there in BMWs and Lexuses, and because we got suspended a lot.

Shawn was older than us but much smaller and frail. But he had a fighting spirit, and when one of my boys tried to extract his cash from his pocket, Shawn punched him. It was a weak blow and hardly noticed, but it ignited us. How dare he fight us back. So we commenced punching and kicking the crap out of him.

When Shawn fell down on the grass, we circled him and were about to deliver a boot party on his legs and ribs when a tall man with this very commanding demeanor seemed to come out of nowhere to protectively straddled the kid. He lifted his palms and told us just above a whisper to stop. That whisper had authority, and his eyes were penetrating and not just a little frightening. The man was Sensei, but I didn't know him then.

"Who the hell are you, old man?" Cal demanded. It was kind of funny seeing him demand anything since Sensei was nearly twice his size and looked like he could eat a nail sandwich.

"Look fellas," the man said, his voice still low but authoritative. "It must be great fun to pick on someone smaller and more vulnerable than you. But right now, he's going to get up and go on his way."

Years later, in the police academy, I'd learn the technique he used was called "fogging," where the speaker agrees about what is going on without escalating the situation. A bully often becomes bored when someone doesn't react the way they want him to, such as disagreeing or fighting back. It's a good technique, but like all techniques, it doesn't always work.

Jerry had been grumpy and quiet ever since we got together that day. It might have had something to do with the fresh bruise on his face, no doubt from his doped-up old man. Anyway, Jerry shot in low to tackle Sensei, but poof, the man evaded it as smooth as can be, and Jerry flew past him. Sensei tripped him as he passed, which sent our buddy ass over teakettle sprawling onto the grass.

Stupidly, Road and I both threw big roundhouse punches at the man, Road first, and me three or four seconds after. But he evaded

Road so quickly it was like he wasn't there. Except for his palm. That he slapped across Road's forehead so hard, it lifted him off his feet. When I started to throw my punch, he did a push-pull technique on my shoulders, as fast as a blur. I mean, I spun around without a chance to react. He pressed behind my knee with his foot, dropping me onto my butt next to Road and his fiery-red forehead. Cal stood his ground, his fist clenched, his face a combination of fear and anger.

"You want to hit me, son," the man said as calmly as can be, "and I probably deserve getting hit, but I'm asking you to sit down with your pals." This time the fogging worked, and Cal, after a moment of hesitation, sat down with the rest of us rubbing our injuries.

Sensei remained standing. "Do me a favor, will you? Sit up straight, cross your legs, and look at me. Cal and Jerry didn't; Road and I glared at him all hard like, at least we thought we were hard. "I'm sorry," Sensei said a little louder this time, looking at Cal and Jerry, "did you think that was a question? Sit up and look at me like men." This time we did, no doubt with a hint of fear in our eyes. I'm sure mine had more than a hint.

"Everyone calls me Sensei. Please tell me who I have the honor of speaking with." He pointed at me.

"Thomas."

"Jerry."

"Cal."

"Road."

Sensei looked at the last boy, the one whose forehead he had smacked. "Your name is really Road?"

"Yes. You're the karate teacher, right. I watched you teach once."

Sensei nodded. "I like your name. I do. Yes, I teach martial arts. I hope you come again. I'll give you a free lesson." Road nodded slightly, then looked guiltily at the rest of us. "Tell me, guys, why were you about to kick the crap out of that little guy?" Sensei's voice was still low, but now it was inquisitive, without challenge or reprimand.

Cal, Road, and I shrugged and looked down. Jerry glared at him.

"Please, men," Sensei said firmly, "look at me. There, thank you. Eye contact is very important, you see. It shows respect to each other. It shows that you're listening. Looking down shows just the opposite. Some people think it reveals cowardice and a lack of intelligence."

That made all four of us straighten and look at him.

"You're an adult," Jerry challenged, "and a big bad-ass karate dude. You knocked us down, and you hit Road in the head. You can go to jail."

"I understand what you're saying, Jerry. But please look up at the corner of the 7-Eleven's roof." They did. "A video camera. It captured what you were doing to that much smaller boy, what you tried to do to me, and what I did to defend myself." He let that sink in while they all exchanged glances. Then he said, "It's one in the afternoon on a Tuesday. Why aren't you guys in school?" No one answered. "Why aren't you in school, Thomas?"

I shrugged, feeling like a wilted tree under his gaze. When Sensei continued to look at me, in that forceful way of his, I said weakly, "I'm suspended for three days."

Sensei looked at Jerry, who only glared back without speaking. Sensei didn't challenge it but instead looked at Road.

"Suspended until further notice," he said.

Sensei looked at Cal, who looked away.

"He doesn't go to school," Road said.

"Shut up, dickwad!" Cal snapped.

"Anyone have a police record?"

"Thomas doesn't," Cal said.

"Anyone have one for assault?" We all shook our heads.

"I got suspended for fighting," Road said. "But it wasn't like assault because we were both doing it. I mean, I didn't attack him or nothing."

Sensei looked at each one of us for a long moment. Jerry looked as if he wanted to leave. I knew the feeling, but something was also telling me to stay.

"Tell me Road," Sensei said, "what do you think Sensei means?"

Road shrugged. "Teacher? Sensei always means teacher in the movies."

Sensei nodded. "Close. It's a Japanese word, and it literally means 'one who has come before in life.' What does that mean to you, Cal?"

Cal thought. "That's easy. You're older?"

"Good. Or to say it another way, someone who is ahead of you in the journey of life." He looked at Jerry, smaller than the others and scowling. "What do you think, Jerry?"

The boy pulled up a fist full of grass, looked at it. And let it sprinkle from his open hand. Pulling up another handful and without looking up, he said, "I think you're holding us hostage."

Sensei looked at the rest of us as if to see if we concurred. But none of us said anything. I actually thought the guy was cool in a badass sort of way, and Cal and Road said the same thing later.

"I just want to talk with you guys, Jerry," Sensei said. "You were all assaulting that kid. That's time in the Juvenile Detention Center off Thompson Street, a police record for a few years, a bad rep, and—"

Jerry stood up quickly. "Then I'm out of here." He looked at his buddies to see if they were going to leave. They didn't.

"Sit back down, Jerry," Sensei said. When he didn't, Sensei looked at the rest of us. "Please. I want to offer you guys something—for free."

‹0›

Thomas took a swig out of his water bottle and looked at the samurai figurine, his mind still back there.

"Did Jerry sit back down?" Grant asked.

Thomas shook his head without looking away from the sculpture. Then he said, his voice low, "My first coach on the job was cold-hearted as he was an excellent cop. It was a defense mechanism, but it often came across as calloused, hard. My second night on the street with him, we responded to a car that ran off Marine Drive into the Columbia River. We both swam out to it and managed to pull a man and woman to safety. When the woman stopped vomiting river water, she screamed that their toddler was in the backseat. We hadn't seen him in the dark waters, and we looked too. Sadly, he had drowned by the time we swam back down. The parents were hysterical, blaming us for his death. "I felt like shit, but my coach just shrugged as we headed back to the precinct to change clothes. 'Hey, we can't save everybody,' he said.

No, Jerry didn't sit back down that day. He ran off and continued to get into trouble. He did time in juvies until he was old enough to go to jail. The last I heard was that he was doing well and living in Seattle completing his studies in the seminary."

Grant smiled. "I see a movie in the works."

"I hear someone is writing a book on him too. Anyway, Sensei offered us a deal. He would teach us martial arts for free, but we had to clean the school twice a week, work in his yard, and that first summer, help him roof his house." Thomas shook his head. "Oh, we rebelled, skipped training, did sloppy work, talked back to him, and all that. But he didn't give up on us. We might have been asshole teenagers in the beginning, but it didn't take long before we saw the light that he cared about us. He gave us more positive attention than we were getting in our homes, you see. I was the first to understand what he was doing; the others eventually caught on. Soon, we all wanted to do good by him."

"Do you credit him with saving you?"

Thomas shrugged. "We were three guys getting a bum deal at home and in need of strong parents. Might we have gone on to more serious crimes?" He shrugged again. "I like to think no…but maybe. But we'll never know for sure because Sensei stayed on us until we saw the light.

"Like I said, we tested him, like kids do to see if their parents really care. But unlike some martial arts teachers, he never punished us with exercise, like pushups or running laps. He did just the opposite. He made us stand at attention while the other beginners did pushups, squats, and planks. He told us that if we wanted to keep up with the rest of the class who were growing stronger from the exercises, we had to do them after the workout or at home. I didn't for about six weeks, but then I could see how the other students were benefitting. So I quit screwing around and was never made not to exercise again."

"You clearly stayed with it, but how about Cal and Road?"

"They stayed until they were brown belts then moved on to work on their education and careers. Road went into the Army, got a degree while serving, and is a major now. He served two tours in Afghanistan. We swap emails every few months. Cal is an assistant district attorney in Bremerton, Washington. His mother lives in Portland, and we have a beer every three months or so when he comes to visit her. Both guys give full credit to Sensei for their life. I do too, of course."

"That's a great success story, Thomas. If I may, could I get Cal and Road's contact info?

"Sure."

"Thank you. How would you call your relationship with Sensei as you got older? Friends? Teacher/student?"

Thomas took another swig of water. "I've thought about that question over the years. I guess he was more of a friend to me than I was to him. I mean that I shared a lot with him, but he didn't share much of himself with me other than his approach to the fighting arts. He also taught me how to deal with the ups and downs of life. He taught me so much, things that I could apply in the dojo and in my day-to-day life outside these doors."

"Could you give me one example?" Grant asked.

Thomas thought for a moment. "Here's one that has always been my favorite. Sensei told me to be cautious about instantly believing what other people tell me is the truth, with emphasis on 'the truth.' He said when you instantly believe what you're told, it's called 'putting another head on top of your own.' He said knowledge is only relevant when you test it in your own life, in your own mind and body. Sensei said, don't believe something just because it comes from an expert or a respected teacher, including him. Instead, apply it to your own life to experience it for yourself. Then you will know; then you will understand if it's usable for you."

"Wow," Grant said, writing. "I like that." When he finished, he looked up at Thomas, who looked lost in thought. "Did Sensei talk much about Vietnam with you?"

Thomas shook his head. "I didn't know he had been in the war until after I'd been training with him for a few years. Sensei revealed that one night when he took me out for a beer to celebrate me getting hired by the police department. I think it came out as a slip because he tried to change the subject. When I asked him about it, he waved me off like it was no big deal, or something he didn't want to talk about. I took it as the latter.

"He then talked to me about the importance of thinking ahead about using deadly force. He said it had been his experience back when he taught in the police academy that too many rookies think abstractly about the possibility that they might have to shoot someone in self-defense. Some even deny it will ever happen to them. He said by not pre-thinking an event, the shock of actually doing it, the trauma to their psyche, could mess me up. Thank God I haven't had to, and I hope I never will, but I have read about it, and we had a class on PTSD in the academy. So I have some idea…"

Thomas trailed off, his attention on the samurai figurine he had been fidgeting with as he had been talking. After a moment, he looked up at Grant and said, lowering his voice, "Leo said for me to be honest with you."

Thomas didn't phrase it as a question, but Grant sensed that it was. "Yes, that's what Sensei wanted, an honest book."

Thomas returned to fiddling with the figurine, turning it clockwise and then counterclockwise. He looked up again as if making up his mind. "Okay. My gut feeling is that Sensei might have been suffering from PTSD."

Thomas seemed to study Grant as if to see how he took that bit of info. When the writer raised his eyebrows, an interviewer's gimmick to encourage the interviewee to keep talking, Thomas did. "I mean, I'm not a shrink, but I took a few psychology classes at PSU, and I've read about PTSD besides what I learned in the academy."

Thomas pondered again for a moment, then, "It's weird, but before I knew Sensei had served over there, I always wondered about something I could never put my finger on." He set the figurine down and picked it up again.

"Could you give an example?"

"Well, again, it was something I sensed more than anything tangible. Sensei was always a quiet man, introverted. In some classes, he was especially so, like he had a big weight on him. Then there were times he seemed really tense. He'd get this faraway look in his eyes, and he'd drum his fingers on his legs when he was standing idly in class. After I got my brown belt, he'd ask me to lead his class whenever he got…tense. I guess that's the best word.

Sometimes I'd take the full ninety-minute session because he never came out of his office. Other times, he'd come out onto the floor about halfway through, thank me, and take over.

"I've read where this isn't too uncommon among vets, but there was something else that I hadn't read anything about. Sometimes he'd get this look. I don't remember seeing it in class, but I'd see him in his office, and he'd be sitting there, his face so tight it looked like it might rip, his eyes narrowed and glaring into space. I never went into his office when I saw him like that; the other students didn't either."

"You think it was Vietnam related?"

Thomas shrugged. "Don't know, but I'd bet it was." He took a deep breath and let it out. "I…" Grant waited for him to continue. He could see the man weighing something in his head. After nearly a minute, Thomas said, "I get it that Sensei wanted everything told…, his good and his not so good."

Grant nodded, wondering how many times he had said that in the past few days.

"Okay. Here's a war story. It doesn't show him in a bad light, I don't think, but it does show his intensity, his mindset.

"I was twenty-three when I finished the police academy, and I turned twenty-four at the end of my probationary period. I was working downtown out of Central Precinct, and I loved it. Patrolling the core area is what I always thought policing should be. A high-energy city, street people, businesspeople, skid row, druggies, shoppers, all mixed into a chaotic stew.

"About my third month by myself, I asked Sensei if he'd like to ride with me one shift. It was like I wanted to show off to my dad so he could see I was grown up and on my own. And I wanted to show him he had produced a good man, someone giving to the community. All that kind of stuff."

"Did he?"

"He did, and he was excited about it. I worked the four to midnight shift then. It's usually the busiest time of the day, plus he picked a Saturday to boot. He got a kick out of all the bantering at roll call, and some of the guys recognized him from his ads; three others had been students at one time. He was fascinated with the car computer and all the bells and whistles. I had been a black belt for a while, and I was training hard for my second degree. He apologized for not having thought about teaching me some techniques with my collapsible baton. I told him our instructors were good, and I worked out with it often at home. He nodded and said, "Very good. Many of the principles and concepts you already know from karate will also apply to the baton. But I have a couple of tricks that I'm sure your instructors haven't taught you. They're good for when the shit hits the fan.'"

"Did he teach them to you?"

Thomas nodded with a smile. "He did. And they were hardcore techniques, so a lot of shit would have to hit the fan before I could use them. The general public doesn't mind cops getting hurt, but they do mind if we hurt a criminal too much, no matter how justified our actions."

Grant nodded. "The general public doesn't like it, and the press loves to run the story ad nauseum."

"Yes. And by doing that, they make our job even more dangerous."

"You said you wanted to 'show off to my dad.' Would you say you and Sensei had a father-son thing going on?"

Thomas pointed at the recorder. "Please don't put this in the book, but I think I was his favorite or one of them. We would talk about a lot of things after the students left, life stuff, but as I said before, he rarely mentioned Vietnam. One time we were in his office, and he kept scooting around in his chair like he couldn't get comfortable. When I asked if he was okay, he said his back was bothering him, which it often did in winter. He said, 'My war injury is reminding me of that day.' But he never said what 'that day' was. He'd say a little about the weather and how miserable the jungle was, but that was it."

Grant started to tell him it would be in the book but decided to let it be a surprise.

"Anyway, my shift began slow, but by seven o'clock, we were rockin' and rollin'. We backed up another unit on a violent shoplifter who had injured two security people. Then we took an aggressive street preacher to jail who thumped a homeless man with a bible.

When we cleared that, this gorgeous woman waved us over to the curb. She had been shopping at Saks Fifth Avenue, and when she came out, she discovered she had locked herself out of her car. It was funny because she was all over Sensei, and she even gave him her number before we left. 'In case I lock myself out of my car again,' she said. Then we got a fight call at a café that was over when we got there, the assailant gone. I called for an ambulance because the cook had a pretty bad head injury."

"Did Sensei flirt with the woman?" Grant asked, remembering what Brooklyn and Miss Graham had said.

"Not at all. He acted a little shy with her, which probably underscored his charm. She was clearly a high-class woman, who was no doubt used to uptown men with hundred-thousand-dollar cars. But she saw something in Sensei."

"Did he help during the calls that were violent?"

"No. I made it clear that he couldn't do anything because the lawsuits could be biblical. Sensei did open the backseat door for me when I arrested the street preacher and the shoplifter before that. And he held doors at the jail. Doors can be a problem when you're by yourself and holding onto a prisoner who doesn't want to go through them. But it wasn't until a call just before quitting time when I absolutely needed him."

Grant made a note, then said, "As you probably know about PTSD, sometimes an event can trigger it. I'm talking about fireworks on July Fourth, war movies, that sort of thing. Did Sensei's demeanor change at all when you made the arrests, say when you went after the violent shoplifter?"

Thomas shook his head. "Nothing other than he looked really focused on the two we took to jail. Sensei was acting like a good backup officer."

"You said something happened near the end of your shift."

"Yes. The call came out as an unwanted drinker at a hole-in-the-wall tavern called Pakistan. It was a dive with a lot of toughs, all of them police haters. The thing is, they had stopped calling us because Oregon Liquor Control had threatened to pull their alcohol license because of the sheer volume of police calls to the place. Plus, several officers had been injured there in the past.

"I was surprised they called for the police this time. But I'd soon find out why."

THE BAR FIGHT

Dispatch: *Eight Thirty-Two, you got an unwanted at Pakistan Bar at Fourth and Ankeny. Male, six-foot, long black hair, black leather jacket, sitting at the end of the bar by the restrooms. Unknown if weapons. Car Eight Thirty-One, you got the cover.*

I rogered the call and flipped on my overhead flashing lights. "This bar can be a rough place," I told Sensei. "The bureau says a ride-along must stay in the car when there is a potential for danger."

"Do you have backup coming?" Sensei asked, apparently not understanding dispatch. I told him Car 831 was on the way. "Then I'll wait outside the bar door instead of going in with you."

I shot him a quick look as I took the corner onto Ankeny. He didn't ask me but told me what he was going to do. I knew he had been in some shit, but this was police work, my world, and he couldn't get involved. Even if it weren't bureau policy that a ride-along remains in a place of safety, I wouldn't want to have to worry about Sensei's safety while dealing with whatever was going on.

Car 831: *This is Eight Thirty-One. Be advised I just got T-boned by a pickup at First and Ankeny. No injuries.*
Dispatch: *Copy Eight Thirty-one. Eight Fifty, are you close to cover Eight Thirty-Two at Pakistan Bar?*
Car 850: *Eight blocks and heading that way.*

"My first cover unit was in an accident, but another is coming my way," I told Sensei. I pointed at the bar's broken sign that read AKISTAN, the P burnt out. "We're here." I stopped at the curb about 20 feet away from the crumbling walkway to the front door. "You never want to park directly in front of the problem location," I said.

A disheveled-looking man stumbled from the front door and stopped in front of the police car, leaning heavily on the hood. "Problems insides Paki," he slurred as I got out. Sensei got out the passenger door. "Theys wants you in theres." He looked at Sensei. "Yous a detective or somethings?"

"What's happening inside?" I asked.

The drunk turned back to me and struggled to refocus his eyes. "Oh, hi cops. Assholes number one hits assholes numbers twos with a glass. Lots of blood."

I extracted my portable and asked dispatch how far my backup was. Eight Fifty said he was about four minutes away.

"Theys be deads by thens," the drunk said, nodding at the radio.

I told dispatch I was going in and to ask 850 to step it up. I looked at Sensei. "I can't wait for my cover. You need to stay—"

"I want a beer," Sensei said. "Let's go."

"You can't..." But he was already ten feet ahead of me.

I walked quickly toward the door and said firmly, "I'm going in first." I must have used my cop voice I'd been working on because Sensei quickly retracted his hand from pushing open the door and stepped back. I'm betting no one had used that tone on him since Army boot camp.

Cigarette smoke and godawful Pakistani music poured out the door. The joint was jammed, and it appeared most were several cheap beers into the evening as they stumbled about, slumped against each other belching their sour breath and incoherent opinions into one another's faces. I made a quick scan of the place, including the bar's far end where the problem was said to be. I didn't see anything out of the ordinary or anyone as described by dispatch or the drunk outside.

The terrible music stopped.

"What are you doing?" It was Sensei's voice.

I turned around and followed his eyes to a man locking the entrance door. I immediately flashed to a story one of my coaches told me over coffee. He got locked into a rough bar in Northeast Portland, and before the chaos ended, he had a broken leg, broken wrist, and a minor concussion. It all went down while his backup was trying desperately to get inside.

I snatched the door-locker's upper arm and started to shove him into the wall, but hands grabbed my upper arms from behind and yanked me backward before I could react defensively. I shuffled my feet to stay upright, but it happened too fast and my balance was too far gone.

I landed hard on my back. At least I tucked my chin so that the back of my head didn't hit the floor.

Still down, I kicked the closest man's leg, landing a solid blow against his kneecap. He yelped and crumpled to the floor, holding his knee. A hard groin kick with the tip of my shoe sent another man down into a screaming ball.

I got just a glimpse of an incoming boot before I felt a rib break. Another one connected with my forehead, fogging my vision and distorting sounds. I didn't lose consciousness, but my eyes and ears were receiving only bits and pieces of the madness.

Shouting.

Flying chairs.

Men crashing to the floor.

Bloody faces.

People fighting to get out the locked door.

I felt hands under my armpits pulling me backward on my butt. I was braced against a wall. Feet moved around me to my front. I looked up…

…and saw Sensei's broad back; to his front, at least a dozen men forming a half circle around him. He didn't wait for them. Instead, he went on the offensive like a really, really pissed off lion.

He used his hands, feet, elbows, knees, and headbutts in a mad assault that was one sided, his side. If I had seen it portrayed in a movie, I would have rolled my eyes and called b.s. But there he was—doing it.

It was at once very, very cool, but also troubling to witness. I knew Sensei was protecting me, but he was obviously in a zone, his face blank, his eyes stone cold, his movements vicious. He was shouting something. It took me a moment to realize it was Vietnamese. I dated a Vietnamese girl for half a year, and while I didn't understand Sensei's words, I recognized the language.

The man was back in Vietnam.

I think I blacked out for a moment because suddenly, police uniforms were streaming into the place through the damaged front door. Three of them took Sensei to the floor and started to handcuff him. I had just enough juice left to call over to them that he was with me; he was my civilian ride-along.

Then all went black. When I came to, I was in the ER. A bunch of cops was there, along with Rhonda, my fiancé, and Sensei. Rhonda gave me a kiss and a hug that hurt my ribs. Sensei nodded, gestured that he would call me, and turned to leave. I tried to ask him to come back, but my voice was too hoarse. I guess I ate a throat punch or something that I didn't remember.

The cops parted to give him a path and patted his back as he passed.

Sergeant Andrews said I had a cracked rib, a concussion, and an injured larynx. He said, "The doc said you could probably return to light duty in ten days or so if your concussion improves as quickly as he thinks it will. Your ride-along did a job on those assholes." He looked guiltily at Rhonda. "Sorry, ma'am."

"I think they're assholes too," she said.

"Sensei pulled me out of the fire," I managed with my rough voice.

"Yes, he did," the sarge said. "And he was taking no prisoners. There just happened to be an Oregon Liquor Control Commission officer in the place when you came in."

"What was OLCC doing there?"

"He was undercover, working a complaint about the place selling to minors. He saw it all unfold when you came in, but when he went to help you, your friend kicked him clear across the room." Sarge dropped his head and laughed at that. "Your ride-along hurt nearly a dozen people; four needed an ambulance. The good news is that OLCC can testify that they were all trying to hurt you and your friend. The only one not trying to hurt you two was the OLCC man. He laughed off the kick and said he's going to try to get a week off to heal and tie it into the two weeks he was going to take off to go to Hawaii."

Sergeant Andrews shook his head. "The OLCC man said your buddy was a tornado. Like he was the Tasmanian Devil with supernatural skills. He also said he'd write the best report he can to show that your friend was justified to use the level of force he did. Hopefully, that will prevent any lawsuits against him and the PD. Like I said, four people were hurt pretty damn bad."

"Thanks," is all I could croak.

The sarge frowned at me. "And when you get back to work, we're going to have a sit-down chat about going into a hot place before your backup gets there."

<0>

"I think I remember this in the news," Grant said, looking up from his notepad. "About five years ago, or so?"

Thomas nodded. "Six. It was something to see. If I may brag for a moment. I'm pretty good, but I'm nowhere close to what he did in that bar. His form was flawless, his speed eerie, and his power, I swear, was that of a two-hundred-and-sixty-pound linebacker. And he was about sixty-five, I think. What he did was so effortless, so smooth. Like a demonstration that he and the others had rehearsed." Thomas looked at his samurai, then back up at Grant. "But…"

"But?"

Thomas thought for a moment, looking like he was trying to figure out a way to express himself. "Like I said before, there was something else going on in that fight. Yes, they were coming at him right and left, and the situation was a desperate one worthy of his intensity, but unless my head kick was harder than I think, he was fighting something else."

Grant watched Thomas toy with the samurai figurine again, not wanting to cut into his thoughts. Finally, the young cop looked up. "I have nothing to base this on other than my gut, okay?" Grant nodded and gestured for him to speak freely. "To repeat what I said before, I really think he was back in Vietnam." He shrugged. Maybe fighting some kind of unfinished business. That's just a gut feeling based on a couple of psychology classes and an active imagination."

Grant's phone chimed.

"I'm so sorry, Thomas," he said, plunging his hand into his pocket to retrieve it. "I forgot to shut it off. Let me just poke—" The screen read "Brooklyn." Why would she be calling? She knew he had the interview. The ringing stopped, then his text tone chimed. Brooklyn: *Call me, please,* the message read at the top of his screen. *It's important.*

"It's okay," Thomas said.

Grant stood, "I'm so sorry. Thank you." He stepped out of the office and moved a few feet into the empty training area. "Brooklyn, Grant," he said before she could say hello. "What's going on?"

Her breathing was ragged, and she sniffed a couple of times before speaking. "My dad… He's really drunk, and he's been snorting coke. He's crying and asking for you."

"What? Coke? I don't understand. Why would he ask—"

"Oh, God… Okay, about once a month, he gets rip-roaring drunk. It's one of the reasons I'm staying here because he's fallen a couple of times and gotten hurt. One time he laid out in the rain all night. But since you were here last week, he's gotten hammered twice and snorting coke again. And he's saying things about Sensei. He's so drunk I don't understand what he's talking about... Oh, God, maybe I do."

"I don't understand."

"She made a sound like a choked sob. "He wants you to come and see him. He said now. I'm sorry… I know you're working—"

"I'll be there, Brooklyn.: He looked at the time on his phone. "Forty minutes tops. Don't let him drink anymore, K?"

"Thank you," she said softly.

CHAPTER EIGHT

LEO ICHIRO

It was getting windy with a threat of rain when Grant arrived at the Watkins Street Dojo earlier, but now his wipers were fighting a losing battle against the heavy wind-blown sheets of water that slapped his windshield and sent street debris streaking past his side windows. The night streets were shiny-slick and dangerous, and his promised 40-minute arrival time turned into over an hour. Brooklyn was waiting for him in her chair on their front porch, her hair dripping from the sideways rain that blew in under the overhang.

"What are you doing out in this?" Grant said, hurrying up the steps. "You're going to get sick."

"He's calmed some," Brooklyn said, reaching up to slip her wet arms around his neck and kissing him. Grant felt it to his toes. "He cursed me for hiding his Jim Beam, so he switched to his beer. I hid the last of those too. He can hold his drink, but he's had a lot, and the coke has made it even worse. He's been cursing and crying since after dinner two hours ago."

"Where is he?"

"Out in the glass room." Brooklyn choked back a sob. "Thank you for coming. I wouldn't have dragged you into my shit, but he's been asking for you."

Grant leaned on her chair arm with one hand and knuckled the tears from her cheeks with his other. They kissed again. "You shouldn't have thought twice about it. Do you know what it's about?"

Her eyes looked into his for a moment. Her lips were trembling, and Grant assumed it was from the damp and cold. "I'm afraid I might."

Grant frowned and shook his head. "I don't under—"

"I'm sorry," she whispered, the words barely audible over the storm.

Grant straightened. "Sorry?"

"Dad will explain. Please, he's waiting."

Still confused, he pushed open the front door. When Brooklyn didn't turn her chair around, he asked, "Are you coming in?"

She shook her head. "He said he didn't want me out there when you came."

"Okay. But you should get some dry clothes on."

The living room lights were off. Grant turned on a standing lamp and headed for the kitchen, where only the small light over the stove cast a dull hue around the orderly room. He pulled open the sliding glass door, startled at how the rush of rain and wind slapped and rattled the tall panes of glass. Grant wondered if it was safe out in the potentially shard-rich space.

Two small lamps on opposite ends of the long room illuminated the setting, which was oddly cozy despite the tempest raging so near. Leo sat slumped in a rocker, his socked feet resting against a window. He didn't look up when Grant entered.

"Leo? It's me, Grant. How are you doing?"

Leo pointed a shaky arm at the chair next to him without turning away from the sheets of rain smacking the windows. "I'd offer you a brew, but Brookie took 'em all. Like I'm a goddamn child." Grant was surprised at how clear his speech was, though he hadn't moved from his slumped position or looked his way yet.

"She's a good daughter who is worried sick about you."

"She likes you, that's for damn sure. You hurt her, and I'll shoot you."

Grant swallowed. That didn't sound like a tease. "I'm not that way, sir."

"I know, goddamnit. That's why I wanted to see you. Now sit down."

"I am, sir. Next to you here."

Leo regarded Grant with unfocused eyes. "You look different. How long's it been?"

"Almost a week, sir. What did—" Leo looked back out the window and, after two minutes, Grant wondered if the man had forgotten he was there. He waited a bit longer then gently cut into Leo's reverie or whatever was going on. "You wanted to see me, sir? Have you remembered something about Sensei?"

"There's no damn remembering," he snapped, "because it's always right there in the front of my forehead. It's there when I first wake up in the morn, it's there all damn day long, and it's there behind my eyelids when I close them at night."

Grant didn't say anything. He had to assume that whatever the old man wanted to tell him, he would get to when he was ready.

Outside, the rain had paused for a moment, though the wind hadn't let up. The yellow corn stalks weren't visible in the darkness, but Grant knew the field was whipping all about.

"Guilt is a hungry son-of-a-bitch, son. It's always gnawing and feeding on your soul." Grant nodded, but Leo didn't see him because he was still looking out the window. "Sometimes the thing causing the guilt is so bad you can't share it with anyone. They say, whoever the damn hell *they* are, that it will be lessened if you share your guilt with someone. 'Pain shared is pain divided,' someone called it. But Sensei is gone now, and I don't have him anymore to share the pain and the guilt. We only talked about it a few times in the years after, but we always knew we shared it.

The rain returned with a hard slap against the tall panes, making Grant jump.

Leo looked at him. "I'm an old man now, Grant, and soon I'll have to answer for what we did."

When he didn't say anything after a half minute, Grant asked, "The robberies? I'm not a religious person, but I would think God understands that you two were young and foolish. On top of that, Sensei was confused and seeking an adrenaline rush. You both saw that it was wrong, and you quit. God has probably forgotten all about—"

"That's not it, goddamnit," Leo said, snapping his head toward him, his eyes wet, large, his mouth open as if wanting to speak but unable to.

For the first time since Grant had been sitting there, car headlights passed behind the blackness where the corn stalks had died after giving up their yield. An old country road, he figured. The brief, moving light passed through long water trails on the outside glass, casting their fleeting shadows on Leo's face to crawl down his cheeks like tears.

Memories of regret? Grant wondered. Is that what this is about? Did he and Sensei do something worse than the robberies?

Leo turned away from him, swiped his sleeve across his eyes, and looked out the window a moment longer. When he turned back to face the writer, his eyes were afraid. Worse, they were terrified.

"Sensei and I…we did something."

Grant waited for Leo to say what it was, but when he didn't continue, he said, "I'm sure whatever it was—"

Leo looked at him and shook his head, then turned away to face the storm. "It was nineteen seventy-six, five years or so since Sensei had gotten back from the war, back when Portland was getting an influx of Vietnamese refugees. You weren't even born then, but hundreds of them, maybe thousands, were placed in Hokum Courts apartments, several square blocks of low rents on Glisan Street in Northeast Portland. There were all kinds of problems for a while, which is no surprise because they mixed Vietnamese people from all walks of life together—intellectuals with uneducated, criminals with former law enforcement people, and South Vietnamese military with North Vietnamese sympathizers. They even mixed some former Viet Cong and regular North Vietnamese soldiers that managed to flee from Vietnam to greener pastures over there in Portland. It was a mess that kept the Portland police hopping as well as social workers, teachers, and a host of other people.

"I hadn't heard any of that. I've driven through that area, and I've seen lots of Asians."

"Vietnamese. Yes, there are still some there, but not like it was. Most have gotten educated, joined the workforce, became hard-working taxpayers, and blended into the neighborhood communities throughout the cities.

"Sometime after our robberies, Sensei got into an apprentice program to be a plumber. He had returned to the martial arts, and he hadn't had a drink for a long while.

"He and his plumbing coach had been in Hokum Courts for a solid week getting the pipes in the apartments up to code because they were expecting a bunch more refugees. Sensei said the sprawling complex was chaotic and getting worse every day because most of the residences were housing two, three, even four families. Most didn't know each other. This was terrible for the people, and it was a miserable time for Sensei. He was spending all day around more Vietnamese than he ever saw during his year in the bush. It was giving him nightmares.

"It was on the third or fourth day when he had his head inside a wall doing whatever with some pipes when he heard some Vietnamese people in the next apartment speaking a little differently. Sensei had picked up quite a bit of Vietnamese from his scouts in Vietnam, and they had taught him the difference between the North Vietnamese language and the South's. The language is similar, see, except for a few obvious sounds.

What Sensei heard in that apartment was North Vietnamese.

"This shocked him because, at that time, no one knew that the North Vietnamese were coming to the states too, the bastards he fought over there. The government probably knew, but they didn't make the information public. Sensei said he began to hyperventilate, and he was shaking so bad he couldn't hold his wrench. He told his trainer he had to get some air for a few minutes.

"He went out onto the balcony and looked toward the apartment where he had heard the voices. The picture window curtains were open, revealing a living room crowded with people. The door opened a moment later, and two little kids came out, both about seven or eight years old. They stared at him for a moment, probably because Americans were still a novelty, giggled, and took off toward the stairs.

"Sensei stood there looking out at the sprawling apartment complex with Vietnamese coming and going. He never told me so, but I'm guessing he was having a whole lot of flashbacks. Then the same apartment door opened again, and two men came out, one with a cane, limping. Sensei told me they looked at him, then at each other. It was as if they didn't know what to do. The crippled man said something in a low voice to his buddy, which made him turn and look at Sensei for a moment longer. He said the man looked surprised, then tried to conceal it by looking up at the wall. A couple of seconds later, both men turned about and headed toward the stairs. He said it was obvious they wanted to get away from him."

Leo frowned as he studied Grant for a moment. "My beloved daughter likes you," he said.

Grant blinked rapidly, not only because of the man's 180-degree topic change but because of what he said about Brooklyn. "Well… sir. Uh, I like her too. We, uh, seem to have connected."

He nodded. "I saw it. But here's the thing. Brookie's a good judge of character. I taught her to be. I also taught her knife skills with that blade attached under the seat of her chair." Leo pointed at him. "Judging by your expression, you haven't seen it, even when she dismantled her chair to ride in your car."

"No, sir."

"Good. A wise eagle hides her talons, no?"

Grant nodded. "I guess." Then he exhaled, "Damn."

Leo looked at the refrigerator but didn't get up to get a beer—thanks to Brooklyn. He looked at Grant for a moment, his face grim, his eyes…pained?

"What I've just told you up to this point, you can use in your book. I suppose you could include it as an example of Sensei's mindset in the early years after getting back from the war—confused, suspicious, alone. It was the same mindset that so many young men had upon their return. But what I'm going to tell you next is not for the book. Can you agree?"

Grant frowned. "What? Well, I don't know. I mean, Sensei wanted the book to show all sides of him and—"

"Not this," Leo snapped, his tone angry. This can't be in the book, for him and me. And for Brooklyn. Even for you."

"Me? I don't understand."

"Of course, you don't, Grant, because you don't know what it is. But I need your word now, without knowing what it is, your word that you won't print it." He studied the writer for another moment. "I think I'm a good judge of men, and my daughter is too. I trust you if you say you won't, and I know she would too."

"Does she know what it is?"

"No. And you will never tell her."

Except for Leo's watery eyes, he didn't appear drunk now or high on coke. He was even sitting straight and tall like a West Point cadet. But he seemed anxious and agitated.

"You're thinking about this longer than I'd like," Leo said, his wet eyes boring a hole through him.

"My concern," Grant cleared his throat, "is wondering how this might affect Brooklyn and me. I don't want secrets between us."

"'Us?'" Leo repeated, studying Grant. "Isn't it a little early to think 'us?' But I like that you respect her feelings. But this is about Sensei and me, our 'us,' you see?"

Grant nodded. "I know you wouldn't do anything to hurt her, so—"

Leo's eyes flashed. "Your attempt at using psychology on me is offensive, son."

Damn, Grant thought, wilting before the man's ire. Coke brings out the psycho in the man. "Sorry, sir. I assure you I don't mean disrespect." He hesitated for a moment, then. "Yes."

"Yes, you won't print it, and you won't tell Brooklyn?"

"Yes, you can trust me. I won't print it. And I won't tell Brooklyn unless it interferes with our relationship. If you think it will, then don't tell me."

"Goddamnit!" Leo growled between clenched teeth.

Outside, the wind gusted, slapping a sheet of rain against the glass. Leo turned away from the writer to watch it. "Since our interview, this thing has torn me anew," he said so low that Grant had to lean toward him to hear. "Like I told you, it's never too far from the forefront of my mind. But there are times it settles back and leaves me the hell alone. Then it comes creeping up again, to interfere with my sleep and my daytime thoughts. But I can't talk about it with Sensei anymore. I can't share it. I thought that by telling you, someone my gut is telling me I can trust with this even though we've just met, it would help me. Sharing it, that's what I'm saying that I need. Sharing."

Another rush of wind and rain hit the windows. "Goddamnit!" Leo said, leaning forward to press his palms against the glass. "Goddamnit, goddamnit, goddamnit."

What the hell have I gotten myself into, Grant wondered. He didn't know if he should feel sorry for him or be concerned that he was mental and might flip out further. Brooklyn hadn't said anything about him being prone to violence. Okay, he was a martial arts teacher, so he was capable. He decided to try a lowkey approach. He touched Leo's shoulder.

The old man turned and looked at him, his eyes unreadable.

Grant searched his face for a moment, then nodded. "Okay."

Leo closed his eyes. "Thank you." He opened them. "Damn, I'm thirsty. Hold on a sec." Leo headed for the kitchen.

Everything happens fast with this family, Grant thought. I just referred to Brooklyn and me as 'us,' and now her father wants to dump something on me I can't use but will somehow lighten his burden. Grant wasn't sure how to wrap his head around all of it yet, but for now, he would let it all play out.

Leo returned with a pitcher of ice water and two glasses. He filled them, chugged his, and filled it again. Then he began.

"Sensei recognized the man with the cane. He told me he was ninety-nine percent sure he was one of those that bayonetted his men, his squad, that day in the jungle. You told me the professor told you the story, right."

Grant nodded grimly. "I'll never forget it." He shook his head. "You're telling me this guy in Portland was one of the—?"

Leo nodded. "Sensei said one of the VC was wounded in the leg, the knee. It was the guy he had watched take great delight in driving his bayonet through his men, many of which might have survived. Sensei was convinced the man did it as much out of precaution as he did for the joy of it. That was the word he used. 'Joy.'

"Anyway, the guy on the balcony had the limp and a cane, and he had the weird eye. Sensei said the man bayonetting had one normal eye, but his other one wasn't as open."

The professor hadn't mentioned that, Grant thought. But in the way he described the scene, he couldn't have seen it because he was facing the other way. Sensei was looking behind the professor, so he could see the VC who were doing the bayonetting.

Leo said, “His eye was sort of a slit, like he had dirt or something in it. Sensei hadn’t even thought of his eye over the years that had passed, but when he saw the man on the balcony, the limp and the same partially opened eye, he knew it was him. And the man recognized Sensei. He was sure of it.”

“The phrase ‘small world’ comes to mind,” Grant said.

“Yes, and Sensei wondered if the other man with him was there in the jungle that day too. Because the side of Sensei’s face was in the dirt while the stabbing was happening, he couldn’t see the rest of the VC very well. But he sensed that the other man was there too. Sensei had nothing to base it on other than a feeling.

“When he got off work, he called me and told me about seeing the man, the two men. He was breathless, and he kept stopping to collect himself. When he got to the place where the two had turned and headed toward the balcony stairs, he stopped talking. When he didn’t continue, I asked if he was okay. He said no, and he said it so faintly I barely heard him. I waited for him to talk some more. When he didn’t, I said, ‘Do you want me to come over and bring some beers.’ He said no again in the same faint voice and said he’d call me the next day.”

The sheets of rain had stopped smacking the windows, but the wind still groaned as if suffering some great pain. Grant said, “That must have been surreal for him. I mean, thousands of miles away from where it happened, then seeing the man right in front of him. Some might say it was like some great plan.”

Leo nodded. “That’s sort of what Sensei said four days later when he called me again. We had been talking, and he said, ‘Some say karma means what goes around comes around. They say it’s residual from a past life that must be resolved in this one. Well, I say it doesn’t have to be something from a past life; it can be a residual from ours, one that must be resolved—in ours.’

“Those were Sensei’s words exactly. I remember them because at the time I thought that to have worked out those definitions, he had to have been thinking about, maybe even planning something. So I came out and asked him what he was going to do. I have to say I was not just a little worried what he might say.

"He said, 'I must avenge my men. That man—that murderer—took their lives. He murdered the ones who were still alive, and they had a party afterward. The ones already dead were killed in a war battle. You understand the difference? The wounded ones were murdered for laughs, and oh, did they laugh. Then they got drunk and laughed some more about it while my men lay dead on the jungle ground. And they shot their dead bodies right from where they were sitting and getting drunk. Where they were having their party.'"

Leo paused and leaned forward to rest his elbows on his knees. It seemed to Grant that he was tiring quickly. It would make sense since he had been drunk and high earlier, and now telling the story was draining what little he had left.

Leo sat up ramrod straight again. "Sensei said he had been watching that apartment from his car. The man with the cane and his buddy took lots of smoke breaks on the balcony. He figured the women didn't want them smoking inside. He said on all four nights, they took their last smoke break out in the parking lot by a beat-up sixty-two Ford, a red one. They'd get in the trunk, retrieve a bottle, and take a couple of chugs.

"I asked him if he had a specific plan.

"I still remember how his words came out as cold as ice. 'I'm going to hurt him, bad. I want him to remember what he did every time he moves. I'm going break his elbows, his knees, his ankles, and his fingers. Maybe his shoulder joints too.'

"I thought for a moment about spouting some inspirational quotes about how revenge is never a good idea, but I knew he was way beyond listening. He had made up his mind. He was good to go.

"So I said I would go with him."

‹0›

Grant was in the kitchen, pouring himself a cup of coffee. Leo had gone upstairs to take a pill. Probably a valium, Grant assumed, judging by how his hands had been shaking.

"How's it going," Brooklyn whispered, wheeling into the kitchen. She had changed into dry clothes and dried her hair. "Dad looked kinda shook when he passed me. I asked if he was okay, and all he said was to stay out of the kitchen when you guys start talking again. I guess he remembered about the vent acting like a speaker."

Grant stole a quick kiss and straightened.

"Are you okay?" Brooklyn asked, taking his hand. "You look a little frazzled too."

He sipped his coffee and leaned back against the counter. He whispered, "I'm afraid where this new information is going."

"I see," she whispered, her expression…worried? Why would she be— "What if it's something bad?"

Grant was in mid-sip when the meaning of her question sunk in. "Why would you ask—?"

"He's coming," she mouthed, nodding toward the doorway. "Are you hungry?" she asked Grant in a normal voice. "Want some soup or something?" He said he was fine, still frowning at her.

Leo came into the kitchen, looking calmer. He no longer showed any indication he had been drinking, and the hand tremors were gone. Whatever he took must be fast-acting stuff, Grant thought. Leo rested his hand on Brooklyn's shoulder and looked at Grant. "Ready to continue? You can bring the coffee pot if you'd like." He looked at his daughter. "And you. Stay out of the kitchen."

As they headed toward the window room, Grant looked back at Brooklyn. Instead of a conspiratorial smile on her face about her dad knowing about the vents, he saw worry and…sadness?

The rain had picked up again and was once more trying to shake loose the floor to ceiling windows. Leo turned on the backyard floodlights, the pale light revealing the thrashing dead cornstalks.

"A scene out of a scary Halloween movie," Grant said, forcing a little humor into the moment. Leo, looking distracted, sat back down without commenting.

Grant retrieved his recorder from his backpack. When Leo shot him a stern look, Grant said, "Sorry. Old habit," and put it away.

Leo leaned over a small table next to him and retrieved a fuzzy blue blanket. "You cold? All this glass defeats our furnace when the wind is blowing hard." Grant said he was fine and watched him drape the blanket over his lap.

Leo leaned his head back against the chair and looked out the window. "Sensei had it all planned out."

OLD ENEMIES?

Sensei drove us to a quiet residential street about three blocks from the west end of Hokum Courts. He turned off the key and looked out the windshield, his hands white-knuckling the steering wheel at 10 o'clock and 2 o'clock. He sat rigidly, his eyes narrowed. He appeared as if every muscle were flexed, including one at the side of his jaw that twitched nonstop. I felt afraid to speak, but I had to.

"You sure you want to do this?"

Sensei didn't answer for what seemed to me like a full minute. Then he said in a low monotone, "From where I lay that night, I could see three of them, their ugly smiles…" He paused, his chest heaving as if he'd been running uphill. "Smiling as they indifferently plunged those blades into my men. My youngest troop that was still alive was nineteen but wounded and unable to fight back. All those who were hurt were so young, so terrified. They begged the murderers not to do it, but their cries went unheard. The ones who pleaded the most, the slower the bastards shoved their blades through their chests."

Sensei's running tears reflected a nearby porchlight; he didn't wipe them away. "I knew how to put my head in a different place and eat the pain of the steel penetrating me. I should have taught my men how to do that before we went out. Before it happened."

"Sensei, you…" I cleared my throat to rid the catch in my voice, but it didn't help. "You…can't blame yourself. You couldn't possibly have known the VC would do something like—"

"I was their leader. They looked at me every time we went on a mission, trusting me to get them back to our unit safely. I didn't like it, but I accepted the responsibility because whatever trait I had been born with or developed made them look to me for guidance. But I couldn't do that this time. Instead, I lay there with those ants crawling in and out of my mouth, and I watched them murder my men, one by one. All except Ben Walters. He avoided getting stabbed because he was lying under a dead man. They stabbed the man on top of him but got distracted when one of my men jumped up. Walters survived by chance. Same with me. The blade went through my back and almost into my lung. I survived it. My men didn't.

"I owe it to them."

I started to say that Ben Walters credited him with saving his life, but it was clear Sensei wasn't receptive to my input.

He turned, his wet face glistening, and looked at me. "This isn't to revenge, Leo; I've thought about it these last few days. No, I'm not here for that."

He looked back out the windshield, then reached for the door handle. "I'm here to *punish.*"

Jesus, I thought.

I got out too.

"Stay in the car, Leo."

"No. I'm coming. Discussion over."

He shook his head, giving in to me. "You're my friend," he said warmly, "and a pain in the ass too. Okay, but I don't want you to take part in whatever goes down. Understood?" I nodded.

The only plan was to split up after we met with the men. Since I didn't know the neighborhood, I was to walk back the way we came, and Sensei would take a roundabout way to the car.

We walked casually without speaking. If Sensei was nervous, the only indication was that he checked his watch twice, the second time less than a minute after the first.

I was surprised at the size of the apartment complex. I could count seven separate two-story complexes, each with 12 apartments. It looked like there were others beyond the ones I could see.

"That old red Ford in the second row by the pickup is the car in question." He looked at his watch a third time, then up at the sky. "It's colder than the nights I surveilled," he said worriedly, maybe thinking the men might not follow their previous routine. "Continue walking until we get to those dozen dumpsters at the end of the lot. We'll stand by there."

I was terrified. I hadn't said a word since we left the car, and I kept questioning my sanity for being there. But I kept coming back to our friendship. It wasn't that I was willing to go to jail for Sensei, but I felt it was my duty to be there and maybe prevent him from delivering a coup de grace on a guy when there was a chance that he wasn't the man in the jungle that day. And he didn't convince me that it was about punishment and not revenge. But whatever the motive, an assault was illegal. I had a good job, and I was thinking about marriage. So why in the hell was I jeopardizing all that for this craziness?

"There they are," Sensei said.

I leaned around the edge of the dumpster and watched two men, Vietnamese, small of stature, both wearing the same color blue winter coats, one man walking with a cane.

"Your taxes paid for those winter jackets," Sensei whispered bitterly, watching them descend the steps. "Yeah, the more I see them, the more convinced I am that the one with the cane is him. Watch, they'll head over to the red Ford… See, there they go. Okay, the one with the cane will open the trunk… Yes, he did it. Now they'll take a few swigs out of the wine bottle… Creatures of habit."

Without looking at me, he whispered, "Stay here."

"Sensei," I whispered, but he launched himself away before I could say anything further. I wanted to tell him it wasn't too late to change his mind. But he was in a zone, in another world.

I slowly walked along the front sides of the dumpsters and watched him move through the lot behind the parked cars, then stealthily approach the men from the front of the red Ford. The upraised trunk blocked my view for a moment; then I saw him inching along the driver's side. He hesitated by the back door.

The upraised trunk also kept the men from seeing him. Unaware there was a threat less than ten feet away, they chatted and swigged from the bottle, their breath forming white clouds around their mouths.

Sensei crept closer, closer still, and then moved into their view.

The crippled man jumped, and the other one jerked the bottle away from his mouth and coughed. Sensei stared at the lame man without speaking. I couldn't tell if my friend was trying to confirm that they were the two in the jungle that day or if he was convinced and deciding how to proceed.

Did the men recognize him from the balcony when he was working next to their apartment? Or from that night in the jungle? Their expressions gave nothing away.

Sensei said something to them in Vietnamese. The last part I understood. "VC."

Both men vigorously shook their heads. I heard the one with the cane say in thickly accented English, "We no VC. We live before in Saigon. No VC."

The one without the cane said something in his language. He didn't appear to be excited but somewhat surprised at the accusation. He set the wine bottle down inside the trunk.

"You VC," Sensei said louder, using pidgin English and jabbing his finger at the one with the cane. He pantomimed holding a rifle and thrusting it like a soldier would when a fixed bayonet protruded from underneath the end of the barrel. Then he pantomimed holding a knife and plunging it downward. "You stabbed many wounded GIs," Sensei said, tightly restraining his voice from shouting. "They die because you are a coward." He jabbed his finger just short of the man's chest. "You are fucking VC," he growled. He pointed toward the man's leg. "You hurt leg same-same day."

Both men had been vigorously shaking their heads at the accusations. The lame man looked stunned. Was it because they had been identified, or was it from the absurdity of the allegations?

"No soldier," the man with the cane said, his tone stunned, I thought. "I drive taxi Saigon. I crash taxi one year ago. Hurt leg." Did that sound believable? I wondered. At first, I thought it did, but then I didn't think so. What I knew for sure is that I didn't want to be there.

I was still standing about 30 feet away by the dumpsters. My eyes were tearing heavily from the cold night or, more likely, from my raw nerves that were jacking up my heart rate and trembling my hands. I remember thinking about how much I wanted to be back in my apartment, sucking down beers and laughing at Archie Bunker on "All in the Family."

Sensei said something which I couldn't hear, and both men vigorously shook their heads again.

"No soldier," the one with the cane said beseechingly. "Drive taxi six years. Drive American GI *beaucoup* before GI go home America." He pointed at the ground when he said, 'America.' "When VC come Saigon," he pointed at his friend, "my friend and me come America." He nodded vigorously. "We *beaucoup* happy be Ameri—"

Sensei slapped him. The man fell against the bumper, nearly falling into the open trunk.

"Damn," I muttered, launching into a hard run toward them.

The lame man delicately touched his palm against the side of his face and cried, "No lie. We no VC."

"No VC," the other man parroted, reaching out to hold his friend up. He extended his open palm toward Sensei. "Please, we no VC."

"You were there!" Sensei shouted, emphasizing the two words. "You same-same VC." Then through clenched teeth, "You *caca dao* my men; now I *caca dao* you."

I stopped two strides behind my friend. "Wait. Don't—"

As quick as a wink, Sensei shuffled his lead leg back, then whipped it into a high arc, slamming the lower part of his shin against the same side of the man's face he had slapped.

"Stop, Sensei!" I blared as the Vietnamese man fell head-first into the trunk as if looking for something. I pulled at my friend's coat jacket. "Come on. Let's get out of here."

The other man was hopping around like a bee-stung rabbit, apparently unsure what was happening and unsure what to do about whatever it was. Sensei reached into the trunk, pulled the groggy man upright by his hair, and slammed a horizontal elbow into the side of his neck. That blow turned off the man's lights and sent him straight to the ground on his butt where his chin dropped forward onto his chest.

I touched Sensei's upper arm, and he snapped his head toward me, his eyes on fire. I took a quick step back, afraid he might hit me.

The lame man's friend had stopped his crazed hopping and stood motionless, looking at Sensei with an expression of fear and disbelief. "We no VC," he managed, his voice shaky. He looked down at his unconscious buddy, then back to Sensei again. "Trung drive taxi. I drive cyclo. We live Saigon. Hate VC." He practically spat the letters, VC.

"Let's leave," I said gently to Sensei, this time without touching him. But he ignored me; his glare was focused on the man who had toppled over onto his face.

The other man bent down to help his friend up, but Sensei palm-slammed the man's shoulder, sending him stumbling back a couple of steps then down onto the asphalt.

"We need to go," I said sharply.

"Not yet," Sensei mumbled.

"I don't know," I said. "These guys seemed confused. It's like they don't know why you're—"

Sensei jabbed his finger at the lame man, now looking up at us as if confused about why he was laying on his belly. "He knows," Sensei said, watching the man laboriously sit up. "He sure the hell knows, and so does the other one."

The other man who was standing now, his jaw trembling, his head slowly shaking. "No soldier," he said again, this time softly as if he realized his words weren't being believed.

The lame man blinked rapidly to clear his fogged head from the brachial stun blow to his neck. Sensei stepped toward him.

"No more," I pleaded. "Let's leave—"

The Vietnamese reached out awkwardly like a blind man.

"We no VC," the other man blared, drawing Sensei's attention.

The downed lame man found my friend's lower leg and quickly wrapped his arm around the calf.

I moved toward him, but Sensei's fast sidestep stretched the man's arm out on the asphalt. My friend snapped his other knee up high and, in one continuous motion, stomped down on the elbow, the sickening sound of the breaking joint loud in the quiet night. When the man opened his mouth to scream, Sensei rammed a kick into his teeth before he got out a single note.

The man groaned and sprayed broken teeth and blood out onto the pavement.

The other man quickly reached into the trunk and grabbed the wine bottle they had been drinking from minutes earlier. He held it by its neck along his thigh, his chest heaving. "Me no VC," he cried, looking down at his friend, tears streaming down his face. "Trung no VC!" he shouted, his eyes angry. He looked at me since I was within arm's reach of him. "You go Vietnam and look for soldier. Not Trung, not me." He snapped the bottle up above his shoulder, as one would a club.

I was getting mixed feels about the men's complicity in that terrible night in the jungle, but that didn't mean I'd let this guy hit me in the head with the bottle. I fired off two palm heel-strikes into his face, exploding his nose into a red spray. I don't know why I hit him twice, but I instantly regretted having to strike him at all. Hell, I regretted being here and part of this night.

The man stumbled back a step, dropping the bottle and whipping his head back and forth like a swimmer emerging out of the water, flinging the blood into the air and onto me. He advanced toward me, though he had to be blind from his heavily tearing eyes. I felt my anger rise. I was sick of this night, angry at Sensei, and mad at myself. I decided to take it out on the man.

I lunged in close, tucking my head next to his ear, wrapped my arm around his chest, and swept my leg back into his. With his support gone, he would have fallen without further help from me. But I used my arm across his torso to drive him down hard onto the concrete, the back of his head, making that distinct sickening sound when skull-meets-asphalt.

I looked away from his fluttering eyes to check on the other man. He was on his back, rolling from side to side, one hand clutching his broken elbow, blood oozing out his shattered mouth. I remembered part of what Sensei said earlier. "I'm going break his elbows, his knees..."

I quick-scanned the yard and the apartment complexes, thankfully not seeing any witnesses.

I looked back at my man.

Shitshitshit.

He was lying motionless, his eyes open and unblinking. They seemed to be staring accusingly at me.

I looked away and started to wretch, but I somehow managed not to. I looked at the man again.

His eyes still stared without blinking.

"Sensei," I said, my eyes unable to look away from the man's face. His dead face?

What have I done?

"We…need to leave," I managed, still looking down at the man. When it sunk in that Sensei didn't answer, I looked over at him.

He was pulling his whimpering man up onto his knees. Blood and teeth oozed down the front of the man's jacket. Sensei pushed his head down so he could wrap his arm under his chin, like a reverse headlock. It was a dangerous hold if the guy could fight back, but the Vietnamese was limp, held in place by my friend's forearm against his Adam's apple.

My God, I'll never forget Sensei's crazed eyes when he looked up at me. Sweat streamed down his tense face despite the cold night, and a bold vein protruded along the side of his forehead.

I knew what he was going to do.

"No, Sensei," I said, reaching toward him, though he was at least six feet away. "Nonono," I begged him. "Let him go, please. Let's leave now. Let's—"

"*Đối với người của tôi,*" Sensei said to the man, his voice low, intimate. He told me later it meant, "For my people."

He adjusted his forearm from the front of the man's neck to his jawline. Then with a powerful rotation of his hips and a vicious crank of his arms, he twisted the man's head beyond its limit.

That break was louder than the crack of his broken elbow joint.

Sensei released him and, without saying a word to me, he walked off unhurriedly across the grounds that would take him through the sprawling complex to the car. I walked fast across the lawn to the sidewalk we had walked on earlier. Halfway to where we parked, I vomited.

‹0›

Leo had slowly turned away until he was once again looking out the window.

Grant was speechless. The writer wasn't much of a drinker, but at the moment, he wanted a triple anything that was 100-plus proof. He seldom cursed either, believing vulgarity should be left to the ignorant who lacked an intelligent command of the English language.

"Holy fucking shit," Grant finally got out, staring in disbelief at the side of Leo's head. When he didn't get a response, he said, "A broken neck. He died?"

Leo's single nod was almost imperceptible. "My man, too, from hitting his head on the pavement when he fell."

"The hell!" Grant nearly shouted. "Did… Did you get arrested?" He knew they didn't, but he was too stunned to think of a better question.

Leo shook his head and turned to look at the writer with pained eyes; the lines in his seventy-plus-years old face had deepened. "Unbelievably, no one saw us according to the news. It was the mid-nineteen seventies, and there were no video cameras on roofs, nothing. We split up as planned, met at the car, and drove off. We got drunk at my apartment. Sensei slept it off on my couch, and I passed out with my head on the kitchen table.

"I felt awful reading the front page of the newspaper about something that was my doing."

Interesting, Grant thought. A couple of seconds earlier Leo said when the man *hit his head on the pavement when he fell.* Like he wasn't responsible. Now, Leo says, *something that was my doing.* He still seems a little undecided about his complicity that night. Or he's having trouble admitting it to himself.

Leo was still talking. "The article named the men and gave an approximation of their ages, but nothing else about them. One person said they were from North Vietnam, but two others said they were from Saigon in the south. The article pointed out that it wasn't illegal to be from North Vietnam once they were here in the states, but it could be a motive for the killings.

"The article said the police were not getting much cooperation from people in Hokum Courts. Apparently, the police over in Vietnam were crooked and brutal, and the people over there both feared and distrusted them. That naturally extended to the refugees viewing the American police here the same way. So the Portland police got very little help. Supposedly, no one saw or heard anything, and no one knew the two men except for the three who gave conflicting information where they were from." Leo looked down as he added, "This was good news for us."

He looked up, but not at Grant. "The police detectives felt it was an internal situation, part of the many problems the Vietnamese were having assimilating into the American mainstream. There was a lot of prejudice among the general public too. American boys had been fighting over in Vietnam since the early nineteen sixties. Now the Vietnamese were in Portland needing food, clothing, and housing, all the while fighting among themselves. So Americans didn't give a shit. About a week later, it was no longer in the news."

Grant was feeling his anger brewing. But he needed more information. "Did you two go hide out somewhere? Go to Mexico or something?"

Leo shook his head. "After that week, we rarely spoke of it, at least for a few years. We stopped hanging together, and I switched to a different martial arts school for a couple of years. It was uncomfortable for me to be around Sensei, plus I thought it best that we weren't seen together." Leo shook his head. "I was acting like a criminal."

Because you were, Grant thought. You were a murderer.

Leo went on. "I know he was tortured about it too, but my sense was then that he wasn't as tortured by it as me. This is what I was thinking at the time anyway. Who knows what's going on in another person's head?" He looked at Grant as if to get a read on how he was taking everything.

The writer took a deep breath in preparation to gather strength for his next question. But Leo beat him to it, his voice lifeless.

"I know what you're going to ask, son." He looked at Grant for a long moment, his head nodding. He turned back to the large window. The wind was no longer slapping sheets of rain against the glass. Now it fell steadily, and the wind only agitated the field of dead corn.

Leo took a ragged breath. "Okay, here it is. About two days after, when we were again drinking hard, I asked Sensei if he still thought the lame guy and the other man were the same VC who bayonetted his squad. I have to say that it took every bit of courage I had to ask the damn question. I knew I'd still feel like shit if the answer was yes, but I was afraid what a no answer would do to me."

Leo's shoulders seemed to slump, and his head tilted back slightly as if sinking into his neck. He closed his eyes. Seconds passed.

When Leo finally spoke, his voice was low and measured. "Sensei looked at me with those penetrating eyes and whispered, 'I don't think so, Leo. Maybe, they were, but I don't…'"

With that, Leo looked down, and his shoulders began to shake. He was crying.

"My God," Grant managed, his voice gravelly. He could feel the adrenaline flooding his body. Hold it in, he told himself.

"Who else knows this? Did you tell your wife? Your brother? A buddy?"

Leo shook his head. "Just you."

"Just me!" Grant shouted, leaping to his feet, his hands fisted at his side. "Are you fucking kidding me! You two killed two innocent men who came here to this country for a new life." He leaned toward Leo, anger trembling his body. "Damnit to hell! No, no," he blared when Leo opened his mouth to speak. "You don't get to talk anymore. What could you possibly say now that you've put this… *murder* into my head to what? To make *you* feel better?"

Grant took two strides down the room, turned, and came back, standing over Leo, who looked small and defeated in his rocker. "You just made me a material witness to this, or whatever it's called. You do know there is no statute of limitations on murder?"

Grant snatched his backpack off the floor. "You had to tell me you killed two innocent people to lighten your burden? What am I supposed to do with it now that you've shared your guilt? Do I just live with it?" He grabbed his coat and walked quickly toward the sliding glass door. He turned back and looked at Leo, sitting small and watching the rain that was once again slapping the large windows.

"Goddamnit!" Grant shouted before turning and sliding open the door.

In the living room, Brooklyn looked up as Grant stormed out of the kitchen, her face pained. "I heard you yelling. Grant? Do you want to talk about it?"

He walked quickly past her.

"Grant? Please talk to—"

"I've got to go," he snapped without stopping until he reached the door. He looked back at her. "I'm sorry, Brooklyn." He opened the door and stepped out into the storm.

EPILOGUE

Grant's brown vinyl recliner faced his second-story apartment window. It didn't offer a view of a cornfield whipping about in a windstorm, but rather the backside of a high school: running track, tennis courts, and a graffitied fence. But it had nonetheless been the unseeing focal point of his out-of-control thoughts for the last 72 hours. He had eaten junk food in the chair, drank beers there, and slept, getting up only to use the bathroom or take a quick trip to the corner grocery to buy more junk food and beer. He hadn't looked at his notes, listened to his interviews, or written a word. Brooklyn had called half a dozen times and texted even more, but he had ignored them. What could he say to her? "Sorry I haven't answered. I'm feeling conflicted about finding out your dad, and the subject of my book are murderers."

He had thought about the book, though; oh, yes, that he had done. Grant thought about it sober, and he thought about it while drinking bottle after bottle of hefeweizen.

His decision changed by the hour as to what to do with the new information. There were three options.

Trashcan the notes and recordings and look for a new project.

Write the book without Leo's shocker.

Write it with the murders included.

What about his word to Leo that he wouldn't put the new information in the book and that he would never tell Brooklyn? But it was a promise made before he knew the gravity of what he was about to be told. Compared to the killings, his word didn't mean diddly-squat. Nada, zero, zilch, nix.

Someone said the best way to keep your word is not to give it. But I did give it, Grant thought.

Two nights ago, he Googled to see how much trouble he could get into by not reporting his knowledge of two homicides.

His findings were inconclusive. Not reporting wasn't a crime in most states, but in a small few, you could be charged with a misdemeanor for not reporting a felony that resulted in bodily harm. Grant assumed that a guy getting his head twisted part way off and another getting his skull bashed into the pavement would fall under the bodily harm category.

Maybe he should inform the police and let them do with it what they will. Or he could take the cowardly way out and call them anonymously. But Leo would know how they found out, and it would shatter Brooklyn's life.

Grant lowered his chair's leg support and stood. He stretched and twisted his torso back and forth to a chorus of spinal clicks and pops. The wall clock read 2:20 in the afternoon. He'd been sitting in the chair virtually motionless since nine this morning. He lifted each knee three times, started to do another repetition but decided that was enough exercise. He went to the bathroom, then to the kitchen to pour himself a glass of orange juice. He leaned back against the counter and sipped.

Until Leo's terrible revelation, Sensei's story had unfolded as he had hoped and as he imagined the teacher saw the finished volume. It was the tale of the many sides of a man—a leader, a war hero troubled by PTSD, a robber, redemption, a hard drinker, redemption again, a return to teaching, a leader, a role model to troubled youth, a sports champion, and a man who had reached the zenith in the martial arts.

Where does a murderer fit into this? Did Sensei factor in the killings when he told Grant and the interviewees to disclose everything?

What if he had mentally shut it out? Grant read once about a tow truck driver who had completely blocked out stabbing a prostitute to death but freely admitted it under hypnosis. Because his crime of passion executed in a moment of rage was just too much for his conscious mind to accept, the act disappeared into his subconscious, where it remained until a hypnotist brought it out.

Could Sensei have done that? Could he have blocked it out after all these years? Leo said they had talked about it, but when was the last time? If several years ago, would a significant passing of time work for the blocking-out theory?

Grant walked over to a small table by his front door and flipped through a short stack of unopened mail. I should pay these bills, he thought, then dropped them back on the pile.

He headed to his chair, plopped down, and cranked the handle to bring up the footrest.

A couple of days after Sensei and Leo had killed the men, Leo asked him if he still thought the two were the same ones who bayonetted his troops. The answer came as a devastating shock to his friend. Sensei said maybe they were, but he didn't think so.

When did his mind change? During the beating? An hour after? Could he have made them the perpetrators in his mind from the first moment he saw them? Everyone Grant interviewed felt the war had affected Sensei. Miss Graham didn't say as much, but the description she gave of how he beat the crap out of the protestor might indicate his inner rage. Yes, the protester had molested Miss Grant by swiping his hand, wet from her salad dressing, across her chest. But Sensei could have restrained him until the police arrived, instead of unleashing whatever was pent up inside of him to the extent that Miss Graham said she almost felt sorry for the unfortunate recipient.

Some of the other interviewees said Sensei seemed to be fighting something else when he got into brawls. Carl Hanes said something like: It seemed like he was trying to punch away the pain he felt. He was so depressed or guilty over what he had to do in Vietnam that he wanted guys to hurt him. Thomas Martin saw something similar.

Grant massaged his temples.

"I should just shitcan the whole project," he said aloud bitterly. "No, there's a book here, but how to write it is the question."

He shook his head. "Maybe it's too soon in my writing career to tackle a book like this." He shook his head harder. "No damnit, I can do this.

He smiled and said aloud, "Talking to yourself is supposed to make you smarter. Well, it's not working."

He scooted his rear to the front edge of the chair, sat up straight, and returned to his rambling thoughts.

So is it a leap to think that when Sensei was working at Hokum Courts, a place with more Vietnamese than he ever saw as an infantry soldier in Vietnam, that his imagination heard what he thought was a North Vietnamese pronunciation of a couple of words? After all, the voice came through a wall while he and his trainer worked on the plumbing. How clear could it have been? Later, when he saw two men exit the apartment out onto the walkway, might his mind have continued to make them the Vietcong he had focused his burning hate on for the past four or five years?

If so, might the delusion have continued right up to the night he attacked the lame man, and Leo prevented the second one from interfering by, well, killing him? Judging by Leo's description of the extreme brutality of Sensei's confrontation, his friend had no doubt at that moment that the man was the one in the jungle armed with the fixed bayonet. That is, his delusion had no doubt. The uncertainty came into play after the adrenaline, and whatever else had been driving him, had dissipated two days later.

Am I grasping at straws? Grant wondered. Am I using my imagination to create a backstory? He sighed and reached over to the table to get his glass of orange juice. "Damn," he muttered. He didn't bring it with him from the kitchen. He tiredly decided it was too much work to get up and get it.

Taking a different angle, what if Sensei wanted his crime told in the bio as a self-punishment thing? Or a confession? Not because the two men weren't the real guys but because they were. By some weird twist of fate or bizarre coincidence, the two enemy soldiers escaped their county to end up in Portland, Oregon, on the other side of an apartment wall that separated them from the leader of the squad of American GIs they murdered. Too much? Sure, it's a lot, but stranger things have happened.

Running with the idea that Sensei wanted his life's story told—the good, the bad, and the ugly—maybe he wanted readers to see the cost of revenge. By Sensei murdering a man for murdering his helpless soldiers, his best friend was drawn into the fray, forcing him to take a life too. In the end, two men died to satisfy Sensei's need for revenge.

In the aftermath, Sensei and Leo were haunted by what they did at those apartments for over half their lives, some 40 plus years. "He who seeks vengeance must dig two graves: one for his enemy and one for himself." In this case, Grant thought, the Chinese scholar who came up with that quote would have to tweak it to read four graves.

Sensei had always been uncomfortable with his students idolizing him. Maybe he felt that way because of what he had done at Hokum Courts so many years ago. At least he was of good enough character, if that was the right term, to feel guilty about what happened. So many idolized celebrities and highly respected politicians say they "made a mistake" when they have been arrested for something. Sensei and Leo actually felt bad about what they did.

Grant returned to the dilemma of revealing the killings in the book. If Sensei wanted his crime exposed, he had to have considered that Leo would be charged with homicide too? Leo sure had, hence his not wanting it told in the book.

Conversely, Grant thought, exhausted from wallowing around in all the possibilities, maybe Leo planned all along to give himself up should Sensei pass before he did. Okay, but what about Leo's request not to publish it?

Maybe the act of Leo confessing to Grant was what he considered 'giving himself up.'

Grant slapped the arm of his chair. Then did it again, harder. Could this get any more convoluted?

Brooklyn loves her father, Grant thought, and Leo loves her. His participation in a murder documented in a book would be there for the world to see. Grant didn't know Brooklyn that well, but he would have to assume that it would destroy her or at the very least deeply hurt and embarrass her.

Grant stood stiffly and walked over to the big window. Two boys, mid-teens, rolled by on skateboards, the one in the lead was arm-dancing hula-like to the music in his earbuds. His friend, a little uncertain on the board, laughed at his buddy's antics.

Grant wondered what they had learned about Vietnam in school. Did they watch the movies or read anything about it? They probably knew some about Iraq and Afghanistan; maybe they had relatives who served over there or are there now. Have the boys been taught anything about the horrific suffering by many of those who served?

The world really sucks sometimes, Grant thought, as he walked into his kitchen. He finished his orange juice and then retrieved a bottle of water out of the fridge. Thinking like an agitating washing machine made him thirsty. He took a long pull, set the remainder back, and commenced thinking again.

He remembered how Brooklyn's expression had changed in the restaurant, and a sort of darkness settled over her. Was she thinking then about him finding out about the murders? If she had even the slightest thought that Grant might learn of it, was she concerned about what he would do with the information? Did she wonder if he would turn her father into the police or keep it a secret?

Has Brooklyn factored in what his knowledge of the murders would do to their budding relationship?

Grant headed back out to his living room, plopped down on his sofa, and stretched out. "What am I doing?" he said aloud. Then to himself, I've jumped from Brooklyn not knowing anything about the crimes to her knowing about them and not thinking through the repercussions of him finding out. Or her dad discovering that she has somehow known for years about what happened. He looked up at the ceiling and blared, "Damn, shit, piss."

His phone sounded. This time he decided to answer it. He needed the distraction. He walked into the kitchen and retrieved it off the counter.

It was Leo. Damn.

Grant hadn't heard from him since that night when he walked out. Was he going to say the whole thing was a joke? Or again tell him not to print it? Or tell him *to* publish it?

"Hello."

"Grant? This is Leo." Grant didn't respond. "You there?"

"I am."

Long sigh. "I'm sorry about the other night. I get crazy sometimes."

"Really?"

"Booze and coke do it every time."

"You're over seventy years old. Isn't that kind of old to be using coke?"

Grant shook his head. The man killed someone and was an accomplice in another man's beating death, and here I am focusing on him snorting some powder.

He heard another long sigh from Leo. "There's no age limit, you know. I've used it since my love-in years in the nineteen sixties. Not as much as I used to, but mostly when that night comes back to bite my ass. Being interviewed, making me think about all that stuff back then, it… Sorry, Grant. I don't mean to say you made me think about it. You know what I mean. Anyway, it brought that night back into my dreams.

"I've tried to block it out over the many years, and I've done a pretty good job except every couple of months or so when I'm tired or sick. And always the date it happened, October fourth, or when I just start thinking about it for a few days. I…" Leo chuckled; it sounded forced. "On second thought, I guess I haven't done such a good job blocking it out."

Grant waited for him to continue. It was his show, one that he laid on Grant.

"I'm not a religious man," Leo said, his voice lower than before. "I'm spiritual, I guess. You can't help but be when you work on a farm and spend time in nature and all. But I do believe we have to pay for our big wrongs, and shit doesn't get more serious than when you take a life."

Leo didn't say anything for several seconds, and again, Grant let him decide when to continue.

"Sensei took a lot of lives in Vietnam, twenty-six, he told me once. But that wouldn't count against him because it was war. But the one at Hokum Courts in the parking lot would, and I know he sweated that. Hell, I've sweated it too, even though I didn't go there with the intention of killing someone. Sensei didn't either, at least that's what he said. His plan was to break the man's bones, but then his rage took over."

Grant took a deep breath and eased it out. "Do you have any idea how learning about this has messed me up, Leo? I mean, the fact I now have knowledge of two murders. What about Brooklyn? How much does she know? How much—"

"She doesn't know anything," Leo cut in. "And you promised."

"Damn you, Leo. Damn you." Grant's phone alerted another call coming in. Brooklyn. He disconnected Leo without telling him.

"Brooklyn," he breathed.

"I'm mad at you." She sounded more disappointed than mad. "I've called and texted you a bunch of times in the last three days. I didn't think you were one of those guys."

"I'm not." Grant rubbed his face as if trying to scrub away the stress. "I'm sorry, Brooklyn—."

"For…?"

"Uh…"

"For acting like a dick?" she suggested without hesitation.

"Uh, yeah, that."

"And an asshole?"

"It's just that—"

"My dad told you something, right?"

"I… I can't talk to you about this. I'm sorry. I—"

"Listen, Grant," Brooklyn said, sounding tired. "I haven't slept since you left… I understand that—"

"I'm afraid you don't understand, and it has to stay that way. I made a promise."

"My dad talks in his sleep," she said. "Sometimes in front of the TV, but mostly when he's out of his mind drunk and high."

"He talks—"

"Yes, in his sleep."

"What are you saying?"

"He went a whole year without drinking before my mom died. After the accident, he started up again. Sometimes drinking hard twice a month, occasionally more. Then snorting coke. Where he gets it, I haven't a clue. He thinks I don't know about it, but when he's drunk and uses it, he often leaves white powder under his nose."

"Can you understand what he says?" Grant asked. "When he talks in his sleep, I mean."

"Yes."

Grant's mind was whirling. What does she know? How much could she understand from a few sleepy, sputtered words?

"You're wondering how much I understand." This time her voice sounded as if on the verge of crying.

"Yes."

"Grant. I appreciate, and it means the world to me, how sensitive you are about me regarding this. But it's okay. I've heard him talk about what happened in bits and pieces for years. Always in bits and pieces, sometimes mumbly but other times clear as a bell. What I've pieced together is that two men died. Sensei broke a man's neck and my dad… He didn't mean for a man to die.

"I heard his ramblings long before I moved out and got married. I would ask mom about it, but she wouldn't ever say anything. Sometimes she would go into the bathroom, and I could hear her crying in there. So I stopped asking her.

"After she and my husband died, dad insisted I move in with him until I got myself 'squared away' as he put it. Since I returned, he's been drinking again, like I said, and snorting that shit. He's been at it especially hard the last six months. I think grieving, if that's the right word, for what he and Sensei did."

Grant's mind was racing in ten directions.

"I don't know what led up to that night," Brooklyn said, her breathing ragged, "what their motivation was, but I know it had something to do with Vietnam. Sensei's experience there. I heard dad mutter 'Hokum Courts' many times. I knew the place because when I was young, dad and I would go to Portland to pick up supplies, and he would drive by it real slow. Sometimes he'd pull to the curb by one of the parking lots, and he'd just look at it. I asked him early on what he was doing, and he said he knew someone who died there. After that, I would sit quietly in the truck until we would be on our way again.

"I don't remember if I knew the name of the place then; I wasn't even in my teens yet. But when I was in my twenties, I worked at a Chinese restaurant on Eighty-Second Avenue, and I'd take Glisan Street and pass by it. That's when I saw the name on the lawn. And I'd remember us stopping there.

"It wasn't until I moved back home and heard him say the name in his sleep that I looked it up on my computer. Some articles on one site told of Hokum's history with Vietnamese refugees. One of the articles told of the violence there for two or three years in the mid-seventies, stuff like shootings, knifings, and gang fights. The article said it was part of the difficulty the people had assimilating into this country. There was this interview with a Vietnamese lady who had lived there since the beginning. She told the reporter of a double murder that the cops never solved. I don't remember now what year, but it was something like nineteen seventy-five or six." Brooklyn paused for a moment, then, "That has to be what dad talks about in his sleep."

Neither spoke for a full minute. Then, she said, "I would have eventually told you. At least what I know. I didn't hear what dad told you the other day, so you probably know more than I do."

"This is so much to absorb," Grant said. "A big part of my concern was you not knowing. I didn't know if I could deal with me knowing and you not knowing. Your dad made me promise not to tell you, and I was going to honor that promise. But I kept wondering how I could keep something like that to myself. The elephant in the room thing and all. I couldn't see how we could…"

"Go on?" Brooklyn finished for him.

"Yes. How we could go on."

"You still wonder now that you know that I knew about some of what happened?"

"I don't know…?" Grant said. Then quickly, "I mean, no. I don't wonder anymore."

"Sweeeet," she said with a small laugh. Then she blew her nose.

"Nice," he teased, snorting a laugh.

"You just snorted."

"Yeah, but you just blew your nose into the phone." This time she laughed, and Grant thought it sounded beautiful. "I want to see you again." Before she could say anything, he added, "But I'm still very confused about all this," he said. "What happened that night. How knowing now involves you and me. And your dad."

"We can be confused together, Grant. We can split it. Thirty percent for me, seventy for you."

He was amazed at how she could joke. But then she has had years to come to terms with it.

"Grant?"

"Yes."

"In case you're wondering, I've been seeing a shrink for the last six years."

"I'll need his name and number."

They talked for a moment longer and made arrangements for dinner at Italy on 4th Avenue. "They got checkered tablecloths," Grant told her, feeling better than he had in three days.

"Love it," she said, sounding elated, relieved. Then softer, "Grant?"

"Yes."

"What are you going to do about your book?"

He didn't answer for a long moment as he thought about the three options: toss away his notes and recordings and look for a new project; write about the man without the murders; or write it with them included.

Which one would give Sensei's restless spirit some peace?

Finally, "Brooklyn?"

"I'm here."

"Sometimes," he said softly, "the hardest thing and the right thing are the same."

"What do you mean?" she asked, her voice close as if they were face-to-face, her eyes looking into his.

Grant took a deep breath then said with total certainty, "I'm going to write Sensei's story."

ABOUT THE AUTHOR

The author with Boot and Pearl

Loren W. Christensen has been involved in law enforcement since 1967. He began as a 21-year-old military policeman in the U.S. Army, serving stateside and as a patrolman in Saigon, Vietnam during the war. At 26, he joined the Portland, Oregon Police

Bureau working a variety of jobs to include street patrol, gang enforcement, intelligence, bodyguarding, and academy trainer, retiring after 25 years.

In 1997, Loren began a full-time career as a writer, now with nearly 60 books in print with seven publishers, as well as magazine articles and blog pieces. He edited a police newspaper for seven years. His non-fiction includes books on martial arts, police work, PTSD, mental preparation for violence, meditation, nutrition, exercise, and various subcultures, to include prostitution, street gangs, skid row, and the warrior community.

His fiction series *Dukkha* was a finalist in the prestigious USA Best Book Awards. He has also written a novella, nearly a dozen short stories, and several omnibuses.

As a martial arts student and teacher since 1965, Loren has earned a 1st-dan black belt in the Filipino fighting art of *arnis,* a 2nd-degree black belt in *aiki jujitsu and, on* October 23, 2018, the American Karate Black Belt Association in Texas, awarded him a 10th-dan black belt in karate. Loren was inducted into the master's Hall of Fame in 2011.

OTHER TITLES BY LOREN W. CHRISTENSEN

The following are available on Amazon, from their publishers, and through the usual book outlets. Signed copies can be purchased at LWC Books, www.lwcbooks.com

Street Stoppers
Fighting In The Clinch
Fighter's Fact Book
Fighter's Fact Book 2
Solo Training **(Bestseller)**
Solo Training 2
Solo Training 3
Speed Training
The Fighter's Body
Total Defense
The Mental Edge
The Way Alone
Far Beyond Defensive Tactics
Fighting Power
Crouching Tiger
Anything Goes
Winning With American Kata
Total Defense
Riot
Warriors
On Combat **(Bestseller)**
Warrior Mindset
Deadly Force Encounters
Deadly Force Encounters, Second Edition
Surviving Workplace Violence
Surviving A School Shooting
Gangbangers

Skinhead Street Gangs
Hookers, Tricks And Cops
Way Of The Warrior
Skid Row Beat
Defensive Tactics
Missing Children
Fight Back: Self-Defense For Women
Extreme Joint Locking
Timing In The Martial Arts
Fighter's Guide to Hard-Core Heavy Bag Training
The Brutal Art Of Ripping, Poking And Pressing Vital Targets
How To Live Safely In A Dangerous World
Fighting The Pain Resistant Attacker
Evolution Of Weaponry
Meditation For Warriors
Mental Rehearsal For Warriors
Prostate Cancer
Cops' True Stories Of The Paranormal **(Bestseller)**
Seekers of the Paranormal
Policing Saigon
Musings on Violence
Street Lessons, A Journey

Fiction

Dukkha: The Suffering **(Best Books Award Finalist)**
Dukkha: Reverb
Dukkha: Unloaded
Dukkha: Hungry Ghosts
Old Ed, Omnibus
Boss, Omnibus
The Reincarnation of Kato the Monk
The Life and Death of Sensei

Short Story Fiction

Old Ed
Old Ed 2
Old Ed 3
Old Ed 4
Old Ed 5
Parts
Knife Fighter
Boss
Boss 2
Boss 3

DVDs

Solo Training
Fighting Dirty
Speed Training
Masters And Styles
Vital Targets
The Brutal Art Of Ripping, And Pressing Vital Targets

Note: On Combat and Policing Saigon are also available in audio from Amazon

YOU MIGHT ALSO LIKE

Knife Fighter, The Omnibus Edition includes Knife Fighter, a short story, and the follow-up, Knife Fighter 2, a novella-sized short story. The omnibus and the short stories are available on Amazon.

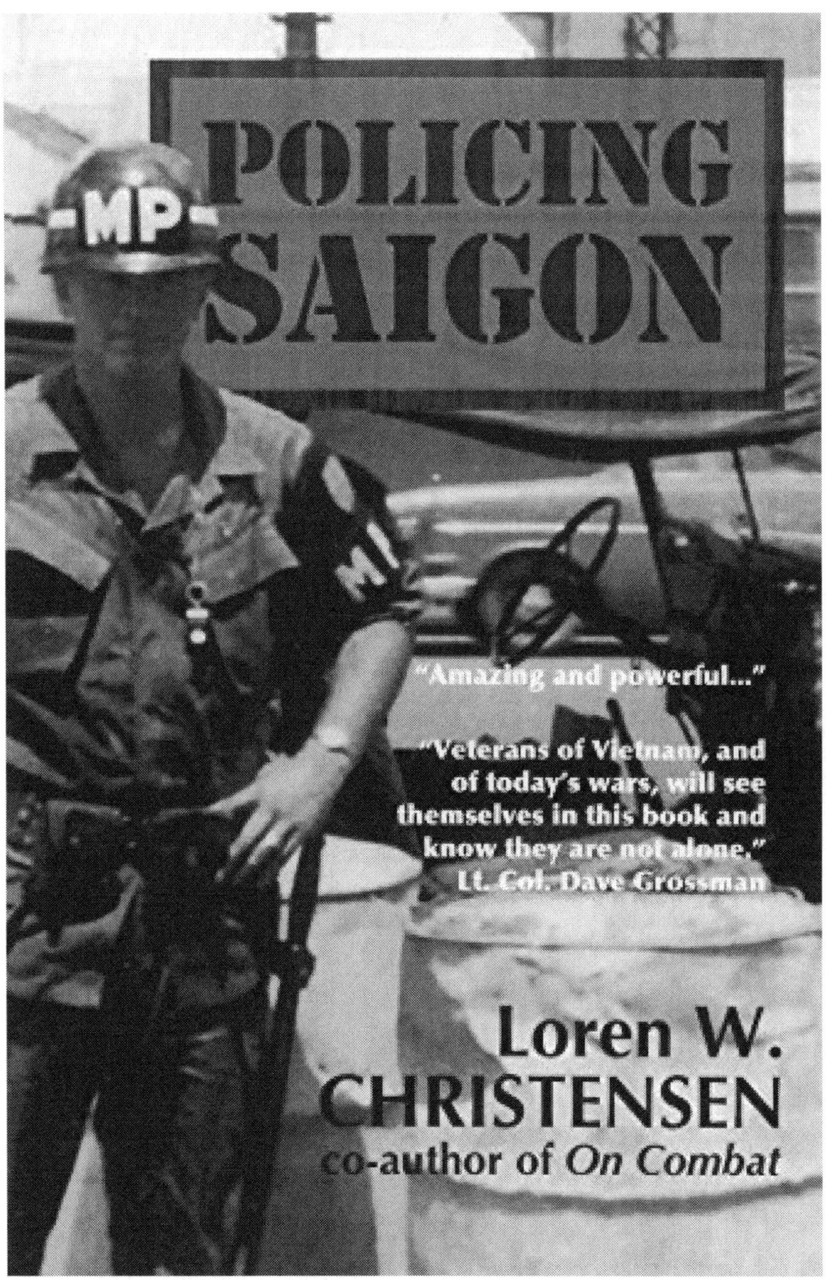

Policing Saigon is the biography of the author's year policing Saigon, Vietnam, at the time considered the most dangerous city in the world. The book is available on Amazon in paperback, Kindle, and audiobook format.

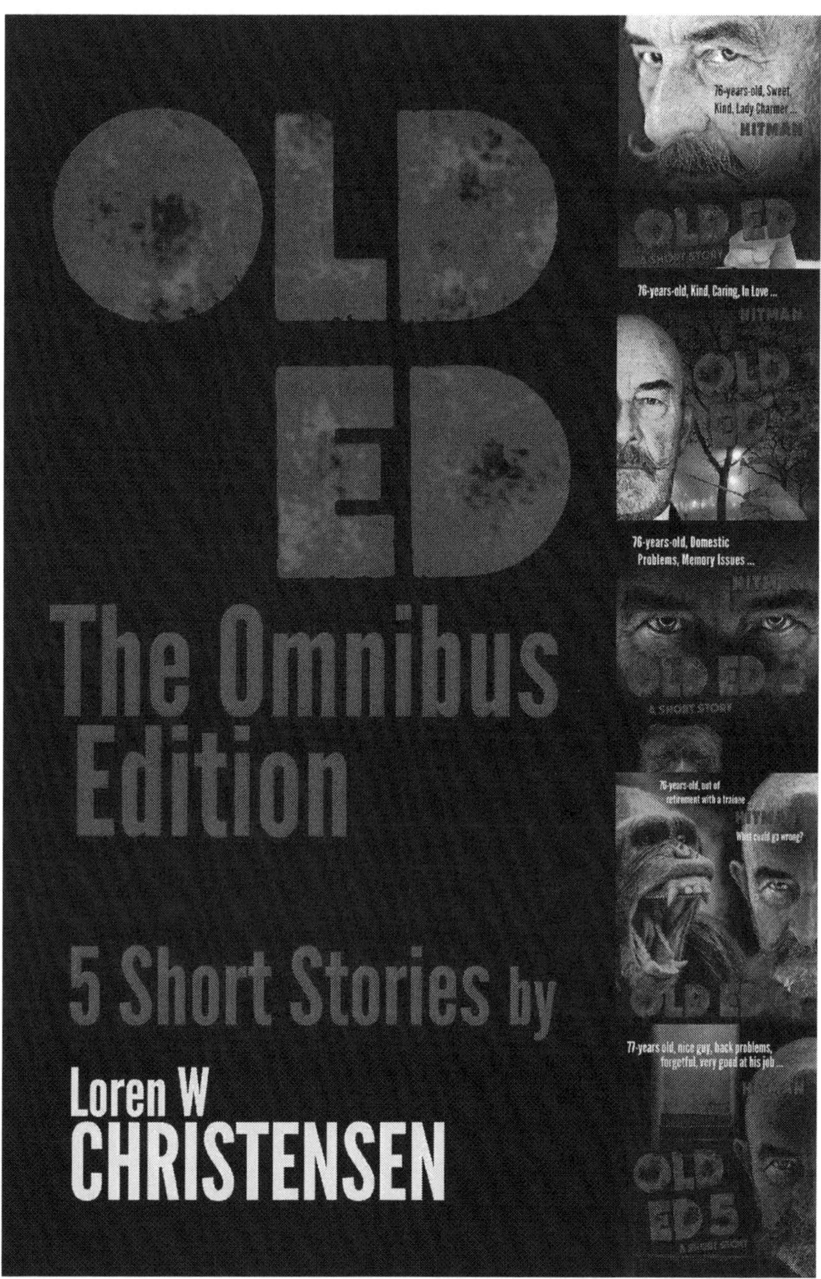

Old Ed, The Omnibus Edition includes all five very popular short stories about the debonair and womanizing Ed, a 75-year-old hitman with a unique philosophy and a deadly set of skills. The omnibus and the individual short stories are available on Amazon.

Printed in Great Britain
by Amazon